Praise for the *Baby Boomer Mysteries*

"Not since picking up one of Janet Evanovich's Stephanie Plum mysteries have I laughed or enjoyed a book as much as Susan Santangelo's *Retirement Can Be Murder.*"
−*Suspense Magazine*

"*Masquerades Can Be Murder* is humorous and delightful. You won't want this one to end."
−Catherine Coulter
New York Times bestselling author

"*Mistletoe Can Be Murder* is a wonderful addition to one of my favorite series."
−Allison Brook, author
Haunted Library Mystery Series

"In *Politics Can Be Murder*, Susan Santangelo serves up a humorous story with a serious underpinning. Highly recommended."
–Leslie Wheeler, author
Berkshire Hilltown Mystery Series

"Susan Santangelo combines humor and mystery to create a great read. What a treat to see a female lead character who's over fifty. *Moving Can Be Murder* is a must read!"
–*Readers' Favorite*

PICKLEBALL Can Be MURDER

Every Wife Has a Story

A Carol and Jim Andrews Baby Boomer Mystery
Twelfth in the Series

Susan Santangelo

BABY BOOMER MYSTERIES PRESS

Copyright © 2026 Susan Santangelo
All Rights Reserved

No part of this publication may be reproduced, stored in or introduced into a retrieval system, or transmitted in any form, or by any means (electronic, mechanical, photocopying, recording or otherwise) without the prior written permission of the author.

Cover Artist and Design: Elizabeth Moisan
Published by Baby Boomer Mysteries Press
ISBN: 978-0-9857-7992-4

This book is a work of fiction. Names, characters, businesses, organizations, places, events, and incidents are the product of the author's imagination. Any resemblance to actual events, locales, or persons, living or dead, is coincidental.

This book is dedicated to Elizabeth Moisan, whose wonderful artwork has brought it to life. Thank you.

Baby Boomer Mysteries

Retirement Can Be Murder (#1)
Moving Can Be Murder (#2)
Marriage Can Be Murder (#3)
Class Reunions Can Be Murder (#4)
Funerals Can Be Murder (#5)
Second Honeymoons Can Be Murder (#6)
Dieting Can Be Murder (#7)
In-Laws Can Be Murder (#8)
Politics Can Be Murder (#9)
Mistletoe Can Be Murder (#10)
Masquerades Can Be Murder (#11)
Pickleball Can Be Murder (#12)

Acknowledgments

Thank you to my wonderful family—David, Mark, Sandy, Jacob, and Becca. And especially to my husband Joe. Your support and love mean everything to me.

A big thank you to the First Readers Club for this book—George Eastman, Marti and Bob Baker, Judy O'Brien, and Mark Santangelo—for their helpful comments and suggestions.

To all my long-time New England friends and my new Florida friends, I appreciate you all so much.

Thank you to all my friends and cyber friends from Sisters in Crime and the Cape Cod Writers Center for sharing your expertise with me.

For the last 37 years, my life has been enriched by the unconditional love of English cocker spaniels. To Tuppence, Tessa, Tillie, Tucker, Lucy, Boomer, and especially, Lilly, thank you for the memories. And a special shout-out to Lynn Pray and Courtney Ross, Pineridge English Cockers, Rehoboth, MA.

To all the bloggers who love mysteries as much as I do and support the mystery genre in so many ways, especially Dru Ann Love, Lori Boness Caswell, Heather Doyle Harrisson, and Shawn Stevens, a huge thank you.

And to everyone who has enjoyed this series—the readers I have met in person or via Zoom book events, those who have emailed me, those who have posted online reviews for the books, and those who have followed me on social media—thanks so much. Hope you enjoy this one too. And keep those chapter headings coming!

Fairport, Connecticut
Late Summer

It's fair to say that Poppy Hollister and I never had a warm, friendly relationship. I would best describe it as two opposites who did not attract.

The first time I saw Poppy Hollister, she was killing her opponent (figuratively speaking) on one of the Fairport Recreation Center's new pickleball courts. I envied her prowess and skill in a sport that I was struggling to master and probably never would.

The second time I saw Poppy Hollister was a few days later in the rec center parking lot. I was trying desperately to avoid a close encounter with the expensive sleek white vehicle next to me while backing out of a tight parking space. I needed help, and Poppy was happy to pitch right in with a loud stream of curse words because, of course, the expensive sleek white vehicle I was trying so hard to avoid hitting belonged to her. She was so angry that I was afraid she was going to smack me. And after seeing her power on the pickleball court, I knew she could knock me out with a single blow.

The third time I saw Poppy Hollister, she and her attorney were standing at the front door of my beautiful antique home on Old Fairport Turnpike. Her look of triumph as she announced she was suing me for $2 million for damage I'd caused to her precious automobile was a sight to behold.

"You're going to regret the day you tangled with me," she hissed.

I already did.

Chapter 1

*Becoming an adult is the stupidest thing
I've ever done.*

A Few Months Earlier

There are few things moms love more than spending quality time with their adult children, especially if the kids live far away from the parental nest. So every time my son, Mike, comes home from Florida for a quick visit, I'm expecting a perfect family reunion where petty disagreements are forgotten and all is right with the world—just like in a Hallmark movie. What I always forget is that, unlike real life, Hallmark movies are only two hours long (including commercials).

    I'm Carol Andrews, and I've been married to my retired husband, Jim, for more than 40 years. Oh, wait. That didn't come out right. Jim wasn't retired when we got married. He was a hard-working intern at a prestigious public relations firm in Manhattan, Gibson Gillespie. Jim and I were both born and raised in Fairport, Connecticut, but I'm one year younger, so we didn't hang out with the same group of friends when we were kids.

Eventually we each moved to Manhattan and ended up living in the same West Side apartment building, right near Central Park. One thing led to another, and after a whirlwind courtship of more than five years (he was a real slow mover in those days), Jim finally popped the question.

I believe his exact words were, "Don't you think we'd save a lot of money if we moved in together?" I took that as a marriage proposal, hemmed and hawed for about ten minutes, and finally said yes.

About a year after our wedding, our first child, Jenny, was born. We were still living in an apartment in the same building, but it had suddenly gotten much smaller with the addition of a crib, baby carriage, and all the other things an infant needs.

We decided to move back to our old home town of Fairport, and with a little financial help from relatives, bought an antique home on Old Fairport Turnpike in the historic district that needed tons of work. It's still a work in progress, and if I'm honest, it always will be. But Jim and I loved it, and we had plenty of room for expansion–four bedrooms and two bathrooms on the second floor, and a master suite on the first. We filled another bedroom about a year after we moved in with the arrival of our second child, Mike, and kept the rest for guests.

Jenny is now married to her grammar school sweetheart, Fairport police detective Mark

Anderson. I'm proud to say that she's also an adjunct professor of English literature at Fairport College, and recently made us grandparents for the first (I hope not the only) time. They live only fifteen minutes away from Jim and me, which is a mother's dream come true.

Mike now lives in Miami, Florida; runs a highly successful bistro, Cosmo's, on South Beach; and was at this very moment taking a shower in our second-floor bathroom. I was thrilled he was home for a few days, and I vowed to do everything I could to make his visit wonderful. I was hoping that if Mike had a fabulous time at home with his loving family, he'd visit more often.

"I won't even complain if Mike leaves his wet towels all over the bathroom floor, the way he used to do when he was a kid," I said aloud to our two English cocker spaniels, Lucy and Ethel. "Everyone has to pitch in to make Mike's visit memorable, including both of you."

Lucy gave me a skeptical look, which I ignored. Ethel was her usual loving, supportive self.

It turned out that the word "memorable" has more than one meaning. Too bad I didn't know that in advance.

Chapter 2

Sometimes I talk to myself and then we both laugh and laugh.

"Morning, Mom." Mike breezed into the kitchen and gave me a quick smooch. "Do you have anything I could grab for a quick breakfast? I'm late already."

My plan for a cozy breakfast with my son vanished before I could even blink.

Don't let Mike see you're upset, Carol. And for heaven's sake, don't interrogate him about where he's going, who he's going with, and when he'll be home. He's not a kid anymore.

I reached into a nearby cupboard and pulled out a box of energy bars I'd bought several months ago and never opened. And probably never would, not that my son needed to know that.

"Fantastic, Mom. This is perfect." Mike grabbed the box as I heard a car horn beeping. "If I eat them all, I promise I'll replace them."

"That's not necessary," I protested.

He gave me another quick kiss. "Gotta go now. I'll see you later."

"Okay," I called after him.

I knew I couldn't get to the living room window in time to see who was picking him up, so I consoled myself with a cup of Jim's excellent coffee and half a blueberry muffin. One of the few upsides to my husband's too early retirement from his public relations job (upsetting my life forever, not that I'm complaining) is that he's taken over making the morning coffee.

Jim was frequently up long before I was, and this morning he had left me a hand-scribbled note that I couldn't decipher, even with my glasses on. I figured I'd hear from him eventually, if only to ask me what tonight's dinner menu was, so I tossed the note into the garbage can.

"You're both lucky you never had puppies," I said to the dogs. "You'd just start to bond with them, and they'd leave you for another home. You'd never hear from them again."

It wasn't any of my business (which has never stopped me before), but I couldn't help wondering if the driver of the car was male or female. Mike was wearing pressed chinos, a starched shirt, and a navy blazer. He was dressed to impress, for sure. But who was Mike dressed to impress? The only person who probably knew the answer, and who might tell me if I begged her, was my darling daughter, Jenny.

I checked the time and realized it might be a little early to text Jenny, especially if CJ had a restless night. I knew he was teething, which can make even the most perfect grandson in the world cross and fussy.

After scarfing down the other half of the blueberry muffin (it would only get stale if I didn't, plus blueberries are a healthy choice for breakfast) and finishing my coffee, I clipped leashes on the two dogs. A brisk morning walk would be a good way to start the day.

The moment the three of us reached the sidewalk, I saw the unofficial gossip queen of Old Fairport Turnpike, Phyllis Stevens, waving and heading across the street for a chat.

Chapter 3

Your secret's safe with me. There's a good chance I wasn't listening.

There may be some of you who haven't yet had the pleasure of meeting Phyllis, so allow me to introduce you. Phyllis and her long-suffering husband, Bill, have been our neighbors ever since we bought our antique house over thirty years ago. Phyllis has appointed herself in charge of the historic district in town and pays particular attention to our neighborhood. She spends most of her time patrolling Old Fairport Turnpike, looking for infractions, like garbage cans left outside too long, grass that needs cutting, shutters that need painting—you get the idea. Since she recently discovered that Bill has an ancestor who fought in our town's American Revolution battle, she's become even more insufferable.

There's been an unsubstantiated rumor floating around the neighborhood for years that Phyllis keeps a telescope in her living room to keep track of the local goings on. Since our house is directly across the street from hers, she has a front row seat for viewing the comings, goings, and frequent infractions committed by the Andrews family.

I was trapped, and it was my own stupid fault. I usually check outside first before leaving the house to be sure the coast is clear of Phyllis. Harsh, but true. I didn't check this morning because I was so preoccupied with Mike.

"Hi, Phyllis. We're just back from a long walk and we're all exhausted." I panted a little to add some credence to my story.

"Today's going to be very hot," I continued. "I should get the dogs back inside, so I can't chat now. Say hello to Bill for me."

I turned to make a break for it just as Phyllis said, "You must be very happy to have Mike home again. How long is he staying?"

Busted. I'd never get away from her now. I was sure she knew I was lying about coming home from a long walk. And annoyed that she already knew Mike was home.

Don't be stupid, Carol. Phyllis could have valuable intel about Mike's early morning departure. See what you can find out.

"Yes, Jim and I are both thrilled, although it's just a quick trip. He was able to spend some time with CJ yesterday. Mike really loves his nephew."

Phyllis's eyes twinkled. "Maybe he'll finally settle down and start a family of his own. Is he seeing anyone special right now?"

Sheesh.

"You probably know as much about that as Jim and I do," I said.

Way to insult the woman, Carol. Nice going.

"Mike keeps his private life very private, even from us," I added quickly.

"He's certainly an early riser these days," Phyllis continued without missing a beat. "Bill was walking by the living room window this morning and happened to see someone driving an official Town of Fairport car stop in front of your house and pick Mike up. What was that all about?"

"One of Mike's high school classmates works at Town Hall now," I lied. "Patty somebody. It could have been her."

"The driver was a man," Phyllis said emphatically. "At least, that's what Bill said."

And she scurried away before I could get anything else out of her.

Chapter 4

It turns out that when someone asked me who my favorite child is, I was supposed to pick one of my own. I know that now.

Any incentive I'd had to take the dogs on a long walk around the neighborhood had vanished. No surprise there, considering how much I loathe exercise in any form and do everything I can to avoid it. The dogs love long walks, however, so I decided it was only fair to let them decide what we should do next.

"Let's walk to the corner and back," I suggested to my canine sidekicks, both busily inspecting something a careless passerby had discarded near my front gate. I bent down and picked up the offending litter, which turned out to be a flyer from our town's new recreation center. I may not be the neatest housekeeper in the world, but I can't stand litter cluttering my yard. I stuffed it in my pocket to dispose of the instant I got home.

"We can either take a walk now, or we can all go home and you two can have biscuits. You decide," I said to the dogs.

Lucy gave me one of her plaintive "I'm hungry" looks. I knew she would. I'd mentioned the magic word "biscuits."

"Good choice," I agreed. "We'll walk to the stop sign at the corner of Beach Road and back home."

I swear, I'd taken barely 10 steps from my house when I heard a woman calling my name.

"Carol, hi! Wait for us and we'll walk together." Stacy O'Keefe, one of the young mothers on our block and a good friend of Jenny's, jogged up beside me. She was pushing a baby stroller with her adorable daughter safe inside.

"I was jogging straight home with Addie, but she fell asleep, and I didn't want to wake her. She's teething, and you know what that's like. I saw you talking to Phyllis, so I waited until the coast was clear to call out your name. Does that make me a terrible person?"

"No more than most of other people in the neighborhood, including me," I confessed.

By this time, both dogs and were straining at their leashes, telling me to cut the chit chat and get moving.

"We're walking one more block, then going home," I said. "I don't know if you've heard the news, but Mike's here for a quick visit. I want to spend as much with him as possible."

"That won't be an issue much longer," Stacy said, pointing to the flyer in my pocket. "I see you got the flyer."

She looked surprised at my confused look. "Uh oh. I guess I spoke out of turn. Me and my big mouth."

Stacy's phone pinged with a text. "Yikes! I'm running late. Bye, Carol. Enjoy your day." She jogged away before I could grill her about what she knew that I didn't.

Lucy gave me one of her plaintive "I'm hungry" looks. I knew she would. I'd mentioned the magic word "biscuits."

"Good choice," I agreed. "We'll walk to the stop sign at the corner of Beach Road and back home."

I swear, I'd taken barely 10 steps from my house when I heard a woman calling my name.

"Carol, hi! Wait for us and we'll walk together." Stacy O'Keefe, one of the young mothers on our block and a good friend of Jenny's, jogged up beside me. She was pushing a baby stroller with her adorable daughter safe inside.

"I was jogging straight home with Addie, but she fell asleep, and I didn't want to wake her. She's teething, and you know what that's like. I saw you talking to Phyllis, so I waited until the coast was clear to call out your name. Does that make me a terrible person?"

"No more than most of other people in the neighborhood, including me," I confessed.

By this time, both dogs and were straining at their leashes, telling me to cut the chit chat and get moving.

"We're walking one more block, then going home," I said. "I don't know if you've heard the news, but Mike's here for a quick visit. I want to spend as much with him as possible."

"That won't be an issue much longer," Stacy said, pointing to the flyer in my pocket. "I see you got the flyer."

She looked surprised at my confused look. "Uh oh. I guess I spoke out of turn. Me and my big mouth."

Stacy's phone pinged with a text. "Yikes! I'm running late. Bye, Carol. Enjoy your day." She jogged away before I could grill her about what she knew that I didn't.

Chapter 5

I just paid for a 12-month gym membership. My bank called to see if my credit card had been stolen.

I am by nature a curious person. I'm always interested in learning something new, which is a good thing.

I am also a person whose feelings are easily hurt, which is not such a good thing. My vivid imagination and habit of jumping to conclusions without any evidence whatsoever usually results in my behaving more like a petulant child than the adult I'm supposed to be.

In other words, rather than discuss with the person who has hurt my feelings by not sharing, for example, his plans to move back to Fairport, my M.O. would be to shut down completely, pout, and refuse to talk about it.

Not this time.

For once in my life, I would behave like a grown-up and give Mike the opportunity to tell me the exciting news whenever he chose. Yes, indeedy.

Right now, my canine companions and I would take a long walk and enjoy this beautiful morning. And we wouldn't go home until I was in a more positive frame of mind.

Yes, indeed. And an excellent plan it was, too.

However... by the time the dogs and I finally staggered to my back door after walking all over Fairport (huge exaggeration), I had worked myself into a classic infantile hissy fit. I stormed into the kitchen, slamming the door behind me. Both dogs scurried to the safety of the master bedroom without even giving me time to take off their leashes.

You are behaving like a complete idiot, Carol Andrews. You're even freaking out the dogs. Focus on the positive. If you understood Stacy correctly, your son is moving back to Fairport. You should be thrilled!

Taking my own good advice, I decided to make some of Mike's favorite food for dinner tonight. I rummaged around in the freezer, looking for inspiration, but came up empty.

I had to go food shopping, a chore I truly detest.

Don't get me wrong—I don't hate the "shopping" part. I have a black belt in all kinds of shopping, from clothes, to shoes and handbags, to food. The part I hate about food shopping is lugging the bags inside and unpacking them.

There may be some among you who are thinking I should just wait for Jim to come home to help me.

Jim's "help" comes with a catch. He's already memorized the latest flyer from the food store and decided which items should be purchased. Woe to me if I deviate from his master list, even if his list includes items that we will never, ever use. I've devised a clever strategy to substitute things we actually need, but in the interests of self-preservation, I have no intention of sharing it with any of you.

"Rats," I said aloud.

I felt a tap on my shoulder, which scared the heck out of me.

"Are you ready to go?" Mike asked.

"Are you trying to give me a heart attack?"

"Sorry, Mom, I didn't mean to frighten you. I told you I'd be back around ten to pick you up."

"When did you tell me that? I hope I'm not losing my hearing like your father."

"I wrote you a note and left it on the kitchen table after you and Dad went to bed. Didn't you read it?"

"The only note I saw this morning was from Dad. I couldn't make out his writing, so I threw it away."

After a quick search of the kitchen garbage can, Mike pointed to Jim's note, now dripping with soggy coffee grounds. "Dad used the other side of my note to write his."

"Don't pick it up!" I warned. "You'll get germs."

Mike rolled his eyes. "Mom, I'm not nine years old anymore." His implication was clear: Back off, lady.

I managed a weak smile. "Sorry. Force of habit."

"I forgive you." He checked the time on his phone. "You have exactly fifteen minutes to get ready."

"Ready? Ready for what?"

"We have a mother-son date today. I guarantee you'll love it. And that's all I'm saying."

"But...."

"I'm changing into shorts, a tee shirt, and sneakers. I suggest you do the same."

Suddenly, I figured out what was going on. Mike thought he was surprising me. But thanks to Stacy tipping me off about Mike moving back, he'd rented a place and was taking me to see it. His insistence on what I should wear was just a way to confuse me.

For a millisecond, I imagined how wonderful it would be if he decided to move back home instead of renting a place, then dismissed the idea. Mike was all grown up and used to living on his own, even though he was still trying to put one over on his dear old Mom.

It wasn't going to work this time. I knew all his tricks.

Play along with him, Carol. And, for his sake, act surprised when he shows you his new digs.

Chapter 6

Don't rush me. I'm waiting for the last minute.

Fifteen minutes isn't nearly long enough for someone like me to choose what to wear. I never leave the house without being color coordinated.

"No time for that today," I muttered as I searched in the closet for a pair of shorts that I could zip up and didn't make my legs look chunky. All I could find were some gray gym shorts that I'd bought for Jim a few years ago and he never wore. It had a drawstring waist, so I was sure they'd fit me.

"Ten minutes," I heard Mike call from the kitchen. "I'm walking the dogs now."

"Working on it," I called. When did my son become so bossy?

Rummaging in a dresser drawer, I found an old tee shirt that I reserve for days when I'm taking care of CJ. It was a darker gray than the shorts, which would normally bother me, but I was in a hurry. I just prayed that I wouldn't see anyone I knew while I was wearing it.

Socks, sneakers—two minutes and done. I congratulated myself on being so speedy. I hoped Mike would be impressed.

I had my hand on the door when—yikes! I had a naked face! Oh, well, there was a first time for everything. I waved goodbye to the dogs and ran out the door.

Mike was pacing in front of my car. "Here I am," I said, panting. "Just give me a minute to catch my breath. I'm not used to moving this fast."

"I know," my smarty pants son said. He opened the passenger side door of my car and gestured for me to sit there.

I had a quick flashback of Mike learning to drive, when he mistook the gas pedal for the brake and ended up taking a door off the garage.

"I'm driving," Mike said, dangling the extra car key in front of me. He was wearing that same stubborn look Jim uses when he's decided to do something I disagree with. "Today, you're my date, and the gentleman always drives.

"Besides," he added, "you have no idea where we're going. I have the whole day planned."

"Where are we going?" I asked, playing along with him as I fastened the seat belt on the passenger side of my car.

"You've got to be the most difficult date I've ever had," Mike said as he adjusted the driver's seat and the rear-view mirror to suit him. "Go along with me for a little while, and then I'll treat you to a delicious lunch."

"Promise?"

"Scout's honor. You're going to have a lot of fun. Trust me."

"I do trust you," I answered. "But your idea of having fun and mine may not be the same. My asking you where we're going is a reasonable question, and I'd appreciate an answer. Please."

"Okay, Mom. But promise you'll keep an open mind."

"You know me. My mind is always open, which is why nothing stays in it very long. At least, that's what your father says."

"We're going to the Fairport Rec Center."

I'd realized the rec center must be near Mike's new place. He was trying to throw me off the scent, so I'd really be surprised. Typical Mike behavior. Little did he know that I was already clued in.

After the longest, scariest car ride I'd ever endured, where I invoked every saint I could think of to keep us safe, we turned into the rec center parking lot and cruised to a stop in front of the building.

"Are you ready for your first surprise?"

I bit my lip to keep from laughing. "I'm ready."

"We're going to play pickleball."

Chapter 7

I never thought I'd be the kind of person who got up early to exercise… and I was right.

"Would you please repeat that? I'm sure I misheard you."

Mike laughed. "This is exactly the reaction I'd expected, which is why I didn't tell you before now. I was afraid you'd jump out of a moving car."

He gave me a sideways glance. "Your hand is gripping the door handle. Just relax, will you? I promise, you're going to have the time of your life today."

"You have your fun playing pickleball and I'll have my fun watching you," I said, folding my arms like a mutinous child. "I'll even cheer you on. But I'm not playing."

"I'm dropping you off here," Mike said, ignoring me. "You won't have too far to walk to get to the pickleball courts."

"I can walk just fine, thank you very much. I am not a doddering old lady yet. As a matter of fact, the dogs and I had a nice walk this morning. We were outside for almost an hour."

Much of that time was spent talking to neighbors, but I saw no need for me to clarify.

Mike shifted the gear into Park, then ran to the passenger's side and opened the door for me. "A gentleman always opens the door for his date," he said, holding out his hand for me to take. "I believe you taught me that."

"Thank you, but I'm still capable of exiting my own car by myself."

Don't be so sensitive, Carol. Mike's just being helpful. We're at the rec center, not an assisted living facility. And who knows? Maybe you'll like playing pickleball. Once.

I hoisted myself from the car with some difficulty. "I'm not used to getting out on the passenger side," I said to squash Mike's concerned look. "Where will I meet you?"

"The lobby is directly inside. I'll see you there in a few minutes."

I nodded and tried not to grimace as Mike drove my car away at a speed that was much too fast for a parking lot. "There's no need to rush," I yelled after him, and he waved.

"I'm driving from now on, no matter what he says," I muttered.

As I opened the rec center door, I heard a series of loud popping sounds, thuds, and yells. If this was pickleball, I was sure I could handle the yelling part.

Mastering the thuds and loud pops, which I presumed occurred when one of the players hit the ball (or each other?), would take some practice.

I vowed that if there was any running required to even reach the ball, the way there is in tennis, I was going home right now.

There was no one at the reception desk, so I made myself at home on a very uncomfortable chair to wait for Mike. Pop. Thud. Pop. Thud. Pop. Thud. Pop. The persistent sounds were driving me nuts. They seemed to be coming from everywhere. And the constant yelling was really getting on my nerves.

"Sorry to take so long," Mike said when he finally showed up. "I had a business problem I needed to straighten out."

"In Miami? Or here?"

Mike gave me a look. "Why are you asking me that? You know Cosmo's in Miami."

I was impressed with his clever way of avoiding my question. Instead of answering, I just smiled.

"Ready to play pickleball, Mom?"

"As ready as I ever will be."

Like, never.

I dutifully followed my son to the rec center's old tennis courts, each of which was now subdivided into smaller courts. Only one was currently being used. I couldn't believe all the noise I'd heard had come from a single court with four players.

The most impressive player of the foursome was a tall, slim, white-haired woman in her late forties, wearing crisp white shorts and a red and white striped top. Despite how strenuously she was exerting herself, she wasn't even breaking a sweat.

Her partner was a man who made a few half-hearted swats at the ball if it came near him, but otherwise he was content to let his partner do all the work. Her opponents were two men and, despite their joint efforts, even I could tell they were destined to lose the match.

I immediately had simultaneous flashes of envy and fear. There was no way I'd ever play as well as she did, and if she was ever my opponent, I'd just concede the game before we started and save myself from public humiliation.

I nudged Mike. "Do you know who that woman is?"

"I think it's Poppy Hollister. Her husband's the chairman of the rec center commission. She's creaming the other two players without any help from her partner."

He's probably too scared to move.

"Game!" the woman announced, approaching the net with her partner to shake the hands of her two opponents. After the obligatory handshakes to show she was a gracious winner, she wiped her hands on her shorts, which I found insulting. Even if the guys were a sweaty mess after all that strenuous exercise and she wasn't, she didn't have to make a public gesture that humiliated them even more.

"Thanks for being my partner today, Tim" she said to her partner. "You're always such a good sport."

"You know you can always count on me to stand in your shadow whenever called upon, Poppy dear," Tim said, bowing, which made her laugh.

When Poppy bent down and began rummaging through her gym bag, I saw him stick his tongue out at her, which made me laugh.

Chapter 8

I was in a job interview the other day when the manager handed me his laptop and said, "I want you to try to sell this to me."
So, I put it under my arm, walked out of the office, and went home.
Eventually, the manager called me and said, "Bring that laptop back here right now."
I replied, "Two hundred dollars and it's yours."

"Are you my eleven-thirty?"

I realized the woman, still going through her gym bag, was talking to us at the same time.

"I'm Mike Andrews, and this is my mother, Carol."

OMG. Had my son booked a pickleball lesson with the person who'd intimidated the living daylights out of me before I even said hello?

Poppy checked out my handsome son from head to toe—if you know what I mean—and gave Mike a huge smile of approval. She turned her attention to me and frowned. It was obvious that my choice of attire didn't pass muster in her "What to Wear When I'm Teaching You to Play Pickleball" department.

"I guess we're both your eleven-thirty," I said. "We came early so we could watch a match. You're a fabulous player. The best one I've ever seen."

Which was completely true, because I'd never seen anyone play pickleball before.

Poppy smiled, and I figured my shameless flattery about her pickleball skills had softened her up a little. "Thank you. I do my best."

My insecurities immediately kicked in. Not only was Poppy a killer pickleball player, she sure looked a heck of lot better than I did. I admit (only to you) that I have a few (well, more than a few) extra pounds which have taken up residence in my body, especially around my middle. Elastic waistbands and comfy overblouses have become my favorite clothing choices.

I automatically sucked in my stomach, hoping Poppy wasn't checking me out as closely as I was checking out her.

Now that we were standing closer, I was sure that Poppy hadn't celebrated a birthday in her forties for at least ten—or even twenty—years. Which would put her close to my age, not that I have any plans to share mine with you.

Then I realized that Poppy must have had cosmetic surgery, even a tummy tuck, to still look this good. Even my best friend, Nancy Green, who exercises daily and uses every beauty cream on the market to preserve her youthful appearance, has never looked this good. (Please don't tell Nancy I said that.)

I was dying to get the name of her plastic surgeon to share with Nancy, but since we were just getting acquainted, I figured that would be a mistake. Besides, since Nancy and her sometimes-yes/sometimes-no husband, Bob, were currently on a cruise celebrating their wedding anniversary, my timing of a plastic surgeon referral wouldn't be appreciated.

"You certainly succeed," my son said. "Maybe you can give my mom some tips."

I stiffened. Was that a crack about how much better Poppy looked than me? The little stinker. I shot him the dirtiest look I could muster. He got the message and quickly added, "But I love her just the way she is."

Yeah. Ugly, fat, and feeble.

"I wouldn't wish my exercise regimen on any other human being," Poppy confessed. "My husband says I'm addicted to exercise. I just can't seem to stop myself."

"And I can't seem to start myself," I said. "We're going to be quite a team."

Poppy laughed at my wisecrack. Her laugh was more of a high-pitched cackle, and it made me cringe.

Note to self: Do not crack jokes around Poppy and risk hearing that sound again.

The courts were starting to fill up with other pickleball players. Poppy pointed to the one closest to where we were standing. "We'll use this one while I explain the basic rules of the game and you can both take practice shots." She handed each of us a paddle. "Get the feel of the paddle in your hand."

I walked toward the court as slowly as I could. Maybe Poppy would forget I was there while she concentrated on teaching Mike, and I could sneak out to the car.

"Come on, Carol. Sister Rose always told us that being successful starts with one small step in the right direction. Remember?"

I froze. "How do you know Sister Rose?"

I heard that awful laugh again.

"I was a year behind you at Mount St. Francis Academy. Sister Rose was my English teacher, too. Don't you remember me, Carol?"

I shook my head.

"Who were you before?" I blurted out.

Boy, was that a stupid thing to say. Way to go, Carol.

"I was born Portia Popovani. I'm Poppy Popovani-Hollister now. I insisted on keeping my birth name when I married Lou, so we put the two names together on the marriage license. Too bad nobody except me remembers that."

She gestured around the courts. "All this property belonged to my family, until my father left it to the town when he passed away.

"Everyone called my father Mr. P. You're the one who nicknamed me Poppy."

Chapter 9

Me: (sobbing my heart out, eyes swollen, nose red....) "I can't see you anymore. I'm not going to let you hurt me like this again!"
Trainer: "You only did one sit-up!"

"I remember you now," I said. "And your dad. He was a wonderful man."

"I never forgot you and your friends," Poppy said.

"I'm flattered."

"Don't be. I'm not giving you a compliment. At first, I thought you liked me when we were in high school. I thought you and your friends started calling me Poppy because of my last name. I was thrilled to have a nickname, like a lot of the other girls.

"Somebody finally clued me in that the real reason you and your gang nicknamed me Poppy was because I reminded you of a melting popsicle, a real drip. You were insulting me, and I didn't catch on."

I remembered how my friends and I secretly gave other students, especially younger ones, unflattering nicknames. I hate to admit this, but I was often the ringleader.

"I hope it's not too late to say I'm sorry." I wasn't sure if Poppy would accept my years-overdue apology or not.

"I suppose I owe you an apology, too," Poppy answered slowly. "Maybe you've forgotten when you worked as a maid for my family, but I never did."

I flushed scarlet as I remembered a long-ago summer when Claire and I worked at the beach for Poppy's family, one of Fairport's wealthiest. Claire got the good job: a tutor to the younger children. I was the one who had to do all the cleaning, dusting, and serving of meals to the family. The oldest daughter made my life a misery every chance she got. And now she was going to teach me to play pickleball.

"I feel better now that we've cleared the air," Poppy said.

"I do, too."

"How about you and Poppy shake hands, and then we'll have our pickleball lesson?" Mike suggested.

I gestured to Poppy, indicating it was entirely up to her if we continued.

"Oh, heck," Poppy said, holding out her arms. "Come here and give me a hug. Then I'll show you the basics of the game."

I was relieved we could let bygones be bygones. Or so I thought at the time.

Chapter 10

If a cookie falls on the floor and you pick it up, that's a squat, right?

The next thirty minutes were chock full of pickleball information I'd never remember, followed by my pathetic attempts to hit the ball over the net.

Mike, of course, caught onto the game immediately. The contrast between Mike and his aging mother was humiliating.

"No, no, Carol," Poppy corrected me for the umpteenth time. "Bring your paddle forward so you can connect with the ball when it's in front of you, before the ball reaches the net. Keep the wrist firm, not wobbly, and allow it to hinge backward just a bit to meet the ball squarely. Follow through to straighten your body and return to the ready position."

I held up my paddle and leaned forward to catch my breath. "Trust me, Poppy," I said, "I will never be in the ready position."

She ignored me and lobbed another shot over the net, which hit my right hip. It wasn't hard enough to make me scream. But it still hurt.

"Sorry," Poppy called. "My mistake."

She made a show of checking the time on her Rolex watch, no doubt hoping I'd notice the timepiece was encrusted in diamonds. "That's it for today, Carol. I have another student coming in five minutes. When do you want to come back for your next lesson?"

When hell freezes over.

"I'll have to let you know. I left my calendar at home."

I must have sounded sincere. Poppy nodded like she really believed me.

"You did great for your first time, Mom," Mike said as he handed Poppy his paddle. "That was quite a workout. How about lunch now? My treat."

I picked up my pace to put as much distance between me, Poppy, and the pickleball court as quickly as I could. "I guess I'll have to eat crow for the first course."

"I can guarantee you that's not on the menu where we're going. And you didn't play that badly for a beginner," Mike said.

"That's not what I mean. I'm talking about Poppy reminding me of how badly I treated her in high school." I managed a small smile. "I guess now you know your dear old mom isn't perfect."

"Nobody's perfect, Mom. But you're the perfect mom for me."

"Thanks, sweetie." I squeezed his hand.

"Now, let's eat." Instead of walking toward the parking lot, Mike took my arm and turned us in the other direction.

I had no idea where he was taking me for lunch, but at this point, it didn't matter. I desperately needed to clean up before I was presentable enough to be seen in public.

"I'm all sweaty, Mike. I don't want to be seen in public like this. Do we have time to go home so I can take a quick shower and put on some makeup?"

"You can clean up at the restaurant. I promise that you won't see anybody you know there except me."

I stood my ground like a stubborn child. "What if someone I don't know stares at me because I look so awful? That'd be even more embarrassing."

"Relax, Mom. We'll be the only guests in the restaurant."

Chapter 11

*I choked on a carrot at lunch today,
and all I could think of was,
"I bet a donut wouldn't have done this to me."*

Short of standing still and holding my breath until my face turned red and I passed out, nothing I did convinced Mike that I was not ready for prime-time viewing.

"I hope you're not this bossy when you have a date," I said as I reluctantly—and slowly—followed him to another part of the rec center.

We passed the men's and women's locker rooms, which I hadn't noticed before. Note to self: On the slim chance you ever return to play pickleball again, there's a women's room with a shower you can use after humiliating yourself again. Or, better yet, a place to hide before you humiliate yourself, and then sneak out from before anyone sees you.

At the end of the corridor, we reached a closed door. Mike stepped back. "After you," he said.

"You must be kidding. I can hear hammering inside." I pointed to a sign taped to the wall: Opening

Soon. "We'll have to find somewhere else for lunch, so I can go home and shower before we eat."

Mike dangled a key in front of my baby blues. "The sign doesn't apply to us."

"I hope you know what you're doing," I said as Mike inserted the key in the lock and the door opened. "I don't want somebody telling us we have to leave. You go in ahead of me."

We were greeted warmly by a man who appeared to be expecting us. "Your table is all ready, Mr. Andrews. Please, follow me."

"Surprise, Mom," Mike said, a huge grin on his face. "Welcome to Picklelilly's. It's my new restaurant. I named it after you."

Chapter 12

I like to hang out with people who make me forget to look at my phone.

I was so stunned, I was at a complete loss for words. (No snarky comments, please. It does happen on very rare occasions.) But I recovered quickly.

"I'm not a huge fan of pickles and my name isn't Lilly," I said. "I don't get it."

"Your name isn't Cosmo, either," Mike reminded me. "I named the Florida restaurant Cosmo's because you used to work at Cosmopolitan magazine. Naming this one Picklecarol's didn't work, but your favorite designer's first name is Lilly. It was the only thing I could figure out. Now do you understand?"

I understood, all right. And reacted by bursting into tears. I'm sure I embarrassed Mike in front of his employee, but I didn't care. This wasn't one of Mike's usual surprises. This was a shocker, but in a good way.

"I figured you might do that, so I came prepared," Mike said, handing me a tissue.

I pushed his hand away. "I don't need that. I'm okay now," I lied.

"I guess my little surprise worked too well," Mike said, holding out a chair for me to sit down. "I'm sorry, Mom."

"Calling this a little surprise is like calling Mount Everest a little hill." I gestured around the space. It was still a work in progress, but enough had been completed that I could tell it was going to be fabulous when it was finished. "How did you do all this from Florida? Or have you been sneaking in and out of Fairport without letting me know you were here?"

That was the only thing that made sense. The little stinker. I wasn't upset anymore. Now, I was furious.

"Did everyone know your secret except me? Dad, Jenny and Mark, all my friends? The entire neighborhood?" My voice was so loud by now that it even scared me.

Yes, I was overreacting. No need for anyone to point that out.

"Mom, please let me explain."

I sat back in my chair and folded my arms. "Go right ahead. I'm all ears."

"I got a tip from a friend that the town recreation commission was including a restaurant in the new pickleball facility and was currently accepting RFPs." At my quizzical look, Mike added, "RFP means Request for Proposals. Because the project is funded using public funds, the town had to go through a bidding process from interested vendors to award the contract for the restaurant. I'm a vendor. Or, rather my business is. Are you with me so far?"

I nodded. "Continue, please." Once again, Mike had referred to a mysterious friend.

"I put together a proposal and submitted it as quickly as I could. I didn't expect to get the project, but I figured it was worth a try. I was shocked when my company was awarded the contract."

Meanwhile, a glass of white wine had magically appeared in front of me. Even though I never drink alcoholic beverages until dinnertime, I took a tiny, tentative sip.

"This is delicious," I said, pushing the glass away. "But it's too early for me to drink wine. I'd rather have unsweetened iced tea."

I swear, the words were barely out of my mouth when the wine disappeared, replaced by an iced tea. "This is some service," I said. "I'm impressed."

"It helps that we're the only people here," Mike said.

"And that you're the boss," I said, smiling. "Go on. I can sip and listen at the same time."

"Things progressed very quickly from there. The rec commission members already had an idea of what they wanted. Something family-friendly for lunch but would also attract an adult audience later in the day and evening. I'm designing several different menus, and I'm not sure yet when the opening will be.

"Once construction's completed, all the town inspections take place. I have no idea how long they'll take. Plus, I still have to hire an entire staff. I've only hired two people so far. You just met Ted, my master chef who's doing double duty today as maître d'. I was lucky to find him."

Mike waved around the room. "The color scheme, décor, and furniture choices were all done by email and text. There's still a lot to do before we open.

"I swear, Mom, the first time I saw the whole thing in person was this morning. And you're Picklelilly's unofficial very first guest. I had to get written permission from the rec center commission and the health inspector to bring you for lunch today. Please don't be mad at me. You should be proud of me." He sat back in his chair and waited for me to respond.

Mike's explanation rang true. Mostly. Except for one thing.

"I just have one question. Can you explain why Stacy O'Keefe told me this morning that you were involved in a town rec center project?"

Mike looked confused. "Who's Stacy O'Keefe?"

"One of our younger neighbors. I assume she's the friend who tipped you off about the project."

"I don't know her," Mike said, shaking his head. "This is weird."

He looked so sincere I had to believe him.

"The way Stacy talked, I figured you'd already moved into a rental here, too. Now, I'm confused."

"I haven't even seen my new digs yet," Mike said. "My friend found a partly furnished sublet for me at her condo complex. I don't want to commit to anything long-term until I see how everything else works out. I figured you and I could look at it together after lunch. I'd value your input."

He frowned. "She must know Stacy."

I took another sip of iced tea, then decided to go for it. "You know I make it a point not to ask nosy questions about your personal life," I said.

Mike rolled his eyes. I ignored him.

"Your personal life is none of my business," I reiterated, "but you've mentioned a helpful friend several times in this conversation. So...."

"So?" Mike answered, pretending not to understand what I was getting at.

"So, it's natural for me to wonder who your very helpful friend is. Assuming you're comfortable telling me."

"All right, but don't get the wrong idea. She's just a friend.

"Her name is...."

At that exact moment, our food arrived. Just when we were getting somewhere.

Our lunch was absolutely delicious. Mike had arranged for a tasting plate of one of the restaurant's sample menus for me to try, including dessert.

Because I want to avoid any jealousy (or drooling) on anyone's part, you'll have to take my word for how good the food was. And don't bother to check social media for photos. I never take pictures of my food.

By the way, Mike has assured me that playing a game of pickleball won't be a prerequisite for dining at the restaurant.

Chapter 13

*The secret to a clean kitchen is simple.
Don't ever cook.*

After the previously mentioned delicious meal, I was ready to go home and take a nap.

Don't give in, Carol! What would you rather do, snooze or check out Mike's possible new digs?

My choice was a no brainer, especially if I also got to meet Mike's mysterious, helpful friend.

Mike excused himself for a few minutes to talk to his two employees, so I made a quick visit to the women's locker room to use the facilities. Just as I latched my stall for privacy, I heard the exterior door open and close, then two female voices in the middle of an argument.

"Mother, please, keep your voice down."

"Why? There's nobody else in here but us, and every time I want to talk to you these days, you shut down. I want to know why. I demand to know why. We've always been so close, Charlotte. Now you're pulling away from me."

The woman stopped talking, but I had heard enough to realize it was Poppy speaking to someone named Charlotte, a person I presumed was her daughter. I didn't want to eavesdrop on what was clearly a private and emotional conversation, but I was trapped. If I opened the stall door now, I'd embarrass them and myself.

"Mother, I'm not a child anymore. The only person in this so-called family who seems to get that is Tim. Thank goodness for him."

"My cousin's going behind my back and turning my own daughter against me?" Poppy screeched. "What happens between us is none of his business."

"As usual, you're missing my entire point and choosing to lash out at Tim instead. For once in your life, listen to what I'm saying!"

The daughter was so angry, I cringed. Thank goodness neither of my children ever talked to me like that.

"All right, I'm listening," Poppy snapped.

"What I'm trying to do is remind you that I'm twenty-seven years old now, not a little girl. I have a decent job and my own condo. I'm entitled to have a private life, and it's totally up to me whether I share anything about it with you. I'm leaving now. I have an appointment."

"Your father and I have talked, and we both agree that you should move back home where you belong."

"You and Dad have talked? And you've both agreed? You expect me to believe that? Give me a break. The two of you haven't had a civil conversation in years, much less agreed on anything. You're not even living together! I'm out of here."

I heard the door slam again, then Poppy sobbing.

My back was starting to hurt from staying in one position for too long, and I was afraid I was going to sneeze. I wondered where Mike thought I was.

You have to stay inside here until Poppy leaves. So what if it's a very small space. Don't think about that.

It seemed like I'd been trapped for at least half an hour, but it was probably only a few minutes. I finally heard water running, and I assumed Poppy was making herself look presentable.

There was a knock on the door, then I heard a man yell, "Poppy, we're waiting for you so we can start the next match. What's taking you so long?"

"Be right out," Poppy answered.

"Well, hurry up."

I held my breath. Was she finally leaving?

"Ready or not, here I come," she called out. I heard the door open, then slam shut.

Hallelujah.

Chapter 14

I'm at the age where I appreciate a nice hand railing.

I thought you were lost," my scowling son said. "Where did you go? I've been waiting for you by the front door for fifteen minutes."

"Would you believe me if I said I'd gone back to the court to get in a some more practice?"

Mike laughed. "Not in a million years."

"How about if I told you I was in the women's locker room and had trouble getting out of one of the stalls?"

"Do you mean you got stuck in there?"

"Sort of," I said.

"I have to report what happened to the maintenance people right away so it can be fixed before opening day. Which stall was it?"

"Mike, let me explain...."

"Never mind. I'll have them all checked. Give me a sec to find the maintenance man. I'll be right back."

"But...."

Good lord. Talk about jumping to conclusions before knowing all the facts.

Who do you think Mike got that trait from, Carol? Not from his father, that's for sure.

I hate it when one of my very few character flaws pops into my consciousness without any prompting. Truth to tell, even the dogs give me the stink eye sometimes for the same reason.

Mike finally joined me, his phone glued to his ear. "I know we're late," he said. "I'm sorry."

He grabbed my arm with his free hand, pushed open the door, and guided me to the parking lot a lot faster than I thought was necessary.

"My mom and I are on our way right now," Mike continued. "I promise, we'll be there in less than ten minutes."

He paused for a minute, then said, "Me, too. See you soon."

I couldn't help but notice the goofy grin on my son's face as he ended the conversation. My son was definitely, positively, without a doubt, totally bonkers in love. And I was going to meet her in less than ten minutes.

Chapter 15

We all know mirrors don't lie. I'm just glad mine doesn't laugh.

I caught a quick glimpse of myself in the car mirror as Mike hustled me into the car. It was not a pretty sight. As a matter of fact, if we were headed to a Halloween party instead of Mike's new rental, I was sure I'd win the "Guest Who Most Resembles a Witch" prize. Ugh.

I'd always fantasized about the woman who'd convince Mike to settle down and trade in his bachelor life for one of marital bliss. Would I like her? Would she like me? What if–gasp–she hated me on sight and convinced my only son to forsake his family in favor of embracing her?

I suddenly realized that Mike's new love wouldn't be coming into our lives as a solo act. She'd bring along a family that Jim and I would be forced to interact with on holidays, birthdays, and other special occasions. What if they didn't like us? What if we didn't like them?

And what if Mike and this girl had children? It's common knowledge that the girl's parents are tops in the grandparents pecking order. What if we (I) were forbidden to have any relationship at all with Mike's children? My heart would break. Especially since we (I) had so much experience already as CJ's grandparents.

Don't go looking for trouble, Carol. Besides, maybe you're wrong, and this girl's just a casual friend. If she's a lot more, then just be happy for Mike that he's finally found someone to share his life with.

I promised myself that I'd be the same mature, loving, supportive parent I'd always been. No matter what.

Chapter 16

As I get older, I realize how important it is to stay positive. For example, the other day I fell down the stairs. Instead of getting upset, I just thought, "Wow! That's the fastest I've moved in years!"

"We're here, Mom."

I snapped out of my stupor as Mike drove into a gated community that looked very familiar.

"I know where we are," I said, surprising the heck out of my son.

"How could you know this is where my sublet is? Even I've never been here before."

"I didn't know about the sublet, silly. Despite what you may think, I'm not a mind reader. Or a stalker."

Mike laughed. "Jenny and I were always afraid you were a mind reader when we were trying to hide something. You always caught on. How did you do that?"

"Mind reading is another of my many maternal superpowers," I said.

Then I grinned. "Mary Alice lives in that unit," I said, pointing to one on the opposite side of the parking lot. "I've been here frequently to visit her."

Mike shook his head. "Of course you have."

I swear, my car engine had barely stopped when Mike jumped out of the car, waving.

This is it! Your future possible daughter-in-law! OMG! I'm so nervous!

I bent my head down and fumbled with my seat belt to give them a little privacy to say hello. After all, it wasn't my business if my adult son gave this woman a passionate kiss.

Okay, I snuck a quick peek. Trust me, neither of them noticed.

Thank goodness they also didn't notice my klutzy exit from the car, which almost ended with my doing a face plant in the parking lot. They were too occupied with each other. In my own defense, I always hang on to the steering wheel for a little extra balance when I'm driving. As I said before, I'm not used to exiting on the passenger side. That's my story and I'm sticking to it.

The couple started to walk away, and I realized Mike had completely forgotten about me.

Remind him you're here, but don't embarrass him, Carol.

I whipped out my cell phone and pretended I was talking to Nancy without turning the phone on. I was running out of things to say when I finally got my son's attention.

"I'm sorry, Mom. I didn't forget you were here. I was getting more details about the rental from Charli." He grabbed my hand. "Come and say hello."

I raised my fingers in a "just the sec" gesture. "Give me two seconds to finish talking to Nancy, and I'll be right with you."

I waited a few beats, then said, "Okay, Nancy. That's great. Let's talk more when I get home."

I ended my pretend phone call and put a big smile on my face. An adorable young woman was coming toward me with an equally big smile on her face. Okay, good sign. We were both smiling.

Mike looked nervous, and I realized he was afraid I wouldn't like her. I couldn't smile any bigger without looking truly stupid so I extended both hands and grabbed hers. "It's nice to meet you, Charli. I hope we're going to be good friends."

"That's so nice of you, thank you," Charli said. "I feel like I already know you."

She dangled keys and said, "Let's go check out the rental to see if it'll work. My neighbor Taylor took a job in London, but she didn't want to sell her unit. She asked me to find a temporary tenant, and I thought of Mike right away. I hope you like it, Mike."

From the expression on Mike's face, the unit could have been a complete disaster and he wouldn't have cared.

I'm embarrassed to admit that I was secretly hoping he'd decide against renting the condo and use his old bedroom whenever he was in town. Stupid and selfish, I know.

But the condo was perfect for him and even I loved it. Charli mentioned that the complex even had a private swimming pool, which was a surprise to me. Mary Alice had never mentioned that.

I wondered if guests of current residents were able to use it. Then I remembered how terrible I currently looked in a bathing suit and decided not to ask.

"Where do I sign?" Mike said. "I don't want to take a chance on losing this beauty." I wasn't sure if he was referring to the condo rental or Charli. Maybe both.

"Taylor trusted me to find the right tenant, and you're it, Mike. Now all you have to do is sign some papers in the office."

"Let's do that right now," Mike said. "Mom, do you mind hanging around here a little longer while I take care of this?"

"Not at all," I said. "Just toss me my keys and I'll wait for you there."

"You might be more comfortable waiting in the condo than the car," Charli said. "I'm not sure how long this is going to take."

"I'll be fine in my car."

Watching Mike and Charli walk away together, I realized what a nice couple they made. And she seemed like a very thoughtful young woman, even if her first name was a little unusual.

And yet…something was bugging me about her. She seemed familiar, though I couldn't figure out why. I knew I'd never seen her before.

Maybe she went to high school with Mike. You didn't know all his classmates. She's an intelligent, bright young woman and she makes your son happy. That's all you need to know, Carol.

Then, it hit me. Charli could be a nickname for Charlotte. OMG! What if Mike's girlfriend Charli and Poppy's daughter Charlotte were the same person?

Before I keeled over right there on the spot, I reminded myself that Mike and I had met Poppy together today. He was the logical one to notice a resemblance between Poppy and Charli, because he already knew what Charli looked like. I slapped myself (figuratively) and ordered my imagination to knock it off.

I wondered if there was a patron saint for people with overactive imaginations I could call on for help, so I checked it out on my phone. The only one that seemed close was St. Francis De Sales, who's the patron saint of writers and journalists. Since Jim frequently says that today's journalists are embellishing news stories to make them more dramatic, I decided to ask him for help rather than bother my usual go-to guy, St. Jude, the patron saint of hopeless causes. I closed my eyes and sent up a quick prayer, which made me feel a little better.

And suddenly, I had a plan of action. It wasn't a perfect plan, but it didn't involve my interfering directly in Mike's life. The important word in the previous sentence is "directly." Please remember it in case Mike gets mad at me and I have to defend myself. Feeling better than I had a few minutes ago, I settled back in the driver's seat, closed my eyes, and enjoyed a little nap.

After a long farewell between the besotted twosome (which woke me up), Mike opened the driver's side door and gestured me back to the passenger's seat again.

"Your dad seems like a great guy," he called out to Charli. "I'll call you later." He adjusted the seat and rear-view mirror again, and I pretended not to mind.

However, when we got home, I planned to hide the extra car key in my underwear drawer.

Chapter 17

Old age is just walking around all day muttering things like: "Where did I put my phone?" "Why did I come in here?" "Did I already take my pill?"

Mike had just given me the perfect opening to ask a few questions about Charli's parents. If I was lucky, I'd have some answers before we got home.

"Let's take a quick ride over to the beach before we go home," Mike suggested after he checked his phone for texts. "It's such a nice day and we're so close. I can spare a little more time before I have to get back to Picklelilly's."

"Great idea. It's like you're reading my mind. I love going to the beach before it gets crowded."

"I remember that, Mom. Jenny and I were always annoyed when we'd get to the beach and you wouldn't stay because you said it was too crowded."

"As I recall, dear," I said as Mike maneuvered into my favorite kind of parking space—the ones I can drive directly through when I'm leaving instead of needing to back up first—"the reason the beach was so crowded by the time we got there was because you were such a slow poke getting ready to leave the house. Forgive me if I hold you partly responsible for my then-cranky mood. Your sister and I wasted hours in the car waiting for you in those days."

"Hours?" Mike questioned. "Me thinks my mother is exaggerating."

"Well, that's what it seemed like to us."

"Okay, Mom. I get it. I'm now so punctual that I'm usually early."

"I'm delighted to hear that my motherly chiding had a positive effect."

We sat quietly and looked at the water for several minutes, then we both started to speak at once.

"After you," Mike said, gesturing me to continue speaking. "I know you want to talk about the same thing I do."

"You mentioned Charli's father a little while ago, and I wondered if Dad and I knew her family."

I held my breath, most of me dreading his answer.

Mike swiveled in his seat and faced me. "Her family. Hmm. That's a new approach for you. I was expecting you to give me the third degree about what's going on between us before I drop you back home."

"I didn't realize you were dropping me anywhere," I said, wondering if I'd ever be able to drive my own car again. "I'm very fragile at my advanced age, so please be gentle. And speaking of age, you're an adult and your private life is just that—private and none of my business." I mustered up a sincere look. "I repeat, none of my business."

Mike burst out laughing. "That may be true, Mom, but that's never stopped you before. Besides, I value your opinion. It's important to me."

"How about we take a quick walk on the beach?"

"Good idea," I said. "But not too quick. I'm more the leisurely strolling type, especially after the unexpected exercise I had today."

"Followed by a delicious lunch," Mike reminded me, opening the car door and taking my hand like the gentleman I raised him to be. "Let's walk to the benches in front of the pavilion. Unless that's too far for you," he added, grinning.

"I believe I can hobble that far."

Let Mike guide the conversation, Carol. And don't interrupt him with a thousand questions when he does. You know that's one of your worst faults.

We strolled in companionable silence for about eight hours – just kidding. It was probably less than two minutes. I wondered if my darling son was testing me to see how long I could hold out before giving him what he lovingly called the "third degree."

Well, if that was what he was doing, I wouldn't say a word. Even if it killed me.

He finally broke the silence. "You liked Charli, didn't you, Mom?"

Careful, Carol. Don't be too enthused. Remember, what you really want to know is who her parents are before this romance goes too far.

"She seemed very nice."

"Do you think Dad will like her?"

Whoa. That question came at me from left field.

"I don't speak for him, as you know," I answered carefully. I think I saw Mike roll his eyes, but I could be wrong.

"How about Jenny and Mark?" he continued. "Do you think they'll like her?"

I stopped, turned, and faced Mike. "I have no idea. I talked to her for only a few minutes, but she seemed nice. As I already said."

"It's important to me that everybody in the family like her. Because I think I'm going to marry her."

Chapter 18

I live my life with no regrets. It's a bonus for having a faulty memory.

We arrived home much too soon after Mike dropped that bombshell on me. My brain must have also been on another planet because Mike had to nudge me and point to our house.

"This concludes today's adventures, Mom. I don't see Dad's car, so you have some time to rest up after my surprises. I hope you're happy about all of them. From the look on your face, though, I guess I sprang too many on you at once."

"I only want you to be happy," I said, evading a direct answer to what sounded to me like an about-to-become-engaged announcement.

Mike leaned over and kissed me on the cheek. "I know that, Mom. You always have."

"When are you planning to share all your news with the rest of the family?"

Mike turned the car key, and the engine roared to life. "I'll take care of sharing the restaurant news. The other part is just between us for now. Especially since I haven't even asked Charli yet. Although I'm sure she'll say yes."

My entire body was flooded with relief. Or maybe it was a delayed hot flash. At my age, it's hard to be sure.

I was also able to exit my car without tripping, which was a miracle. The Good Lord was clearly on my side right now.

"One more thing, Mom. I have a ton of work at Picklelilly's, so if you're tired, go to bed. I don't know how late I'll be."

I nodded, which meant nothing. I'm his mother, and I'll always wait up. I'd probably watch a movie until Mike came home tonight, but he didn't need to know that. Once a mom, always a mom.

"And don't say a word about Charli!"

Mike roared out of the driveway in my car.

Chapter 19

I'm always surprised when a liar's pants don't catch on fire.

I don't keep secrets from my husband.

I bet some of you are either rolling your eyes or snickering, so permit me to explain.

Jim had a mild heart issue a few years ago that landed him in the hospital. Perhaps some of you didn't know that. In that case, I forgive you for doubting my veracity. As a loving wife who wants to keep her equally loving husband around as long as possible, I keep peace in the house by carefully editing anything that could upset him or make him angry. I provide ongoing support for his mental and physical well-being through my creative twists on reality. I think of myself as a medical professional without a medical license. However, I do have a marriage license, and after over forty years of marriage, I have a good idea of what might set him off. Although every now and then, he surprises me. (Not in a good way.)

I really wanted to tell Jim every detail of today's adventure with Mike, but I had been ordered to keep my motormouth shut when it came to his new love interest. I wasn't entirely clear on what I could say about Picklelilly's either. What if Jim was upset that our son had told me things before sharing the same news with dear old dad?

I prayed that I'd give Jim enough information so he was in the family loop without breaking my son's confidence. What I didn't want—besides my husband keeling over in front of me—was for him to interrogate me for more details like he was researching an article for our town newspaper.

I was so concerned I'd inadvertently let something slip that I didn't even share my day with Lucy and Ethel, both of whom registered their displeasure by shooting me dirty looks and making themselves comfortable on our king-sized bed. (Out of courtesy, the dogs usually wait for at least one human to get there first.)

You can do this, Carol. You've had years of practice.

I wished I believed me, but I knew I was lying.

Before I had a chance to come up with one of my creative approaches to the truth, I heard a car in the driveway. Yikes. Not only was I plan-less, I had no idea what we were having for dinner. And I still really needed a shower!

Knowing my husband's priorities, he wouldn't care if I hadn't showered. But he would care—a lot—if I hadn't even started to prepare his evening repast.

I sent up a quick prayer for a miracle to St Lawrence of Rome, the patron saint of cooks. I'm not going to tell you why he was given that assignment because it's so horrible. Check it out for yourself if you have a sturdy stomach and don't mind gory details.

I opened the refrigerator door and got a big surprise. To paraphrase a much-loved Christmas story, "What to my wondering eyes did appear?" No, not a miniature sleigh and eight tiny reindeer. A turkey meatloaf surrounded by fresh carrots and potatoes, ready to pop in the oven to cook. And I didn't remember making it.

Chapter 20

*I was watching a television show and the host was listing all these great things to do.
Then I realized I was watching a religious channel and he was listing sins.*

OMG. Was I losing my precarious hold on sanity? Had the visitor from the other side, who'd turned my life upside down a few months ago, made another appearance? (If you don't know who I'm talking about, we'll chat another time.)

I slammed the refrigerator door shut and took a moment to compose myself. Was it possible I was hallucinating? I'd read that it's possible for a person to look at an object without the brain registering what she's seeing. Could the same phenomenon work in reverse?

I opened the refrigerator again, and the meatloaf was still there. As I lifted the pan to move it to the oven, I noticed a scribbled note tucked underneath.

"I was checking out coupons from the local supermarket and found this recipe. It looked pretty easy, so I thought I'd surprise you and try to make it.

I hope it tastes good, but otherwise we can order takeout. Jim."

I was so surprised, I almost dropped the meatloaf right on the floor.

"I hope it's okay that I made dinner," Jim said. My husband was standing at the kitchen door, an unsure look on his face. "I expected to be home before you so I could put the meatloaf in the oven."

"Of course it's okay. This is the nicest thing you've ever done for me."

Jim wiggled his eyebrows, which made me laugh. "The nicest thing? Are you sure about that, Carol?"

"Okay, one of the nicest things. But what, pray tell, inspired your sudden burst of domesticity?"

"I figured with the busy day Mike had planned for you, deciding what to cook for dinner tonight would be the last thing on your mind. Did you have a fun playing pickleball?"

"I wasn't too horrible, considering this was my first time," I said. "And how did you know Mike was taking me to play pickleball?"

Jim assumed a look of innocence and failed. "I guess he mentioned it to me last night. I honestly don't remember." He gestured toward the meatloaf. "Don't we have to preheat the oven first?"

"Never mind about that," I said, pulling out a chair and pointing to it. "Sit. Now. And talk."

"I admit that Mike told me last week he was surprising you with a pickleball lesson, and he asked me to keep it a secret. I didn't want to spoil your surprise."

"Hmm. How thoughtful of you to do that. Thank you."

"I was glad to do it," Jim said. "I'm glad you had fun."

"I didn't say I had fun playing pickleball," I corrected. "I said I wasn't too horrible at it. It was an experience I plan to avoid for the rest of my life. If I change my mind, you'll be the first to know.

"I have another question," I continued, following my husband into our bedroom. If he thought he was off the hook with me, he was sadly mistaken. "Is it possible you knew about Mike's new restaurant for an entire week and kept that a secret too? Fess up. It's true confessions time."

Jim sat down on our bed and faced me. "All right, I'll tell you. But you have to promise not to be mad at me. Or tell Mike that I squealed."

It took every ounce of self-control, but I nodded, which encouraged Jim to continue.

"I've known about Mike's restaurant plans for two months. I'm the one who tipped him off when the first bidding process fell apart."

Chapter 21

Wife: "I have a bag full of used clothing I'd like to donate."
Husband: "Why not just throw it in the trash? That's much easier."
Wife: "But there are poor starving people who could really use all these clothes."
Husband: "Honey, anyone who fits into your clothes is not starving."
Husband is recovering from a head injury now.

"Say something, Carol. Don't just sit there and give me the silent treatment."

Bearing in mind that I keep things from him on a regular basis (for his own good), I chose my response with care. "I'm glad you're telling me now. Thank you. You and Mike certainly love to surprise me."

Jim looked relieved. "You can't imagine how hard it was for me to keep this from you. Lou Hollister, he's the chairman of the town recreation commission, mentioned at an FBA meeting that the original contract to run the new rec center restaurant had fallen through. They were desperate to find a replacement pronto."

At my quizzical look, Jim clarified, "Fairport Business Association.

"Lou cornered me after the meeting and asked about Mike. He remembered that Mike owned a restaurant in Miami and suggested he submit a proposal to run the restaurant here. I figured there was no way Mike could handle running two restaurants simultaneously, but I shared Mike's contact information with Lou anyway. The two connected, and Mike ended up winning the contract."

"The chairman of the recreation commission is Lou Hollister," I repeated.

"Yes. He's a heck of a nice guy."

I just sat there, trying to process this new information on top of everything else that had happened today.

"Is that all you have to say, Carol? Aren't you going to scream at me or cry because I've kept this news a secret for so long?"

I looked at my husband and didn't say a single word.

"I haven't been inside the restaurant if that makes you feel any better. Mike wanted you to see it first. He also said he named it in your honor, but he completely lost me when he tried to explain why."

I pushed my hurt feelings aside (temporarily). Right now, I had other priorities. "I'm trying to behave like an adult. It would be nice if you supported my efforts."

Jim looked skeptical, and I couldn't blame him. After forty plus years of marriage, we've both developed predictable behavior patterns.

"What do you know about Lou Hollister? Is he married? Does he have a family?"

"I know Lou has a company that specializes in building and managing high-end condos. But I don't know anything about his personal life. Why?"

"Hollister isn't a very common surname. I think I met his wife today at the rec center. She was my pickleball teacher."

Jim laughed so hard he had tears running down his cheeks.

"What's so funny?"

"You are. I just had an image of you engaging in any sports activity whatsoever, especially one that involves running...." He stopped speaking (and laughing) when he saw my expression.

It took every ounce of self-control for me not to sock him. After all, he did make the meatloaf.

Chapter 22

Advice to husbands everywhere: Laughing at your own mistakes lengthens your life. Laughing at your wife's shortens it.

All things considered, Jim and I had a pleasant dinner, which translates to my complimenting him on his first try at making meatloaf (it wasn't too bad) and suggesting that if he made it again (heaven forbid!), he should use the measuring spoon to portion out the spices correctly.

"I didn't know where you kept it, so I had to guess" he said defensively.

I pointed to the measuring spoon, clearly visible on a counter next to the spice rack.

"Oh. I guess I didn't notice it."

I resisted from making one of my usual snarky comments. Points for me, right?

"Did Mike say when he'd be home tonight?" Jim asked as he rearranged the dirty dishes in the dishwasher to his exacting standards. I hate it when he does that, but in the interests of behaving like an adult (better late than never, right?), I didn't try to stop him. If loading a dishwasher ever becomes an Olympic event, Jim's a cinch to win the gold medal.

"He wasn't sure."

"Did he mention when he's going back to Florida? I don't know how he'll be able to manage two restaurants at opposite ends of the country at the same time."

"I'm sure he already has a plan in place," I said, crossing my fingers so Jim couldn't see them. Mike was a seat-of-the-pants kind of guy when he was younger, but, as I constantly remind myself, he's an adult now and capable of making adult decisions.

"I hope his plan includes getting a place of his own in Fairport," Jim said. "It wouldn't be good to have him living with us again. He'd be coming and going at all hours of the day and night. We'd never get any sleep."

I figured I was safe to mention that Mike already had a new place to live, as long as I skipped any reference to his new lady love.

"As a matter of fact, this afternoon Mike took me to see a condo he liked. I thought it was very nice. Mary Alice lives in the same complex."

"Those condos are pretty pricey because they're near the beach," Jim said. "Since he'll only be living here part-time, Mike should rent in a less expensive part of town. I hope he hasn't signed a lease yet."

You're just annoyed because Mike didn't ask your advice first. Not that you'd ever admit it.

"Mary Alice loves it there," I said. "I think Carla Grimaldi has a condo in the same complex. Even if Mike's only in Fairport part time, he should live in a nice place. Who knows? Maybe he and our First Selectwoman will become good buddies."

"I think Lou Hollister's company built that complex," Jim said. "Maybe Lou could get Mike a great deal." He made a note on his phone.

I knew Jim wanted to help, but in this case, his help would only complicate things.

"The unit we saw today is a sublet while the owner is away," I clarified. "Mike isn't committing to a long-term lease. He's being smart about this, the way you would be. If he decides on a long-term commitment, I'm sure he'd involve you, the way he did in the restaurant deal."

I waited a beat, then added, "The one you didn't share with me."

"Okay, okay. I get it and you're right. How often are you going to remind me of how I screwed up?"

"I have no idea. But I do know who's cleaning up the kitchen for the rest of the week. I'll check on your progress later." I rose from my chair like a queen from her throne, kissed my husband on the top of his head, and exited before he could respond.

Chapter 23

Without coffee, I'm always going into rooms and forgetting why I went in there.
With coffee, I still don't remember, but at least I have something to sip while I'm trying to figure it out.

While my husband continued his domestic chores, I took advantage of my temporary solitude by finally taking a long shower. Lord knows, I needed it. I knew I'd be stiff in the morning after today's unusually strenuous activity.

I never understood why anyone preferred to soak in a bathtub. After a few minutes, the bath water starts to cool, so you have to add more water and then more water and pretty soon, unless some of the water is drained out of the tub, you'll have a flooded bathroom. What fun is that?

Now that I'd gathered more facts about a family I never knew existed before today, I had to figure out some way to get on Poppy's good side (assuming she had one). Mike's had his heart broken before. I didn't want to be responsible for another one.

To be completely honest with all of you, I was still reeling over Poppy's earlier accusations of my cruel high school behavior. True, I had apologized, but I wasn't sure that was enough to smooth over our relationship. I hoped Poppy had really put our past history where it belonged—in the past—or my son would never have his happy ending with the (current) girl of his dreams.

I stewed about a variety of groveling solutions while I put on my favorite pair of Lilly Pulitzer pajamas, the ones I got at the thrift shop for only five bucks several years ago.

Wearing Lilly usually cheers me up, but not today. Nor did the fact that my steamy bathroom completely hid the chubby body and face of the old woman I see in the mirror every day.

You always thought you were such a nice person, Carol. How could you have been so cruel to a classmate?

What if Poppy started to spread the word around town about what a mean person I was? My whole family and all my dearest friends would turn against me, and I couldn't blame them.

A rational person might argue that, since Poppy had kept mum about my horrible behavior for several decades, the chances of her spreading the news now was pretty remote. Unfortunately, I am not a rational person in moments of stress. This whole day had been one anxious moment after another, so I hope you'll cut me some slack.

What really bugged me was that I had absolutely no memory of the interaction that Poppy claims scarred her for life. Did I treat other people this badly and block out the memories because I was subconsciously ashamed of my behavior?

"Do you think I'm a terrible person?" I asked the dogs, now snoozing comfortably on the bed. Lucy, my number one canine critic, shook her head and Ethel licked my hand. Honest to goodness, that's what they did.

"Thanks for the vote of confidence," I whispered, hugging them both. "You two know me better than most humans and love me in spite of my faults. Just like Nancy, Mary Alice, and even Claire."

It suddenly dawned on me that I wasn't in this situation all by myself. Maybe I was the mouthiest one in our foursome, but there were three other people who would have been part of Poppy's so-called humiliation in one way or another.

While I was waiting up for Mike to come home (assuming he was coming home and not having a sleepover at his new condo), instead of stewing about my possible guilt, I could text my pals to see what they remembered about our high school shenanigans. Brilliant.

Then I realized my brilliant idea wasn't so brilliant.

Intruding on Nancy's anniversary trip with Bob was out, even if I was her maid of honor. Claire might still be awake, but Mary Alice's schedule varies, depending on whether she's doing private duty nursing or not. And she gets very grouchy if anyone wakes her up when she's enjoying a few hours of precious sleep.

Rats. I knew I'd never get any rest tonight with Poppy's accusation weighing on my mind. Or if I did, I'd probably have nightmares. I wondered if I could draft a text to everybody tonight, save it, and not send it until tomorrow morning. I had no idea how to do that, but with any luck I'd figure it out.

I tiptoed out of the bedroom so I wouldn't wake my snoring husband (dishwasher re-loading really wears him out), then walked quietly into our rarely used living room, cell phone clutched in my hand. The dogs followed and made themselves comfortable on my matching wing chairs. Lucy gave me a doggy stare, daring me to shoo them off.

"I'll let you stay this time," I said aloud. "Don't get used to it. Right now, I have more important things to do. And don't interrupt me. I have to think about how to word this text without sounding like a desperate housewife."

I heard the kitchen door open, then close, which derailed my tenuous train of thought. Then, a familiar voice. "It's me, Mom. Don't call 911. I figured you'd still be up waiting for me, so I got home as early as I could."

My son joined me in the living room and sat next to me on the coach. "For the record, Mom, I never thought of you as a desperate housewife."

"I wasn't waiting up for you," I said. "I had to send a text, and I didn't want to disturb your father."

"Yeah, like pushing buttons on a cell phone would wake him up," Mike said. "Not." He reached out and rubbed the dogs' heads. "I miss being met by these two. They're always glad to see me."

"Are you hungry?" I asked, hoisting myself to my feet and prepared to whip up some sort of miracle meal in the kitchen. "Do you want something to eat before you go to bed. You look tired."

"Charli made dinner for me, Mom. She's a pretty good cook."

"That's nice," I said, ignoring the snarky comments that had popped into my head.

"Did you tell Dad about your day?" Mike asked. "How did he react when you told him you'd played pickleball."

"As expected," I answered. "He thought it was hilarious.

"I also told him about your renting a condo. I hope that's okay. But I didn't mention anything about Charli, per your request."

"Thanks, Mom. If everything goes the way I want, I'll be introducing her to the rest of the family soon." He yawned. "I need some sleep or I'll be no good for work tomorrow."

I gave him a gentle kiss and turned him in the direction of the stairs. "Sleep well. Do you want me to wake you at any special time tomorrow morning?"

"I'll set the alarm on my phone." Mike blew me a kiss. "Good night, Mom. See you in the morning."

After a quick romp around the yard (the dogs, not me), I banished all negative thoughts from my head and crept into bed.

Chapter 24

If I waited until I had all my ducks in a row to do something, I'd never get anything done.

I tried to sleep. I really did. But sleep wouldn't come. I was wide awake, like I'd just swallowed an entire pot of coffee. Plus, one of the bedroom windows was open too much. I hate that.

Suddenly I heard a noise and poked my snoring husband. "Wake up. I hear someone walking around outside."

Jim, of course, pretended he didn't hear me. What a stinker.

I sat up in bed so I could see what was going on, which was a very bad idea. Every inch of my body was sore, including some areas I never knew I had.

Note to self: This is what happens when you exercise only once a decade.

Bright lights flashed into the bedroom windows, and I heard a car racing down our driveway toward Old Fairport Turnpike. "Someone's stealing my car!" I yelled. "Call the police now and report it while I see if I can catch him."

Jim grabbed me and pulled me down on the bed. The sudden movement darn near killed me.

"Relax, Carol. Nobody's stealing your car. It's probably just Mike getting home."

"The car was headed away from the house, not toward it. And Mike's been home for a while."

"Then he's going out for some reason. Calm down, for heaven's sake. It's the middle of the night." Jim yawned. "Or maybe you were dreaming."

"Something's wrong. A mother always knows."

My heart was beating so fast that I couldn't catch my breath. "I'm having a heart attack."

I sat up in bed again (I only winced a little bit this time, in case you were concerned), switched on a nearby lamp, and glared at my husband. "I'm having a heart attack and you don't care. My mother was right about you. I should have listened to her and never married you. I want a divorce."

"Carol," Jim said in that patient tone of voice he uses that drives me nuts, "your mother loved me. You know she did."

"She loved you because you fixed anything in her house that she asked you to, not because she thought you were such a wonderful person."

I grabbed the ratty bathrobe that the dogs were sleeping on and wrapped it around me, earning a dirty look from Lucy, which I ignored. My heart was beating normally now, not that I intended to tell Jim that.

"I'm going to read my new library book. If you hear a loud thud or a scream from the direction of the office, I hope it doesn't disturb your sleep. I'll try to collapse quietly."

Jim yawned. "Whatever you say, Carol." He leaned over and turned off the light. "Good night."

I grabbed my phone and the book, waiting for Jim to try to stop me.

He didn't, of course. And who could blame him. My raving childish behavior hadn't gotten me anywhere. Maybe Jim was right—I had been dreaming. There was only one way to find out.

I snuck out of the bedroom, opened the side door and counted the parked cars. It didn't take me long. There should have been two, but there was only one. My car was missing. Tire tracks in our driveway confirmed a turnaround and a speedy exit. And the gate to Old Fairport Turnpike, which we always keep closed to prevent a doggie escape, was wide open.

Chapter 25

Just once, I want the prompt for user name and password to say, "Close enough."

I forced myself to think of the situation reasonably. Despite my disagreeing with Jim a few minutes ago, I knew he was right. Mike had taken my car (again) and driven off into the night. I hoped that in the morning he'd tell me the reason for his speedy exit.

Did he and Charli have a fight, and he was desperate to apologize? Or had my possible future daughter-in-law texted him professing her undying love and devotion, and he had rushed to her side?

I nodded my head and agreed with myself. Both scenarios made perfect sense, especially if he was as crazy about her as he claimed to be.

Face it, Carol, if you go to bed now, you'll only toss and turn for hours and keep Jim awake. Read your library book for a while. Or check your email.

If Mike came home and found me reading a book instead of in bed like a normal person, I'd tell him I was in pain and having trouble sleeping. I knew he'd figure out why without my adding any details.

Then I had a fabulous idea. I'd take advantage of my temporary insomnia and do an internet search about pickleball. I was confident (okay, hopeful) that my thirst for knowledge would be helpful if/when I subjected myself to another lesson. Perhaps I could even find some online tips about dealing with pickleball pain.

Sometimes I marvel at my own brilliance.

I woke up the computer and ignored the siren call of my email. Instead, I typed "Pickleball" in the search engine and was overwhelmed with all the sites I could explore. If I checked them all, I wouldn't get to bed for two solid days!

For those of you who have no clue about the sport, I am happy to share my newly acquired knowledge. Pickleball is sort of a combination of tennis, badminton, and table tennis. It's played on a badminton-sized court with a net, like tennis, uses a paddle instead of a racquet, and a plastic ball with holes. Despite its rather cutesy name, the sport requires a general overall level of fitness and became really popular during the pandemic when people sought safety in outdoor activities.

My general overall level of fitness is zero, but I was sure that's not what the post meant.

Moving on.

I scrolled aimlessly for a few minutes, then clicked on a medical website, "How to Play Pickleball Safely." Please don't suggest that I should have read this post before I went on my adventure with Mike earlier today. In case your memory is as bad as mine, allow me to remind you (gently) that my dear son gave me no hint about where we going and what we'd be doing before the start of yesterday's adventure.

For those of you who are into statistics, I'll share a few tidbits from WebMD. An insurance company quoted in the site's 2023 post predicted that, by the end of that calendar year, pickleball was projected to result in 67,000 hospital emergency department visits, 366,000 outpatient visits, 8,800 outpatient surgeries, and 4,700 hospitalizations.

I stopped reading the post at that point. Did I really want to subject myself to more of this so-called "sport" and hasten my journey into infirmity and old age?

When I find myself in a desperate situation, I always look for a saint who specializes in my emergency-of-the-moment. I did another internet search and, to my horror, found there was no saint assigned to pickleball! I was on my own, unless I asked St. Jude for help again.

I decided not to risk it, fearing that I might need him later for something really serious, like discovering another murdered body. Since Jim retired several years ago, that's been happening to me with alarming frequency. In case you didn't know that.

Correction: Jim was the one who discovered the first dead body and was almost arrested for murder.

Naturally, it was up to me to prove his innocence, not that I'm bragging. Any other loving wife who found herself in a similar situation would have done the same, right? Of course, right. And you know the old saying, one murdered body leads to another.

Chapter 26

Kids today don't know how easy they have it. When I was their age, I had to walk nine feet through the shag carpet in the living room to change the TV channel.

I was getting a little tired from reading about all this exercise. I yawned, then carefully stretched. My body was no longer screaming in pain! It was more like a dull whimper now. Definite progress. Maybe if I stayed up even longer, I'd become pain-free.

Sister Rose always told us that knowledge is power. I reminded myself that Poppy Hollister's family and mine might be joined together by matrimony one of these days. Therefore, it was a smart idea that I (the mother of the groom) learn enough about pickleball, the favorite sport of Poppy (the mother of the bride), so we would have something positive in common before the nuptials took place. Who knows? Maybe we'd become best buddies. Or at least not hate the sight of each other.

Humming "The Impossible Dream" from Man of La Mancha, one of my favorite Broadway musicals, I settled back in the chair and continued my internet search.

This time, I ignored any sites about potential medical issues resulting from playing the game. Instead, I clicked on a link promising a history of how the game began.

I laughed when I found out that pickleball was invented in the summer of 1965 by three fathers who came up with the idea to entertain their sons. As a parent myself, it was easy to picture three desperate dads on vacation in a rental house in charge of their kids for the afternoon while their wives went food shopping.

The kids were bored, the dads were getting desperate, and one of them picked up a wiffle ball and a table tennis racket. The house they were staying in had an old badminton court, so they began to hit the wiffle ball back and forth over the net. Presto! Like magic, the kids really got into it, the dads were thrilled, and pickleball was born. (That may not be exactly what happened, but it's close enough.)

I was so engrossed in my research that I didn't even notice car headlights coming into the driveway. Nor did I hear my son walking through the kitchen and into the office. So when he whispered, "Hi, Mom," I hope I can be forgiven for screaming.

"I'm sorry I frightened you. Why aren't you in bed?"

"I was in pain after playing pickleball today and couldn't sleep. I got up and spent some time on the computer." I gestured to the screen. "I'm doing a little research on the game."

What I really wanted to say was, "I heard you drive out of here like you were in the Indy 500 and it scared me. Where have you been?" But I didn't.

"I guess my great idea wasn't such a great idea," Mike admitted. "I didn't expect Poppy to be so tough on you. She came highly recommended as a teacher."

"I just did too much too soon," I said, to make him feel less guilty. "I'll be more careful the next time." Assuming there is one.

"And you had no way of knowing that Poppy and I had a history. I didn't remember her at all. Lunch was delicious, and I enjoyed meeting your new girlfriend. She seems very nice."

I stood up and gave him a kiss on the cheek. "I'm very proud of you."

"Thanks, Mom. That means a lot to me. For the record, I think I owe you an explanation about why I tore of here so fast a while ago."

"I didn't even realize you'd left," I lied.

"You always were a rotten fibber, Mom. But please don't overreact when I tell you what's happened. Promise?"

"I'll try," I said, fearing the worst, whatever that was.

"I have an app on my phone that's connected to Picklelilly's. It alerts me if there's a problem. Tonight it went off for the first time, so I drove over there as fast as I could. The fire trucks were already there."

"Fire trucks?" I repeated. "There was a fire?"

"It was just a small grease fire in the kitchen. I took some pictures in case I have to file an insurance claim. Fortunately, it was caught early so there wasn't much damage. Small kitchen fires can happen in restaurant kitchens.

"It's weird, though. I can't figure out how this one started. I checked everything before I locked up tonight and everything was fine."

Chapter 27

I might wake up early and go running. I also might wake up and find out I've won the lottery. The odds are about the same.

I stumbled into the kitchen after a restless night of tossing, turning, pillow pounding, and horrible dreams. My most vivid one was of me frying something on the stove and setting the kitchen curtains on fire. I woke up shaking after that one.

Why is it that I can always remember every detail of the really scary ones and forget everything about the happy ones?

Jim didn't even look up from reading The Fairport News, our local newspaper, when I joined him at the table. Maybe he was checking to see if his weekly column was in today's edition. Or maybe he was waiting for me to apologize for my over-the-top behavior last night.

Only one way to find out.

"Is your column in today's paper? I'd like to read it when you're finished."

Silence.

Oh, boy. This was really bad. Jim always wants me to read his column so I can tell him what a good job he'd done. Time to drop to my knees (figuratively speaking) and beg for forgiveness.

"I'm sorry about last night," I said.

He didn't reply, even though I knew he'd heard me. Instead, he turned the paper to another page and continued reading.

I held up my coffee mug. "Thanks for saving me some coffee. It tastes extra good this morning."

Grunt.

"Thank you," I repeated.

Silence.

I couldn't take it anymore. I grabbed the newspaper as hard as I could, but Jim wouldn't let go. The predictable end result was a newspaper torn in half, with each of us holding a piece. Jim started to laugh, and in a few seconds, I joined him.

The laughter didn't last long.

"I appreciate your apology, Carol. I definitely deserved one. Some of the things you said to me last night hurt me, especially about my relationship with your mother. I thought she loved me. I certainly loved her. Did she really not want you to marry me?"

Jim's sad expression reminded me of how the dogs looked when I'd neglected to buy their dog treats. How could I have said such hurtful things to my husband?

"I don't know how you put up with me," I said, my eyes filling up with tears. "When we first started dating, Mom told me you were the best thing that ever happened to me. And she was right. A mother always is."

Which brought me right back to what started our argument last night.

I pressed my lips together. No way was I going to start the whole thing all over again, even though I was right.

I heard a discreet cough, then Mike's voice. "Is it safe to come in now? I didn't want to interrupt, but I have to leave."

Cue mortified Carol and Jim. We were so used to having the house to ourselves that we'd forgotten the "no arguing in front of the children" part of parenting.

"Dad, are you still planning on meeting me later? I want to show you around the restaurant, then take you over to my new condo. I won't force you to play pickleball, though. Unless you want to."

"I'll pass on the pickleball," Jim said. "The rest sounds fine. I'll stop by around eleven o'clock."

"That should be fine, assuming everything is okay after last night's fire." He waved his phone. "The building inspector is stopping by this morning to check for any damage. It shouldn't take long."

"Fire?" Jim repeated. "You had a fire in the restaurant last night?"

"Just a small one in the kitchen. I'm surprised Mom didn't tell you.

Mike bent down and gave me a kiss. "I'm picking up a rental now, so I won't need to borrow your car, Mom. I'll grab something for breakfast on the way. See you both later." And he was gone.

Jim crossed his arms and glared at me. "When were you planning on sharing this news, dear?"

"As soon as you were finished making me feel terrible about my behavior last night, dear."

"Touché. So...."

"I really don't know much," I said, taking a large swig of coffee to fortify myself for the day. "Mike told me he got an alert on his phone that there was a problem at Picklelilly's. He drove there as fast as he could, and there was a small grease fire in the kitchen. He claims it's not an unusual occurrence at a restaurant, but I don't know if he was telling me the truth. Maybe he just didn't want me to get upset."

"You were awake when he got home?" Jim asked. "Why?"

Trust him to miss the point of my story and focus on the least important part.

"Because I heard a car leave our driveway in a hurry. Don't you remember?"

Jim gave me his Long-Suffering Husband look, then sighed. Deeply.

"How could I forget? You woke me up because you thought someone was stealing your car. I told you it was Mike, not a car thief. And I was right."

I decided in the interest of maintaining marital harmony to ignore that remark. Definite points for me.

Jim wasn't finished with me yet. "And then you started ranting about how I didn't love you because I didn't believe you, etc., etc."

"Please let's not go through all of that again."

"I'll change the focus of our conversation as soon as you admit that you overreacted and I was right about who was driving the car."

"All right, already. You were right. I overreacted."

"Thank you."

A few cups of coffee later, Jim's phone dinged with a text. He read it quickly and fired off an immediate response.

"I hope we're finished with this silly argument because Mike needs me at the restaurant right now. The health inspector is there and found more violations that he claims Mike overlooked. He won't sign off on the opening until they're all rectified."

"All these violations can be fixed, right?" I asked, following Jim into our bedroom.

"I have no idea how serious they are, but I'm sure they can be. I've interviewed the health inspector, Barney Moss, a few times for my Fairport News column. I think Mike's hoping I'll be able to help ease today's situation."

Jim grabbed a blue oxford cloth shirt and gray slacks from his section of our shared closet. "And now, dear wife, I'd appreciate your giving me a little privacy so I can shower, shave, get dressed, and get over to the restaurant as quickly as possible."

I opened my mouth but before I could speak, he cut me off. "Yes, I promise I will keep you updated on what's happening as best I can. Okay?"

I nodded like a good little wife. "Okay. Thank you."

Chapter 28

When I was young, I was scared of the dark. Now when I see my electric bill, I'm scared of the light.

Jim was showered, dressed, and gone in ten minutes flat, not that I was actually counting the time until he left. It took me the next hour to bring order back to our bedroom and bathroom from his whirlwind departure.

"Why are men so messy?" I asked Lucy and Ethel, who'd finally shown up after what I suspected was a nice nap upstairs on Mike's bed. I suddenly realized that Mike's bedroom this morning was probably a mirror image of ours before I waved my magic wand and brought order back into what was chaos.

I promised myself that under no circumstances would I take this opportunity to invade Mike's privacy, even though the siren song of an empty bedroom where I could nose around and discover things I had no business discovering was almost irresistible.

"Mike has a lot more on his mind than making his bed and picking up wet towels from the bathroom floor right now," I informed the dogs. "We shouldn't be too hard on him. He's a grown man, in case you two have forgotten that."

Both canines followed me into the kitchen and immediately sat by their food bowls. To be sure they agreed with me, I poured some kibble into their dishes and gave them fresh water. A leisurely stroll around the yard took care of doggie needs.

Too bad a human's needs aren't as simple to satisfy as a canine's.

My phone pinged with a text from Jim. I grabbed it so fast I dropped the darn thing on the kitchen floor. (No damage done, thank goodness.)

Jim: Everything okay here, although fire damage may take longer to fix than expected.

Me: How long? How's Mike?

Jim: Not sure yet.

Me: About fixes or Mike?

Jim: Met a friend of yours here, Poppy Hollister. Lovely woman. Says you went to the same high school.

Cue Carol rolling her eyes before responding.

Me: Yes.

Jim: She's married to Lou Hollister. We should get together with them sometime.

No way, José.

Me: Gotta go. Talk later. Thx for update.

Chapter 29

Did you ever get the feeling that your fairy godmother stepped out for a smoke?

Lucy gave me one of her famous looks. She hates it when I don't share family news with her right away, though how she'd figured out it was Jim texting me is a mystery.

"Everything is going to be okay at the restaurant," I told Her Majesty. "The fire damage wasn't nearly as bad as it could have been."

"Fire damage!" a female voice repeated. "What fire?"

My darling daughter and the most perfect grandchild in the world had surprised me with a visit.

"Did someone get hurt? Dad? Mike?"

"I can see that you take after me in the jumping to conclusions department," I said as she handed CJ off to me.

"How's my favorite grandson today?" I kissed the top of his head and inhaled his wonderful baby scent.

CJ answered me with a four-tooth grin. I love it when he does that.

"Talk," Jenny demanded, grabbing a kitchen chair. "I want details. And don't leave anything out."

"I am talking," I said. "You're Grandma's ray of sunshine," I cooed. "That's who you are." CJ snuggled closer in my arms.

"Very funny. Talk to me, your daughter, not your grandson." Jenny reached out her arms for her son, and I reluctantly handed him over.

"Spoil sport."

"You can hold him again after you tell me about the fire. And anything else you'd care to share."

Where to begin?

"Did you and Mark know about Mike's new restaurant?"

Jenny looked guilty and nodded.

"I won't ask you when he told you. It's obvious I was the last person in this family to hear his news."

"He wanted to surprise you, Mom, and swore us to secrecy. Please don't be mad at me. I hated to keep it from you, but a promise is a promise."

"I'm not mad."

I'm hurt, but I'm not mad.

"Did you know Mike was taking me to play pickleball yesterday, too?"

"I tried to talk him out of it," Jenny said. "I thought you'd hate it. And I was worried you might even hurt yourself."

CJ squirmed in her arms, momentarily distracting both of us.

"Clearly I survived. As a matter of fact, I really enjoyed it and plan to take another lesson. So there."

Liar, liar, pants on fire. And to your own daughter. Carol Andrews, you should be ashamed of yourself.

Jenny rolled her eyes and refrained from commenting.

"Tell me about the fire."

"You should have been a prosecuting attorney," I said. "Keep hammering the witness until she tells you what you want to know.

"There was a small grease fire in the kitchen late last night. Nothing serious, but the repairs might delay the restaurant opening."

Jenny handed CJ back to me, and he snuggled on my shoulder and sighed. Or maybe the sigh came from me.

"I'm trying to tell you things in chronological order, but you keep interrupting me," I continued. "I have big news from Mike I'm not supposed to share, so this is just between us. You know how he loves his secrets."

"I'm glad the fire wasn't serious," my daughter said. "I'll be quiet now. Go ahead."

"The restaurant will be wonderful when it's finished. You and Mark will love it."

"We're both looking forward to a date night there right after it opens. Assuming you and Dad will babysit, of course."

I grinned. "You know we will."

"So, that's your big news?"

"Not exactly. There's more."

I paused. "Although I was sworn to secrecy. Maybe I shouldn't tell you. After all, a promise is a promise."

"Mother! Quit fooling around and get to the point. You know you're dying to."

Oops. I'd gone too far in my teasing. When Jenny calls me "Mother," not "Mom," she means business.

"Mike's in love. I met her yesterday and really liked her. Charli's adorable, and he thinks he wants to marry her."

"Charli?" Jenny repeated. "That's Mike's new girlfriend? And he's thinking of marrying her?"

I nodded.

"Over my dead body!"

Chapter 30

Telling an angry woman to calm down works as well as baptizing a cat.

Jenny's face was beet red. I'd never seen her so angry before.

CJ started to whimper. I was sure he wasn't used to hearing his mother talk like that and it frightened him.

"*Shhh*, sweetheart," I said, patting his back and kissing him to calm him down. "Mommie's not mad at you. She loves you very much."

"I'm sorry, Mom. I overreacted."

"We all do that sometimes," I said. "Even me.

"Oh, heck. Especially me."

By this time, CJ's eyes were drooping, and I figured a quick nap was next on his baby agenda. "How about I put him down for a snooze in the porta crib and then maybe you can tell me why you're so upset."

"Thanks, Mom. He was just fed and changed before we left home, so he should be okay for about an hour."

Lucy and Ethel were snoozing on the bed, and for once, I didn't chase them off. Lucy raised her head to see why her nap was being interrupted, then rolled over and went back to sleep.

It didn't take me long to settle the baby and his favorite teddy bear in the crib. He was fast asleep in no time.

Too bad I didn't have a teddy bear to give my daughter.

Jenny was texting furiously when I walked back into the kitchen. She clicked off when she saw me. I was relieved to see she looked calmer.

"I didn't mean to interrupt your texting."

"It's okay, Mom. I didn't mean to go off the deep end when you told me about Mike's new girlfriend. You surprised the heck out of me, though."

"And vice versa," I said. "Want to talk about it? I've never seen you react that way before."

"Is CJ all right?" Jenny asked.

"He's fine. Sound asleep. Lucy and Ethel are babysitting."

That got a faint smile from my daughter, which was progress.

"I was texting Cindi Page," Jenny said. "She confirmed what I remembered about Charli and added a few tidbits of her own."

"Cindi Page? Why?"

Jenny sighed, and for a split second she sounded just like me when I tell her father something and he doesn't get it.

"Cindi and I were in the same high school class, although we weren't best friends," she explained. "I've lost touch with my close high school friends for one reason or another, and I miss having the tight bond you have with yours."

"I know I'm very lucky. I don't know what I'd do without them."

Jenny gave me a knowing smile.

"Cindi was one of my nurses when CJ was born. We reconnected, and now we're good friends.

"A girl named Charli was in our high school class, and I texted Cindi right away to see what she remembered about her. Cindi said Charli was a stuck-up snob who got a kick out of making other people feel inferior to her every chance she got. That's what I remember about her too."

Wow. Those were pretty damning words. I still wasn't convinced, though.

"Cindi also reminded me of how Charli could be sweet as sugar if she wanted something but vicious if she didn't get her own way. She gave me a few examples, which I didn't know about."

"Maybe we're not talking about the same Charli," I said, grasping at straws. "It's possible Mike's Charli didn't go to Fairport High School."

Jenny raised one eyebrow, a trick I've never mastered.

"Mom, get real."

"Okay, smarty pants. Charli is an unusual nickname. It's still possible we're not talking about the same person." Miracles do happen, right? Of course, right.

"What's her real first name?"

"Charlotte. But she hates it."

I had a flashback of the angry exchange I overheard between Poppy and her daughter. No doubt about it. Poppy had called her daughter Charlotte.

I was doomed. And even worse, so was my son.

Chapter 31

Lazy is such an ugly word. I prefer the term "selective participation."

"I thought they'd never leave," I confided to Lucy and Ethel. Even Ethel looked shocked at my remark (she's not usually so critical).

"You know I love having Jenny and CJ visit. But today was a little different."

You're doing it again, Carol. You don't have to explain your behavior to a dog.

In my own defense, please understand that I can't stand having anyone criticize me or be mad at me. Even if they have four legs and a tail.

Both dogs still looked doubtful, which was beginning to irritate me.

"I don't need both of you to criticize me. I have enough problems dealing with Claire."

Both dogs nuzzled me, then gave me doggy stares.

"What's up with you guys? Why are you looking at me like that?"

After a few seconds more of canine-human staring, the lightbulb in my brain switched on. To be sure I was on the right track, I knelt in front of my two dogs and double checked. "Are you telling me to reach out to Claire?"

Lucy and Ethel both jumped on top of me and started licking my face.

For those of you who are skeptics (or new readers), this may be hard for you to believe, but it's true. My dogs are brilliant, and they often communicate with me. Sometimes, I swear they're smarter than I am.

After a few minutes spent hoisting myself up off the floor (no more details will be given, but it was not a pretty sight), I grabbed my cell phone and sent an SOS text to Claire.

Chapter 32

I try to take one day at a time. But lately, several days have attacked me all at once.

"I got here as fast as I could," Claire said, sliding into the Fairport Diner booth. She fanned herself, leaned back, and caught her breath. "Your text scared me half to death."

I nudged a glass of cold water in her direction. "Drink this and you'll feel better. I didn't mean to scare you."

Claire gulped the water, then gave me a suspicious look. "How come you look so calm? I thought you said there you had a family emergency and needed help. What's the emergency? Where are the others?"

"Nancy and Bob are away on a cruise celebrating their thirty-sixth wedding anniversary, and I didn't invite Mary Alice because I figured she was either working at the hospital or sleeping. Today it's just you and me."

"Hold it, Carol. Before you go into the gory details of your emergency, kindly explain to me how Nancy could be celebrating a thirty-sixth wedding anniversary when she was married two years before you and Jim, and you just celebrated your fortieth. She's been married forty-two years to Bob, whether she wants to admit it or not. That makes no sense."

I grinned. "It does in Nancy's mind. You know hers doesn't work like anybody else's. She told me that even though she and Bob were married two years before me, she calculated the times that Bob had cheated on her or they weren't living together and subtracted those from forty-two. Six years from forty-two equals thirty-six."

Claire didn't respond. She just rolled her eyes.

"After that crazy explanation from Nancy, I'm almost afraid to hear about your latest crisis. It better be worth my risking my life and a possible speeding ticket to get here so fast."

"I'm sure you'd never end up in jail," I countered. "That hot shot lawyer you live with is sure to get you off."

Claire laughed and I relaxed.

"Are you ready to order?"

Rats. Usually I have to strip naked to get a server's attention (only kidding—I'd never do that!), and today, when I wanted to keep Claire's attention focused on what I had to talk about instead of food, here she was.

Before Claire could speak, I held up my hand. "This is my treat, so I'll order for both of us. We'll have two cheeseburgers, mine well done, hers medium rare. One order of onion rings and one order of French fries. We'll share them. And two Cokes."

The server nodded and scurried away.

"Are you crazy? You just ordered two heart attack specials? What are you trying to do, kill us both?"

"Hardly. I'm trying to get you in the right mood."

Claire clutched her chest dramatically. "For what? A coronary? I haven't eaten anything that rich since…I really can't remember when."

"I can. It was the summer between our graduation from high school and freshman year of college. The one we spent together at the beach. It was our go-to meal every Sunday night when we got off work. Do you remember now?"

"Oh, my goodness." I couldn't tell from Claire's expression if she was happy or angry. I soon found out.

"Do you mean to tell me that you got me here to reminisce about old times?"

"Sort of. But not completely. I really have a family emergency, and I need your help. So be quiet and listen."

I cleared my throat. Where to begin?

"You know Mike's been home, right?"

Claire nodded, then paused and gave me a dirty look. "Although I haven't seen him, myself."

I ignored her dig. "Mike's running a new restaurant here in Fairport. He's also madly in love.

Jenny hates his new girlfriend, and I'm not thrilled with her mother either. Mike doesn't know how we feel, and when he finds out, it's going to tear our family apart."

Chapter 33

*Managing your weight requires careful planning.
For example, I took the batteries out of the
bathroom scale this morning.
Follow me for more helpful weight-loss tips.*

"I'm sure you're exaggerating," Claire said. "You always had a flare for the dramatic, even when we were kids. You need to talk to a family counselor, not me."

Our order arrived, and we immediately dug in like we hadn't eaten in years. Why does food that's unhealthy always taste more delicious than anything that's good for you?

Between bites, I gave Claire a succinct (for me) synopsis of yesterday, including my experiment with playing pickleball, who my teacher was, the argument I'd overheard in the women's room, Mike's new condo, and his new girlfriend. For once, Claire didn't interrupt me. I'd like to think she was quiet because I gave such a clear and concise summary, but it could have been because she was too busy eating.

I saved sharing Jenny's comments until we were served dessert. And I'm not telling you what our dessert was, so don't ask me. However, I now know what I want for my last earthly meal (should I be given a choice) before I'm on my way to the pearly gates.

"This whole meal was delicious," Claire said. "Let's do this again in ten years. Our cholesterol levels should be lower by then."

"It's a deal," I said. "When we come again, let's have milkshakes instead of Cokes."

Claire groaned. "I don't think I can wait ten years if we add milkshakes to the menu. You know those were my absolute favorite."

"Ask our favorite nurse for help if you start to weaken," I suggested. "If Mary Alice finds out what we ate today, she'll be lecturing us for the next decade!"

Claire reached across the table and grabbed my hands. "All kidding aside, I have a feeling we haven't gotten to why you insisted we have lunch today. You know you can trust me, and I promise I won't criticize you if you take too long to get to the point."

"I'm going to hold you to that.

"Okay, here goes. What do you remember about that summer at the beach? Especially about our interaction with Mr. and Mrs. P and the kids."

"I haven't thought about that summer for years," Claire said. "I remember how the kids loved playing tricks on me when they were supposed to be studying. Once somebody short-sheeted my bed. Do you remember that? None of them would ever admit which one of them did it." She laughed at the memory.

"I'd forgotten about that. They did the same thing to my bed the night after they did yours," I said. "I remember Mr. P punished all of them because they wouldn't snitch on each other. And made them apologize."

"I don't think their punishment was that bad. No ice cream for a week, or something like that."

"He was a wonderful man," I said. "He and his wife treated us like members of the family."

"Good memories," Claire said, smiling.

"What do you remember about the oldest daughter, Poppy? Did we have much interaction with her while we were at the beach?"

"I don't think so," Claire said. "Her parents treated her and her two best friends to a trip to Europe that summer. I remember how jealous I was of that. She didn't come to the beach until late July. We were the hired help that summer, and she took every opportunity to remind us of that. Even though we'd gone to the same high school."

"When I saw Poppy yesterday at the pickleball court," I said, "she accused us of being mean to her in high school. She said I was the worst one of all. And that we gave her the nickname Poppy as a joke."

"I would say that woman has a huge imagination," Claire said.

"To make matters even worse," I added, "Poppy made all these horrible accusations in front of Mike. She deliberately humiliated me in front of my own son!"

"Maybe she's jealous," Claire said, looking thoughtful.

"Jealous? Of me? Why?"

"You have to admit that Mr. P really took a shine to you."

"I was a girl who had no father," I said, my cheeks getting red. "He felt sorry for me."

"Yeah, so he kept in touch with you during all four years of college." Claire said. "Plus, he arranged a job for you in New York City after graduation so you could move there and not starve to death. He didn't do that for me."

"I'm not even going to dignify that remark with a reply." I grabbed the check and pushed it in Claire's direction.

"I can see now that inviting you to lunch was a very bad idea. I reached out to you for help, and all you're doing is criticizing me, just like you always do. I thought we were friends. I guess I was wrong. You can pay the check. I'm leaving right now."

I was so mad I didn't even look right or left as I stormed out of the diner, which was a huge mistake. I should have checked out who was in the booth behind ours and overheard every word we said.

Chapter 34

I miss the old days when "new hip joint" meant a cool place to go with my friends on a Saturday night.

I sat in the privacy of my car and ordered myself to calm down. Easier said than done.

Please, don't remind me how often I'd ordered myself to do the exact same thing in the last few days. Nor do I need any reminders about how often I'd failed.

I heard a tap on the window. Claire was beside my car, holding up a sign she'd made on the back of a diner takeout menu. It was a drawing of a female face, her mouth slashed with a black X. Underneath the drawing she'd scrolled, "Please forgive my big mouth."

I unlocked the door and patted the passenger seat. "Sit. I promise I won't yell or cry anymore."

"We'll both get cricks in our necks if we try to talk that way. I just wanted to tell you how sorry I am that I teased you about you and Mr. P's relationship. I'm ashamed for what I implied, especially in a public place. I know there was nothing inappropriate going on between the two of you."

"Thank you. And I apologize for overreacting, storming out the diner, and leaving you to pay the check. It was supposed to be my treat." I grabbed my purse. "Let me reimburse you. How much do I owe?"

"Save your money. You can pay the check ten years from now when we have this lunch again. It'll probably cost much more money by then, with inflation."

I smiled a little, but I wasn't feeling any better.

"Mr. P did kiss me once," I admitted. "I'd forgotten all about that. Thank goodness nobody in the family saw what happened between us."

"Nothing happened," Claire said firmly. "Nothing you have to be ashamed of, anyway."

"You're right," I said. "But what am I going to do about Poppy? And Mike's girlfriend? Jenny's never been so negative about anyone else before."

"The situation will resolve on its own," Claire said with the confidence of someone who wasn't emotionally involved and could afford to be blasé about my family's potential heartbreak. "Trust me. Give it some time."

"I hope you're right," I said. I was unconvinced, but in the interests of not starting another argument, it was easier for me to agree.

"I love you, Carol, even though you drive me crazy sometimes."

"Ditto," I said, laughing. "Go home. I promise I'll keep you updated."

After Claire drove out of the parking lot, I texted the rec center and signed up for six weeks of pickleball lessons with Poppy, starting the next day. By the time the six weeks were up, I'd either be crippled and in the hospital or have a new best friend.

I hoped it would be the latter.

Chapter 35

I'm starting to realize I'll never be old enough to know better.

I was in a positive frame of mind the next morning. Jim's snoring hadn't kept me awake, and the two dogs hadn't hogged my side of the bed. I felt ready to take on whatever the universe planned to throw at me. I stretched, and my back didn't protest as much as it usually did. A good omen, for sure.

I greeted the old woman who lives in my bathroom mirror with a cheery hello, and she smiled back at me. Another good omen.

When I sat down at the kitchen table with a cup of delicious coffee, Jim grunted and rattled the newspaper he was reading. I took the hint: rattling the paper in "Jim talk" means "There's nothing really interesting in the paper today. Feel free to interrupt me."

The kitchen table was a mess of toast crumbs, a half cup of coffee, and a plate decorated with the remnants of scrambled eggs, probably courtesy of my husband, who was ignoring the mess. Yuck.

There was no way I could sit and enjoy my breakfast until I cleaned up first.

Just as I was about to chastise Jim for being so sloppy, I heard Mike's voice. "I'll meet you at Fairport Furniture at eleven o'clock."

Pause.

Laughing.

"Yes, I promise."

Pause.

Voice lowered so I had to strain to hear it.

"Yes, me too."

My son appeared in the kitchen with a big smile on his face. He leaned over and dropped a kiss on my cheek. "Good morning, dear Mother. How are you today?"

Hmm. Tough question. Currently annoyed? Anxious? Curious? All of the above?

"Give me fifteen minutes to take a quick shower and then we can be on our way," Jim said. He gave me a kiss on the top of my head and shuffled in the direction of our bathroom.

"Are we going somewhere?" I yelled after him. "I don't remember having plans this morning."

"You don't, Mom," Mike said, gathering up the dirty remnants of breakfast and rinsing them in the sink faster than a speeding bullet. Or something like that.

"Sorry about the mess. I should have cleaned up after I ate." Mike served me another cup of piping hot coffee and joined me at the table. "I'd load the dishwasher but I know that's one of Dad's favorite jobs and I don't want to spoil his fun."

"It sounds like you and Dad have plans together for today," I said, sipping the coffee while figuring out how nosy I could be and get away with it. "I overheard you talking on the phone about going to a furniture store this morning. Are you and Dad meeting someone there?"

Mike laughed. "Hardly. Dad's coming with me to Picklelilly's to supervise repairs of the fire damage, which frees me up for a quick trip to pick out some furniture for my new condo."

Don't react negatively, Carol. Be a supportive person.

"How are the repairs coming along?" I asked, realizing it was safer to talk about the restaurant first.

"They should be done by the end of this week, but then the inspectors have to come to sign off on everything all over again. I'm hoping we'll finally be able to open in another month, but I think I'm being optimistic. The fire wasn't my fault, but it delayed things even more."

My Mom-O-Meter immediately went into overdrive. "You don't mean you're being blamed for what was clearly an unfortunate accident. That's outrageous!"

"Take it easy, Mom. I haven't been accused of anything. It's just a feeling I have, and I'm probably overreacting. Do you think that could be a hereditary trait?" He gave me a pointed stare.

"You got that personality trait from your father, not me," I said with a deadpan expression. We both started laughing.

"Mike gets what personality trait from me?" Jim asked. "What's so funny?"

"Nothing," I said, pressing my lips together to stop giggling.

"What Mom said," Mike echoed.

Jim shook his head. "I give up." He jingled his car keys. "Ready to go?"

"I'll follow you in my rental car. I have an appointment at eleven, and I don't like driving your car."

"I have a pickleball lesson this morning," I yelled as they were leaving, earning no reaction from either my husband or my son. They were too busy squabbling about the necessity of driving two separate vehicles to the same place when they'd both be there at the same time as they headed outside. In the end, I heard two separate car engines roar to life, so I knew Mike had won.

I figured I'd get a lecture from Jim when he found out I'd driven to the rec center today too. Well, tough. I told him and he didn't hear me.

It wasn't until I was stacking the dishes in the dishwasher that I realized I hadn't been able to get the details of Mike's shopping excursion.

Curses, foiled again.

Chapter 36

Lack of planning on your part does not constitute an emergency on my part.

Today's pickleball lesson was scheduled for 11:30. I briefly toyed with the idea of rescheduling to the next decade, but even my fertile imagination couldn't come up with a plausible way to pull that off. As I was searching my closet for the appropriate attire to wear, it suddenly dawned on me that the longer I waited to take lessons, the older I would be. Ergo, the pathetic physical shape I was currently in was the best I would ever be. It was now or never.

I decided to wear one of my all-time favorite Lilly Pulitzer outfits (a blue print polo top with matching slacks) that's comfortable, slimming, and makes me feel happy. After getting approval for my fashion choice from both dogs, and their outdoor needs taken care of, I laced up my sneakers and I was ready to leave. Or as ready to leave as I ever would be.

I marched outside to my car, opened the door, made myself comfortable in the driver's seat, adjusted the mirrors, adjusted the seat, started the motor, realized I had to open the front gate before I drove out of the driveway, exited the car, walked slowly down the driveway, opened the front gate, returned to the car, and finally–lacking anything else to do to waste a little more time–turned the ignition key. The car roared to life without a single hiccup. Traitor!

It was only 10:45. If I left home right now, I'd arrive at the rec center way too early for my lesson. Although, perhaps my being early would earn me brownie points with Poppy.

I crawled down the driveway at a snail's pace, hoping to see a line of traffic on Old Fairport Turnpike to delay me.

What's the rush, Carol? You've got oodles of time. Take Fairport Turnpike instead of the back roads. It'll be an easy drive this early in the day.

Sometimes I give myself good advice.

Sadly, this was not one of them.

The rec center was five miles from my house. The first half mile (give or take) was pleasant. I cruised right along at 25 miles an hour, for once not inching over the speed limit.

And then I saw the ROAD CLOSED sign ahead of me. Traffic was being diverted back to the main road because of construction, so I wasn't so smart after all. It was too late to turn around. I was stuck.

Forget about being early. I doubted I'd even be on time, earning the wrath of Poppy before I even picked up a pickleball paddle.

I crawled for the next quarter mile, then spotted an alley next to Maria's Trattoria that I knew led to a small side street. A few other people had the same idea, but I persevered and finally arrived at the rec center five minutes before my lesson was to start. Yay!

The parking lot was jammed with cars. I spotted Jim's car in a prime location, which made me mad. Irrational, I know. The guy had left home a few hours before I did, and that's why he got such a choice parking spot.

I finally found a spot that would be a tight squeeze, but if I was really careful and inched my way in slowly, I was confident I could make it work.

And I did.

The space was perfect except for one teensy thing. No matter how I tried, I couldn't open the driver's side door wide enough to get myself out of the car.

Too bad my car didn't have a sunroof. Maybe I could've used it to free myself. I could feel my claustrophobia start to kick in and forced myself to ignore it.

Before you have a breakdown, Carol, text Poppy and cancel the lesson. Tell her a family emergency came up and apologize profusely. Then carefully back the car out of the space and get the heck out of here.

I was so nervous by now that I was sweating. To make matters worse (if at all possible), my cell phone slipped out of my hands and ended up under the passenger's seat. I had to hoist myself over to the other side of the car and feel around underneath until I found it.

Then I heard a woman screaming at me.

Chapter 37

The worst thing about parallel parking is the witnesses.

The screaming was coming from Poppy (who else?), who was totally out of control. She called me every curse word I'd ever heard, plus several other brand new, creative ones. Of all the parking spaces in the entire town of Fairport, Connecticut, I had to get stuck in the one right next to her car. And it was my own fault.

I slid down in my seat and prayed she didn't realize it was me inside the car. I didn't think even St. Jude could get me out of this situation, unless he knew how to back a car out of an extra tight parking space.

I closed my eyes and started to cry. I couldn't help it.

You're doomed to be trapped in your car until all the others around you are gone. When you're finally freed, you'll still have to deal with Poppy.

On the positive side, I wouldn't have to take any pickleball lessons.

I opened my eyes and screamed. A strange man was kneeling on the hood of the car, looking at me through the windshield. He gestured at me to put down a window so I could hear him.

"I think you can get out on the passenger's side if you're really careful when you open the door," he yelled. "Then maybe I can wiggle inside and move your car."

I shook my head. "I don't think it'll work. Especially with Poppy still screaming at me."

The man nodded, turned around, and screamed, "Poppy, for the love of heaven, shut up! It's going to be okay, but not if you keep yelling like that. You're making everything worse!"

To my astonishment, the screaming ceased. Just like that. Whoever this guy was, if he could get Poppy to be quiet, he could do anything!

I have no intention of giving you a blow-by-blow description of my auto escape. It was a very tight squeeze, and I had to hold my breath and pull in my tummy (no comments, please), but I finally did it.

My hero was able to take my place in the driver's seat and back my car out without a hitch. He drove it to the rear of the parking lot and pulled into a spot marked "Reserved."

"Don't worry about the sign," he yelled. "It doesn't mean anything."

"Are you sure? I don't want to have my car towed."

"Trust me, it's okay," he said, jogging up to me. "The person who runs Picklelilly's uses the sign to be sure he always has a parking spot. I don't think he'll mind if we borrow it for a little while."

"He'd better not," I said, laughing. "My name's Carol Andrews. I'm Mike's mother."

"I thought you looked familiar. I remember seeing you with Mike a few days ago when you came for a pickleball lesson."

At my confused expression, he clarified, "I was Poppy's pickleball partner. We were in the middle of a game when you got here."

"Now I remember you. We were never introduced, though." I also remember that Poppy was telling you what to do and you didn't like it.

"I'm Tim Peterson," he said, smiling. "I'm glad I could help."

"It's wonderful to meet you, Tim. Thank you for coming to my rescue. If you hadn't come along, I'd still be trapped in my car, and Poppy would still be screaming at me." I wanted to throw my arms around him and hug him but restrained myself.

"Poppy's always screaming about something. I've been tuning her out since we were kids. After a while, she moves on to another life crisis. That's just how she is. And she's used to having things her own way, in case you haven't figured that out yet."

"You seem to know her very well."

Tim grinned. "I should. I'm her younger cousin. She's only five months older than I am, but she's been pushing me around since I was born."

"Let me get this straight. You're Mr. P's nephew. Is that right?"

"Yes. My father was the older of the two brothers. When he and my mother got married and started their law firm, he changed our surname from Popovani to Peterson."

"I remember their ads in the local paper," I said. "And their slogan."

"Frick and Frack, we've got your back," Tim said.

"I thought it was really cute. Although I could never figure out which one was Frick and which one was Frack."

"I hated it. Imagine being their son. I was constantly teased about those stupid ads. After I graduated from law school and joined the firm, my parents finally changed the slogan. Now they're both gone and the firm has only one lawyer—me. I handle all the family's legal business."

Tim checked his phone. "Poppy should be calmer by now. It's safe to go inside."

"Not me! No way."

"You're probably right to hold off for today. By tomorrow, trust me, she'll have another meltdown and somebody else to yell at."

"In that case, I'll hold off indefinitely. I'm not a masochist."

"I guess I must be," Tim said. "Or maybe I'm just used to it after all these years." He tossed me the car keys and jogged back inside.

Chapter 38

In my mind, I'm still 24. But my back is 55, my knees are 67, and my left hip turns 81 next week.

I drove so slowly going home that I could have walked there faster. My chosen speed earned me several one finger salutes and horn blasts on the way from impatient drivers as they finally passed my car.

"I hope you all get speeding tickets," I yelled out the window.

It's hard to see clearly when your eyes are filled with tears. Trust me, I know this for a fact.

I was so nervous I was going to make another stupid driving mistake on the way that I wished I'd left the car at the rec center and asked Jim or Mike to drive it home for me. But if I involved either of them, I'd have to explain why I was leaving the car. No way was I doing that.

To add to my depressed state, I could swear both dogs gave me dirty looks when I finally arrived home, instead of greeting me with the doggie love I was craving. A quick run in the yard and a few dog biscuits won them over. Too bad it wasn't that easy with humans.

"This has been one of the worst days in my life," I told my two canines. "But I'm not going to tell you why. With my bad luck, you'll blab to Jim, and I'll never hear the end of it."

Would you be surprised to learn I have the local autobody repair shop on speed dial? No, I didn't think so. The owner, Rick Anderson, and I are close buddies. I've spent so much money in his shop over the years that I'm sure at least one of Rick's kids was attending college on me. I grabbed my phone in case I needed to beg Rick for help and walked outside to check for any evidence of today's parking lot debacle.

There were already two small dents on the passenger door, the result of a runaway shopping cart rolling into my car at a local market. When Jim saw that damage and began lecturing me for being careless, I told him with a clear conscience that the dents were not my fault. I'd been loading groceries for his dinner into my car when the shopping cart attacked my car. If he wanted to sue the shopping cart for damages, that was entirely up to him. And that, as the old saying goes, was that.

This time, I had no shopping cart to blame.

I carefully surveyed every single inch of my car with my glasses on, so I'd see even the tiniest dent. I even took a few pictures with my phone. Except for my old shopping cart souvenirs, which even Jim said were too small to fix, all was pristine.

Yippee! Thanks to the Good Lord and Tim Peterson, it looked like I was off the hook.

Jim arrived home a few hours later and found chicken with Chinese fried rice, onions, and broccoli simmering on the stove. Believe it or not, I made it all by myself, using leftover chicken that we'd had for dinner recently and instant rice mix.

Needless to say, my husband was surprised, impressed, and grateful. Between bites, however, he questioned me casually about how my day went. Innocent questions, to be sure, but they freaked me out so, of course, I overreacted.

"It went fine," I answered quickly. "Absolutely fine. One of the best days I've ever had, in fact. Why are you asking me?"

Jim looked startled. "I figured you'd be a little nervous about your pickleball lesson with Poppy."

"I didn't realize you heard me tell you about my lesson." I mentally chastised myself for being an overly sensitive jerk. "Something came up at the last minute and we had to reschedule. Poppy will let me know when she has another opening for a lesson."

"I checked out the pickleball courts, but you weren't there," Jim said. "Now I know why."

Not really. And if I'm lucky, you never will.

"Jim Andrews, were you spying on me?"

"I wasn't spying," he answered defensively. "I was curious to see how you were doing. And I wanted to cheer you on. I'm proud of you for trying something so much out of your comfort zone."

"That's really sweet. Thank you.

"I was disappointed I couldn't have my lesson today. I was looking forward to it."

Carol Andrews, you are such a liar! You should be ashamed of yourself.

"How was your day?" I asked, turning the focus of our dinner conversation onto him. "Do you know Mike's schedule? I haven't heard from him all day."

"He was moving into his new rental," Jim said between bites. "He said he texted to tell you."

"I've been too busy cooking to check my phone for texts." (I was not lying; I was exaggerating. The two are completely different.)

"That's not like you at all."

"You're right," I said, unsure if Jim was referring to my cooking dinner or neglecting to check my phone for texts. Either way, he was correct, but I'd never admit that to him.

"I'm sure Mike will spend the night at his new place," Jim continued.

I felt a pang in my heart. My baby boy was leaving the nest. Again. For some reason, it didn't bother me (much) every time Mike went back to Florida. Having him living in Fairport again, but not sleeping in his own bedroom in our family home, was going to be a major adjustment for me.

I know. I was being stupid again. All of you should be used to that by now.

"Why don't you get caught up on all your texts and I'll clean up the kitchen? You deserve some time to yourself after slaving away making that delicious dinner."

"It really wasn't that difficult," I protested, feeling guilty about receiving such high praise when all I did was use the recipe on the back of a package of brown rice.

Then I realized that my dear husband was reminding me that there was no point in my rinsing the dirty dishes and loading them in the dishwasher when he would just re-arrange them more efficiently (in his opinion) later on.

"That's very nice of you, dear. Thank you."

"You're welcome," Jim said, handing me my phone. "Now go and catch up with your life."

I nodded and headed for our bedroom. Knowing Jim's nightly routine so well, I was sure that after he finished in the kitchen, he'd park himself in front of the television in the family room, turn on the news, and chill out by disagreeing loudly with the opinions expressed by the so-called experts on various news channels.

We all relax in different ways, right? Of course, right.

I scrolled through my texts and deleted the spam ones immediately. It's unbelievable how many of those I get in my in-box on a daily basis. Then I was free to concentrate on the important ones: four from Mike and one from Jenny.

My daughter's text made me smile. She apologized for her outburst about Mike's new girlfriend, and reminded me that she was dropping CJ off here two days later for several hours so she could teach a class at the college. Another date with my adorable grandson—I could hardly wait!

The first three texts from Mike contained all the information Jim had already given me. His fourth text was the one that truly gladdened my heart. I read it again to be sure I understood it correctly.

Mike: Mom, I want you to see my new place tomorrow. You may have some decorating suggestions. Would appreciate it if you'd pick me up behind the restaurant at 1:00. I don't want to move my car. Somebody stole my reserved parking spot today and I don't want it to happen again! Thx. Love you.

Me: See you at 1:00 tomorrow. Love you, too.

I closed my eyes and said a prayer of thanks to the Good Lord for getting me safely through such a stressful day. I was sure the rest of the week would be better. Or so I thought.

Chapter 39

Not in jail, not in the hospital, not in a grave. I'd say I'm having a good day.

The following morning, I was actually in a happy frame of mind. (Not for the usual reason, in case any of you got the wrong idea.) Even Jim's cross-examination of my plans for the day didn't annoy me, and that's saying a lot. In "Jim speak," he was testing the waters to see whether he could look forward to a home-cooked meal two nights in a row. After all our years of marriage, wouldn't you think he'd know better by now?

"I'll be out with Mike part of the day," I said. "He wants me to help him decorate his new condo."

Jim looked surprised, which annoyed me. (I know, it doesn't take much to set me off.)

"The place looked fine when I saw it yesterday afternoon," he said. "Mike and his new girlfriend are doing a nice job. She sure is a cutie. I think he's finally found a winner."

I set my coffee mug on the kitchen table and looked at my husband. The look I gave him would have struck fear into most ordinary mortals, but not him. He just looked puzzled and said, "What?"

"What?" I repeated after him.

"I can tell from that look on your face that you're mad at me, and it's not even nine o'clock yet."

"I'm not mad," I said with great restraint. "But inquiring minds want to know why you failed to mention anything to me last night about visiting Mike's condo, plus meeting his new girlfriend."

"That's easy to explain. You didn't ask me." Jim looked like he'd just answered the final clue on Jeopardy! and won the Tournament of Champions.

Consider your reply carefully, Carol. You have to admit, the guy is right. You didn't ask him.

"It never occurred to me to ask you," I finally admitted in the interests of keeping peace in the household and saving my marriage.

"Well, there you are," Jim said, looking very pleased with himself.

I pushed aside all the negative remarks that were swirling in my brain and got right to the point. "What did you think of her?"

"Who?"

"Mike's new girlfriend," I said.

"Oh, her. I figured you'd be more interested in the condo than the girlfriend." He took a slow sip of his coffee, then took a good look at me.

"Okay, I'm teasing you. I'm sorry."

"I only talked to her for a few minutes," Jim continued. "She stopped in to give Mike some sheets and towels. They hadn't bought any when they'd been shopping."

"Mike could have taken some of ours," I muttered.

"She seems like a very nice girl, and Mike clearly adores her. I'm sure she'll be a perfect addition to our family. They're talking about the first Saturday in May next spring for the wedding, when all the dogwood trees in town will be blooming. We should think about throwing an engagement party for them soon."

"Sure," I replied automatically. "Whatever you think."

was in shock, hence my reaction. Or lack thereof. In case none of you understood that. Jim certainly didn't.

"I need to leave now," my clueless husband continued. "Mike has another contractor coming to the restaurant this morning, and he wants me there for the meeting. Maybe I'll see you when you pick up Mike."

I finally came to my senses. "Before you leave, we need to talk more about...."

Jim planted a quick smooch on my cheek and then was gone.

I raced out after him. "Wait a minute! We haven't finished talking! I have things to tell you about Mike's girlfriend and her family. It's important!" I screamed, waving my arms like a maniac.

I was too late. Jim waved back and drove away.

Men!

I stomped back into the house. It was crystal clear that I'd have to deal with this crisis all by myself.

"I thought today was going to be a good day, but it's starting out to be even worse than yesterday," I said to my canine support group. "And Jim's hearing loss doesn't help the situation."

Ethel licked my hand in sympathy, and I stroked her head. "I appreciate the moral support. Maybe I'll think of something brilliant to fix this potential family fiasco." And then, just like a miracle, the clouds parted and I realized what I'd said.

Jim's hearing was getting worse. He realizes it but won't admit he needs to get professional help. Therefore, what Mike actually said about any wedding plans and what my dear husband repeated to me must be radically different because Jim didn't hear it correctly.

"Phew," I said to the dogs. "Don't worry. I'll talk to Mike today and get this whole thing straightened out.

"Cross your paws and wish me luck."

Chapter 40

Have you ever noticed the universe often puts you in the same situation again to see if you're still stupid?

I showered and dressed in record time. For me, that is. It took me only 45 minutes to find an appropriate outfit to wear on the off chance that Poppy saw me (heaven forbid!) when I was picking up Mike. I finally decided on a comfortable dress rather than anything sporty that might give her the idea I wanted to atone for my recent parking transgression by suffering through another pickleball lesson with her.

After a few dog biscuits for Lucy and Ethel, I grabbed my purse, phone, and car keys. I was ready to go.

"I won't be gone long," I said. "Behave yourselves."

Lucy started to bark.

"Give me a break," I told Her Majesty. "I have to meet Mike. I won't be gone long. Honestly, I won't."

Then I heard a knock on my front door. Lucy barked again, probably telling me that she was barking for a reason and I owed her an apology.

The knocking persisted, louder and louder. I knew who it was. There's only one person in my life who insists on using the front door to announce her presence, rather than the side door like everybody else.

I snuck a peek out the dining room window and confirmed my worst fears: Phyllis Stevens was standing on my front stoop with a determined look on her face.

Cursing my bad luck under my breath, I pulled open our creaky front door. "I can't talk now, Phyllis. I'm late for a very important meeting."

"That's fine, dear. This will only take a minute." Phyllis thrust a clipboard into my hands and pointed to the first line. "Just sign here, and I'll be on my way."

I squinted to decipher the printing without my glasses. It might as well have been written in hieroglyphics.

"I can't read this. And if I can't read this, I can't sign it." I gave the clipboard back to her.

"What's happening in Fairport these days is outrageous," she continued. "Our town fathers must be rolling in their graves. People can't get a decent night's sleep with all the noise. It's absolutely, positively disgraceful, and we have to stop it."

She shoved the clipboard toward me again. I was impressed with how strong she was at her age.

"We're getting nowhere, Phyllis," I said. "And I have to leave."

I turned to go, and she grabbed my shirt. Sheesh. This was getting ridiculous. Where were Lucy and Ethel when I needed them?

"All right," I said. "Tell me what this is all about. But be quick about it. I'm going to be late as it is."

"People in town turned to me for help after getting no satisfaction whatsoever from our elected officials," Phyllis continued. "None whatsoever! Can you believe that? How would you feel if you hadn't gotten a good night's sleep in weeks?

"During the day, the noise is even worse," she continued without giving me a chance to answer. "I've heard it for myself, and I knew I had to do something. The citizens of Fairport are depending on me."

"I'm getting a headache," I said.

"That's exactly my point! And you don't even live close to the pickleball courts! Just imagine if you lived right next door!" Phyllis was so angry, she was foaming at the mouth. She was not attractive to look at, believe me.

"I wanted to give you the honor of being the petition's first signer. I know you love our town almost as much as I do. Thousands of our residents will follow your shining example. You'll go down in local history as Fairport's own John Hancock. We'll ban pickleball from our beautiful town once and for all!"

"I don't want to be Fairport's own John Hancock," I protested. I was desperate to get her to leave, but how?

My fertile imagination did not let me down. Instead of continuing to argue with her, I grabbed the clipboard and pressed it close to my heart.

"Phyllis, you've given me so much to think about. I want to share the petition with Jim, if that's all right with you. He may even want to do a feature story about your efforts in The Fairport News."

I knew Jim would probably scream at me for getting him involved, but desperate situations call for desperate solutions, right? Of course, right. Or maybe I'd get lucky and he wouldn't hear me.

"Do you really think he would, Carol? That would be so wonderful. I knew I could count on you to help." Phyllis was pathetically grateful, which made me feel guilty. But I soldiered on.

"It would be best if I talk to him first, so I suggest you stop canvassing for signatures until we get his input.

"And now, I have to go." I slammed the door before she could say anything else, texted Mike I was running late, and was finally on my way before I had still another calamity to deal with.

Phyllis's unexpected visit had added even more to my already long list of Things I Need To Worry

About. Right at the top of that list was "Avoid any interaction with Poppy today."

My drive was peaceful until I arrived at the rec center. I was sure Poppy had stationed herself at the front door so she could start screaming at me all over again once she saw my car.

You can do this, Carol. You're a good driver. You know you are. Don't let one tiny mistake in judgment rattle your self-confidence.

I switched the left turn blinker on and slowly drove into the parking lot. Thank goodness there were fewer cars to deal with than yesterday. I was relieved that Poppy's fancy car was nowhere to be seen. Phew. I was safe for today.

I had to focus on today's primary goal – to find out if my son and Poppy's daughter were really planning their wedding. And how to stop it.

Chapter 41

*The older I get, the more I appreciate staying home, doing absolutely nothing.
I get in less trouble that way.*

I immediately had second thoughts. I had to trust Mike to tell me whatever he had to tell me whenever he was ready to tell me. Until then....

"It's none of my business," I said aloud.

"What's none of your business?" Mike asked, startling me.

"Phyllis Stevens," I blurted out without even pausing to take a breath.

I hope you're all impressed with how fast I came up with an answer to Mike's question. It can be handy to have more than one crisis happening at the same time. I can dodge a tricky question like Mike's without even trying.

"She caught me this morning as I was leaving, and I couldn't get rid of her. You know how she can be."

Mike rolled his eyes and nodded.

"It might be better if I drive today," he said, holding out his hand for my keys.

He knows what happened yesterday in the parking lot! Tim must have told him. What a rat. Or else, Poppy did. That's even worse!

"Why?" I snapped, holding onto my keys for dear life. "What have you heard?"

"Nothing, Mom. Take it easy. I'm not criticizing your driving. I've found a few short cuts from here to the condo. It's easier if I drive myself instead of giving you the instructions."

"In that case, okay" I said, handing him the keys and moving over to the passenger seat of the car with great difficulty. "I'm a little shell shocked from my Phyllis encounter."

Focus on your mission here today, Carol. Did he and Charli set a wedding date? But do not force him or trick him into telling you.

My possible future daughter-in-law was waiting for us at the condo complex along with a handsome older man wearing a Fairport Country Club golf shirt and khaki slacks. I tried not to stare at him, but it was a real effort. With his thick blonde locks, ocean-blue eyes, and megawatt smile, he could have been Robert Redford's twin. I had a brief image of me instead of Barbra Streisand playing the object of Redford's affections in one of my favorite movies, *The Way We Were*.

Charli had a big smile on her face, which I was sure wasn't directed at me. When Mike stepped out of the car, she threw herself into his arms, almost knocking him over.

"Hey, take it easy. You know how fragile I am."

She pulled back a little bit. "I'm just so glad to see you. I missed you."

"I missed you too. But we've only been apart two hours."

A warning sign flashed in my maternal brain. If Charli was this possessive now, what would she be like if they got married?

"Hi, Charli," I said, giving her a big smile. "It's nice to see you again." How about backing up a little and let my son catch his breath?

"Mrs. Andrews, how rude of me to ignore you. It's great to see you, too. I hope you approve of what we've done inside. I can't wait for you to see it." Charli's cheeks were pink with excitement.

The handsome object of my fantasy standing next to her turned his attention to me and held out his hand for me to shake. I tried not to swoon. He really was very good-looking.

"I'm Lou Hollister, Charli's father. It's a real pleasure to meet you, Mrs. Andrews. I understand from my daughter that you and my wife Poppy know each other from your high school days. I'm sure you're both happy to have reconnected after all these years."

I almost said, "You must be kidding," but stopped myself.

"Poppy spends hours every day at the rec center," Lou continued. "Daily exercise has always been her passion."

"Please, call me Carol," I said. "I believe you know my husband, Jim. He speaks very highly of you."

Lou nodded. "Jim's a great guy. I feel like I already know you, Carol. He often talks about you."

I wasn't quite sure how to take that comment, so I changed the subject. "My dear friend, Mary Alice Costello, lives here too," I said, reaching inside the car and grabbing my purse.

"I believe we've met," Lou said. "She's a lovely person."

"Mary Alice has often said how much she likes living at this complex."

I was running out of small talk, which is unusual. I can always think of something more to say. The problem is usually getting me to stop talking.

"That's nice to hear," Lou said. "We certainly do everything we can to keep our owners happy."

"We?" I questioned. "I understood from Jim that your company built the complex."

"That's true. But my company has the controlling interest in the property. We also own several units and use them as rentals.

"Poppy once said that, once I get a hold on something, I won't let it go." Lou's face darkened. "I think it's the other way around."

Chapter 42

I'm starting to realize how much I have in common with my computer. We both start out with lots of memory and drive. Then we become antiquated, crash unexpectedly, and eventually need to have our parts replaced.

This conversation was getting really weird. And we were both still standing in front of my car.

"The kids are already inside," I said. "Charli's waving at us."

"After you," Lou said as we walked toward the unit. "Charli's done an amazing decorating job in such a short time. It looks like home already. She really has a flair for that kind of thing."

Don't think for one minute that I'm letting your daughter get away with doing all the decorating. After all, whose condo was it?

I realized instantly that I'd hit on the million-dollar question. I wondered if handsome Lou had the answer, because I certainly didn't.

"Mike's always been very creative," I replied. "He already had a vision of what he wanted his new condo to look like. We discussed it over breakfast this morning. He values my input."

Okay. Part of that was a tiny exaggeration. Or an enormous stretch of accuracy. But if we'd had a chance to talk at breakfast this morning, this is what we would have talked about. Give me a little maternal leeway, okay?

"Here we are," Lou said.

Mike was at the door, looking a little nervous. "I sure hope you like it, Mom. Please, be honest."

"Oh, my goodness," I said as I got my first peek at his new digs.

"Does that mean you approve?" Charli asked.

"It's very nice," I said as I walked from room to room. "And it's certainly a lot neater than your bedroom at home."

Notice how I threw in that reference to "home."

What it looked like now was a model unit that had been furnished by an interior designer. It was an impersonal collection of furniture and accessories that I was sure Mike hadn't picked out himself.

There was nothing warm and friendly about it at all. Everything was white. White sofa, chairs, lamps, tables, bed, window treatments – get the picture? It made me cold, literally, and I shivered. Perhaps Charli was pioneering a new HGTV design style, Early Igloo.

This would never feel like home for Mike. Where could he sit and relax after a hard day at Picklelilly's?

Heck, where would Jim and I sit and relax if/when we visited? I'd be worried about getting a tiny spot on the furniture. And forget about bringing Lucy and Ethel with us. I could imagine the outcry from Charli if the dogs jumped on the sofa.

Perhaps we could give Mike a Siberian Husky for a housewarming gift. A sled dog would be the perfect pet to match the décor.

I know. I'm a bad person.

Charli threw her arms around me and gave me a huge hug. "I'm so happy you like it, Mrs. Andrews. Mike was worried you wouldn't." She had a goofy, dreamy smile on her face.

"Mrs. Andrews. I just love saying that. I can't wait to have that last name, too."

I was stunned. But not for long.

"I think it's wonderful that you want us to be lifelong friends," I said, returning the hug a little more forcefully than necessary.

Give me some credit. I knew that's not what Charli meant. I just chose to deliberately misinterpret her.

I snuck a quick glance at my son. He looked shell-shocked at Charli's comment. Lou, on the other hand, was beaming from ear to ear.

Suddenly I wondered how much Lou really knew about my history with his wife. Did he realize how our recent interaction could negatively impact any permanent plans our kids may have?

My imagination went into overdrive. I couldn't stop myself.

Was this handsome man devious enough to support Charli and Mike's relationship just to make Poppy angry?

To drive an even larger wedge between Charli and her mother?

Or, even worse, to force the kids to choose which parents to support?

All of a sudden, I didn't find him attractive anymore.

Chapter 43

My therapist set half a glass of water in front of me. He asked me if I was an optimist or a pessimist. I drank the water and told him I was a problem-solver.

We didn't talk much on our drive back to the rec center. Mike parked in front of the entrance, turned off the motor, and offered his hand to help me out of the car.

"I'm not that old," I snapped at him, refusing help like the stubborn stupid woman I can be. "I can do this all by myself."

Predictably, my grand exit ended abruptly when my right foot went into a pothole and I stumbled.

"I just did that to make you feel needed," I said, grabbing his hand to steady myself.

"Sure you did," my smarty pants son said. He wouldn't let go of my hand. "So, Mother dear, what did you really think of the condo? The truth."

"It's difficult for me to put my feelings into words right now," I said.

Mike released my hand. "Try. Please. It's important that you be honest with me."

"I think it could use some personal touches," I said, choosing my words with care. "The furnishings themselves are truly lovely. I was very impressed."

"It doesn't look like my place though, does it, Mom? It's nothing like the condo I have in Florida."

"Here's the thing. You and another person are choosing furniture together. You're combining what she likes and you like into what you both like. In some ways, it's almost like an engagement, to see if you're really suited to spend the rest of your life together. Because a successful marriage is always a compromise. This is the first test. Think carefully before you make a decision. About decorating or anything else."

I held my breath. Had I gone too far?

"Thanks, Mom. I appreciate your advice. I love Charli, and I think I want to marry her, but I don't want to be rushed into anything. She went a little too far today, and that freaked me out. We'll talk tonight and straighten a few things out."

"Great idea." I gave him a quick smooch, he waved, and I was on my way home.

I was proud of myself for handling what could have been a touchy situation without losing my cool. I thought about texting Jenny with an update but decided against it. No use adding more fuel to that particular fire.

My stomach grumbled, reminding me I hadn't had lunch. I was mentally inventorying the contents of my refrigerator as I turned onto Old Fairport Turnpike and slammed on the brakes. There was a strange car completely blocking the entrance to my driveway. How rude!

I beeped my horn and flashed my lights repeatedly, but the car didn't move. Now I was really getting steamed.

I pulled in front of the vehicle, jumped out of my car, and starting yelling. "You're blocking my driveway! Move your car right now! I'm not kidding. I'll call the police!"

"Oh, I don't think so, Carol," said Poppy, exiting on the driver's side with a triumphant look on her face. "But you may want to call your attorney.

"Tim, please give Carol the necessary paperwork. I want to capture the moment with a photo from my cellphone."

"Are you sure you want to go through with this?" Tim asked Poppy.

"Absolutely. Give it to her right now and I'll get a photo for posterity. Then we can leave."

"I'm really sorry about this, Carol," Tim said, handing me an envelope.

"What's this?" I asked. "An invitation?"

Poppy laughed. "Not exactly. I'm suing you for $2 million for damaging my car and causing me tremendous pain and suffering. See you in court, Carol. And I don't mean the pickleball court.

"Come on, Tim. Get in the car and let's go."

I just stood there, holding the envelope, and didn't react as Poppy and Tim drove away. I could hear Poppy's horrible laugh, and then she blasted the horn.

I don't think I'd ever hated anyone more in my life than Poppy Hollister. Now I could really understand how Charli felt about her mother. What an evil person.

"She's not going to get away with it," I fumed as I drove into the safety of my driveway.

The reality of the entire situation came crashing down on me. "Oh, my gosh. She could end up being Mike's mother-in-law!"

Chapter 44

I tried starting the day without coffee once. My court date is pending.

By the time I'd reached the kitchen door, I'd calmed myself down. No need to frighten Lucy and Ethel.

After a quick run in the yard and a few biscuits (for the dogs), I polished off the rest of the mint chocolate chip ice cream I keep hidden for my lunch.

The infusion of chocolate did wonders to sweeten my mood. I was finally sweet enough to give my two canine advisors a summary of Poppy's tirade and see whether they had any suggestions for revenge.

Oops. I didn't mean to let that slip. Not revenge. Of course not. Just...an appropriate way for me to handle the situation.

Both canines made it crystal clear by settling down for another snooze while I was still talking that I had to solve this crisis on my own. Oh, well. It was a long shot.

I knew the first thing I had to do was tell my husband about the lawsuit. Jim was guaranteed to scream and yell, especially since I hadn't told him about what happened in the rec center parking lot yesterday. Then I'd cry and try to explain, emphasizing that I was innocent of any major wrong-doing. He wouldn't hear a word I said and zero in on the amount of the lawsuit. It would be awful. Maybe he'd even want to divorce me!

"Oh, Lord, I wish I could avoid that." I licked the spoon again, hoping for divine inspiration. And suddenly, I had the perfect solution. Larry McGee.

Perhaps some of you haven't met Larry McGee, otherwise known as Claire's husband and the most boring man to sit next to at a dinner party. His social skills are lacking, to put it mildly.

Larry and Jim commuted together to the Big Apple back in the good old days. He's also a retired New York attorney; I've been told he has a legal mind as sharp as the proverbial steel trap.

Although I've known Larry for almost 40 years (I was a bridesmaid in his wedding to Claire), I'm sure we've never had a single one-on-one meaningful interaction or conversation. That was about to change.

I desperately hoped I could reach Larry directly, without having to go through Claire first. She's been criticizing my driving ever since we both got our learner's permits back in high school. No way did I want her to know why I was begging her husband for help. Even after I was proved innocent (which I was certain to be, because I was!), she'd never let me forget it.

I searched my contact list for Larry's information but came up empty. The only email address and cell phone number I had were Claire's. The Good Lord was certainly testing me today.

Priorities, Carol! So what if Claire gives you grief? You've handled her before, and you can handle her again.

Then I remembered our recent "Honey Don't" pact. We'd each made a list of the other's habit that drove us nuts. The idea was to refrain from this habit for as long as possible or suffer a punishment we'd mutually agreed on in advance. I chose Claire's consistent criticism of me, and if she strayed, she had to clean my house, including bathrooms, cellar, and garage. So far, we'd both behaved ourselves. Today would be a true test.

Feeling confident, I fired off a quick text to Claire.

Me: Is Larry home?
Claire: Yes.
Me: In the house?
Claire: Nope. In the garage tinkering with his new love.
Me: Woman or classic car?
Claire: Very funny.
Me: Thanks.
Claire: Why all the questions?
Me: Jim wanted to know.

I clicked off before Claire could question me further.

With any luck at all, I could sneak into the McGees' garage, tell my sad tale to Larry, get his advice, and sneak out without Claire catching me.

Fortunately, the McGees only live a few miles from us, so I got there in less than ten minutes. Their comfortable home was built in the early 1900s on an acre of land, and Larry's lair, as Claire calls the detached garage, is at the far back of their property. Larry claims he only uses the garage to work on his classic car collection, but Claire suspects he hides out there longer than necessary whenever he wants privacy.

I'm sure she's right. But because I'm such a good friend, I never told her so.

I parked my car around the block so Claire wouldn't see it, then cut through a few back yards to my destination. Rock music was blaring out of the garage. As I got closer, I realized the song was Steppenwolf's "Born to Be Wild." Larry was busy polishing the headlights of an antique car while harmonizing (badly) with the band.

I wasn't sure what to do. I hated to interrupt him while he was having so much fun. I also didn't want to embarrass the guy, especially because I needed a huge favor from him.

Oh, what the heck. I joined in on the chorus, and we finished the song together.

"I guess I'm born to be wild, too," I said, laughing. "That was lots of fun."

"Shhh," Larry said. "Don't tell Claire. She may be jealous." His brown eyes twinkled, and I realized he was kidding me. I also realized Larry had very nice eyes.

What is wrong with you? You never noticed his eyes before. Get to the reason why you're here, goofus.

"I won't tell Claire if you won't tell Jim," I said.

"About us singing together?"

"No. About this." I fished around in my handbag and pulled out the envelope from Poppy. "I have a big problem, and I need your advice. I didn't know who else to turn to." I could feel tears spill over onto my cheeks, which embarrassed the heck out of me.

"Hey, let's have none of that," Larry said, offering me his polishing rag to dry my face. (I declined, in case you were wondering.)

"I got this about an hour ago." I shoved the envelope into his hand. "This person claims I damaged her car and is suing me for $2 million!"

Larry whistled and opened the envelope. "Wow. That's an impressive figure. Did you do it?"

"Of course not! Poppy's lying. She hates me."

Larry opened the car door and gestured for me to sit inside. "Give me a while to go over this, and then we'll talk, okay? At first glance, I think this is only a nuisance suit. Whoever this person is, she's trying to scare you."

"She's doing a damn good job.

"Excuse me. I didn't mean to swear. I never use that word. Please don't tell Claire I...."

Larry held up his hand to silence me so he could concentrate on the letter. I'm one of those people who tend to chatter about silly things when nervous, like I was then. It took every ounce of self-control I possessed to zip my lips and not distract him.

After waiting about three hours (only a slight exaggeration) during which I mentally went through my closet deciding what to wear to my trial that would convince the jury I was innocent, I heard Larry say, "I've never seen one of these. Ever."

I was doomed. Forget the trial. I was going right to prison.

"What kind of a car did you hit, Carol?"

"I didn't hit any car!" I said. "There's not a single new scratch on my car, which proves it. That's the whole point. I'm innocent!"

I started to tell Larry the whole sorry story, but he interrupted me.

"Can you describe the other car for me?"

"I think it was white."

"That's all you remember?"

"Yes. Why?"

"According to the lawsuit, the damaged vehicle was a vintage Shelby Mustang valued at more than one million dollars."

"That can't be right," I argued. "Who in their right mind would pay that much for a car?"

Larry favored me with a stare that jarred me. Here I was, sitting in a classic antique car that he'd obviously paid big bucks for. Not a million dollars, though. Although, what did I knew about classic cars?

"Just between us, my new beauty cost me more than our Florida condo did. That's all I'm saying."

"Just between us," he repeated for emphasis.

"I get it," I said, crossing my heart for emphasis. "I've made a few expensive purchases over the years that Jim knows nothing about."

Larry laughed. "Someday, we'll have to share our techniques. Maybe we can help each other.

"And speaking of that," Larry said, "do you have a dollar bill in your wallet?"

After longer than I'm willing to admit to any of you, I came up with a crumpled bill that had probably been resting in my change purse since late last year.

Triumphant, I waved the bill at Larry, who immediately snatched it out of my hand. "My retainer," he said. "Now, I'm officially representing you in this lawsuit."

I laughed out loud. "I didn't realize your rates were so reasonable."

"Let's just say, these are special circumstances, okay? Don't worry."

I started to protest, but my lawyer interrupted me. "I'll call Jim now about the lawsuit and reassure him that I'm handling it. I'll also tell him that I'm one hundred percent certain this ridiculous lawsuit will be dropped before it goes any further. After I've calmed him down, I'll text you. Got it?"

I wanted to throw my arms around Larry and give him a big thank you smooch. I nodded instead.

"Wait until you get my text, then go home. This lawsuit is going to disappear faster than you can imagine. This isn't the first nuisance case like this I've handled.

"One more thing," he added as I was about to make my getaway. "Under no circumstances are you to have any contact, whatsoever, with either the plaintiff in this lawsuit or her attorney. If either of them reaches out to you in any way, you are to let me know immediately. Understood?"

"Yes."

I wondered if Larry's no-contact order also applied to the plaintiff's daughter.

Chapter 45

*I decided to stop calling the bathroom the "John"
and start calling it the "Jim."
I feel so much better saying I'm going to the "Jim"
now.*

Per Larry's orders, I didn't rush to get home. Instead, I drove to the beach where a few hardy souls were enjoying the late afternoon sun.

At least there are plenty of open parking spaces here, Carol.

At first, that random thought made me laugh. But not for long. Despite Larry's assurance that we really weren't going to lose our life savings and our home because of a fender bender that never happened, I was still very nervous. I prayed that he was right.

Soon the rhythm of the waves and the warm sun calmed me. Despite all my pent-up anxiety, I could feel my eyelids getting heavy. What I deserved now was a quick nap.

Why fight it, especially since you might not be able to sleep a wink tonight?

Why, indeed? I was just starting to doze off when I heard a man and a woman in the midst of a heated argument. My car windows were open so I could hear them clearly. I knew it was Mike and Charli.

"We just started dating!" Mike yelled.

"I'm sorry," Charli sobbed. "My father already knew about us, so I wanted to tell my mother, too."

"In case I haven't been completely clear before," Mike said, "I'll say it again. You never should have told your father, or anybody else, that we were getting married!"

"My father already knew about us," Charli insisted.

"He knew we were dating! Which is all we've been doing! You're the one who told him we were already engaged!"

"You're right. I made a mistake."

"I'll say. Telling my mom we were planning to get married was bad enough. You made an even worse mistake by telling your mother the same thing."

"You're right, Mike. I should have known how she'd react. I never should have done it. We had a terrible argument. She told me I'd marry you over her dead body. And I told her that was fine with me. Then I left, and I thought that was the end of it. I guess I was wrong."

"Now you tell me your mother's suing my family for over $2 million, probably just to break us up. Look at all the trouble you've caused. What's the matter with you?"

"Please, Mike. Give me a chance to make it right."

"How do you plan on doing that?"

"I'll give her a day or so to cool down. Then I'll tell her we've decided to take things slower for a while. We'll hug and make up, the way we always do after we have one of these fights. Trust me. It'll work out fine."

"It better," Mike said. "Right now, I'm going back to Picklelilly's."

I slid down in my seat as they both turned in my direction. I prayed Mike wouldn't notice my car.

"Mike! Can we talk again later? Please, Mike. I'm begging you. Please stop. Wait for me!"

Mike ignored her. He was stalking back to the condo parking lot at warp speed, probably muttering to himself. I hoped he was calmer by the time he got back to the restaurant.

My phone pinged with a text from Larry: "All okay."

That's what you think.

I sent back a thumbs up emoji, girded my loins (figuratively speaking), then headed home.

Chapter 46

Every wife's dream is that her husband will take her in his arms, carry her to the bed, and clean the house while she sleeps.

I'd barely turned into my driveway when Jim burst out of the house. The expression on his face was scary. It made me want to turn around and leave without getting into the altercation that was about to happen as soon as I opened the car door. Larry's assurance that everything was okay at my house was a big fat fib. Another example of male solidarity united against a helpless female.

"This is not my fault. I am innocent!" I told myself. "If Jim doesn't believe me, that's his problem, not mine." I wrenched open the car door and stood, tall and proud, to face my husband.

"I am woman," I yelled as he walked toward me. "I am a good driver. And I know how to park a car safely!"

"Oh, Carol, sweetheart, what an awful ordeal for you to go through," Jim said, crushing me in an unexpected embrace. He kissed me, then kissed me again. Which made me immediately suspicious.

I turned to collect my purse and my thoughts. This was not at all what I'd expected. Maybe Larry had done a good job after all.

"It's been quite a day," I replied, allowing Jim to lead me into the kitchen, where I was welcomed by our two canines.

"Sit here," he said, pulling out a chair. "I poured us each a glass of chardonnay." He raised his own glass. "Let's both enjoy the wine. Then we'll talk."

I took a tiny sip, and was surprised. This was the good stuff, the kind we save for when we have guests. What was my husband up to?

"What are we celebrating? I've had a terrible day."

"I know all about it," Jim said.

Oh, boy. Here it comes.

I drained the remainder of my wine, then took a deep breath. "Go ahead. Say what you're thinking. I can take it."

"I think you are the bravest woman I ever met. And the smartest."

Say what?

"Larry called and told me about the ridiculous lawsuit. He said that woman had the nerve to hand the legal papers to you in person, just to see your face. But you didn't flinch for a second."

"I didn't?"

"You knew right away what to do."

"I did?

"I mean, I did."

"You had the presence of mind to immediately contact our attorney. And Larry took it from there.

"Any other wife would have immediately called her husband, hysterical, and gotten the husband all upset. But not you. Instead, you handled it exactly the way I'd handle it. That's what lawyers are for, and we're lucky Larry is such a good friend. If he assures me the suit is nonsense, then it's nonsense."

"What about the money? I thought you'd be hysterical when you saw how much Poppy was suing me for." Jim's reaction was too good to be true. Had a complete stranger taken over my husband's body?

"No big deal," Jim said. "It'll never come to that. Besides, my dear wife, your husband is once again gainfully employed. And I don't mean my freelance job at The Fairport News.

"As of today, I have a full-time job. Mike's hired me to manage Picklelilly's."

Chapter 47

Maybe if we tell people the brain is an app, more of them will use it.

"I don't understand. That's Mike's job. How can he hire you to do his job, when he's already being paid for that job? Isn't that against the law?" I rubbed my forehead. I could feel a massive headache coming on, and not from the chardonnay.

Jim grinned. "I may have exaggerated, just a bit."

There was a discreet cough from the direction of the door, then Mike joined us at the kitchen table. "You sure did, Dad."

Mike gave my hand a squeeze. "Hi, Mom. I know you've had quite a day."

I refused to give in to the immediate urge to sob hysterically. "Quite a day is an understatement, believe me. I'm frustrated, angry, confused, upset—pick one. And I'm also hungry! With everything else going on, I never had lunch."

"Food first," Mike said, presenting me with a shopping bag filled with goodies. "We're continuing to test new recipes at the restaurant before deciding on the final menu. Help yourself."

"I'll get some plates," I said.

"You stay put, Carol," Jim said. "Let me wait on you for a change. I'll get the plates, knives, forks, and napkins."

"And spoons," I added.

Jim sighed. "And spoons.

"You see what I'm up against, Mike? Even when I'm trying to wait on your mother, she has to tell me how to do it correctly."

Mike laughed. A true belly laugh.

"I needed a parent fix today. The way you two play off each other is hilarious."

"Years of practice," I quipped. Jim just rolled his eyes.

After several minutes of companionable eating, I put my fork down and addressed my menfolk. "I want to know what's going on with you two, including all details. Did you really hire your father?"

Mike nodded. "Yep. Dad's going to be my eyes and ears at Picklelilly's whenever I fly to Florida to check on Cosmo's. He's been around the restaurant enough to know the workmen and the preliminary staff I've hired. I trust him to keep me updated on exactly what's going on whenever I have to go out of town. I've already told everyone that whatever he says, goes. He's the boss in my place."

"I start tomorrow," Jim added.

"Does that mean you're leaving tomorrow?"

"Actually, I'm leaving tonight. I managed to get the last seat on a late flight to Miami. I'm heading to the airport from here. I have a driver picking me up in about half an hour."

"Isn't this trip awfully sudden? Are you sure you have to leave now, when there are so many things you have to sort out?"

"That's exactly why I'm leaving now, Mom. I saw you at the beach a few hours ago, so I know you heard the awful fight I had with Charli."

"I didn't mean to eavesdrop," I said.

"I know, Mom. When Charli and I started dating, I knew that Dad and her father knew each other. That's how I got the tip about bidding for the restaurant in the first place. I didn't know anything about her mother, who turned out to be somebody who knew you a long time ago.

"All of a sudden, Charli started talking about us getting married. I went along with her, a little. In retrospect, I shouldn't have. I knew it was much too soon for us to make that kind of a life commitment. But it was just talk between the two of us. Truthfully, I fell head over heels with her as soon as I met her. At least, I thought I did. But marriage! The more I thought about it, the more I realized I was stupid to rush things until I was really sure."

I was so relieved I almost started clapping. Instead, I continued to enjoy the delicious dinner I hadn't cooked.

"Charli had already told her father about "us." Then she said something to you today, Mom. I know that must have been a huge shock."

"Don't forget what she told me," Jim added.

Mike nodded. "That's when I began to realize things were getting out of control. I should have spoken up then, but I didn't.

"Then she told her mother. And when she did that, all hell broke loose. Her mother went ballistic, which is exactly what Charli knew she'd do. Charli told me she hates her mother. They've never gotten along.

"I was furious when I found out her mother was suing you about that stupid fender bender you supposedly caused in the parking lot of the rec center. This lawsuit is all Charli's fault."

"I thought you and Poppy were high school friends," Jim said, looking confused.

"We knew each other in high school, and one summer, Claire and I worked for her parents at the beach," I clarified. "But we were never really friends. When I saw Poppy at the pickleball court, I didn't even remember who she was."

"So, to be clear, this nuisance lawsuit is happening only because you and Charli are supposedly thinking of getting married, Mike?" Jim asked. "That's nuts."

"Yes. So I decided the best thing I can do right now is make a quick trip to Florida and check on Cosmo's while you hold down the fort here. Maybe the situation will improve if my absence gives Poppy a chance to cool down. Charli says her mother will decide not to sue you when she has a chance to think about it, Mom."

"I hope you're right," I said. "We don't happen to have a spare $2 million lying around that we could use to pay her off."

"I guess that would really put a dent in Jenny's and my inheritance," Mike said, a deadpan expression on his face.

"Maybe you should send off a text to Larry and fill him in on what Mike's told us," Jim suggested.

"I don't think so. Not yet. What if the situation doesn't change? What if it gets even worse? I don't want to confuse him. After all, Mike, this is all speculation on your part. You don't know that's what really happened."

"I guess so. But it sure makes sense to me.

"Anyway, thanks to this latest crisis in the Andrews family, you now have a job that will keep you occupied and feeling useful, Dad. Thanks for giving me some space to straighten out my head and my life. I really appreciate it."

"I'm glad I could help you," Jim said. "And that you have so much trust in my ability to do a good job. I'll try not to let you down.

"I'm sure your mother's also happy because I'll be out of the house and not bugging her for at least a few days, right, Carol? I'll try to bring home dinner every night, so you won't have to cook another meal for a while. It's a win-win situation for everybody."

Except, as things turned out, it wasn't a win-win situation for anybody. Not by a long shot.

Chapter 48

Think you're old and you will be old. Think you're still young and you will be delusional.

The next two days were drama-free for me. I thanked the Good Lord for giving me a much-needed break after all I'd been through.

Jenny's teaching schedule became more demanding, which meant more time for me to spend taking care of the most perfect grandchild ever, my darling CJ.

Mike checked in frequently from Florida. I was glad he sounded better after distancing himself from the romantic drama. I wasn't thrilled, however, when he said he and Charli were working on repairing their relationship. I tried to be supportive, but I secretly hoped they'd break up permanently. So, sue me. I'm his mother and that's how I felt.

Even better, Jim was busy at his Very Important Job, leaving home before the sun was up and not returning until dusk. It was just like the good old days BJR (Before Jim's Retirement), when he commuted to his public relations job in Manhattan and I was on my own every day. What bliss it was to be able to spend my days any way I wanted without him standing over me all the time.

On second thought, my life was even better now than BJR. In the old days, when Jim arrived home from the city, I always had a home-cooked meal waiting for him. Believe it or not, I had actually cooked the meal myself, from scratch, as opposed to ordering take-out from a local restaurant and passing it off as my own culinary effort.

Per his promise, when Jim arrived home from Picklelilly's every day, he always had samples of whatever new recipes the chef had tested for our dinner. What a treat!

There was no further interaction of any kind with Poppy. To be safe, I avoided the rec center and the pickleball court like the plague, even driving miles out of my way to avoid going anywhere near them. Jim reassured me my nemesis hadn't been seen on the premises for a while, and I briefly wondered what she was doing with herself these days. I hoped she wasn't figuring out another way to torture me.

On the third day, a text came from a number I didn't recognize. I usually assume messages like this are spam and delete them immediately. But the first two words, "I'm sorry," stopped me.

Only one person owed me a huge apology: Poppy Hollister. Intrigued, I read the entire message.

Poppy: I'm sorry about the lawsuit. Meet me at the pickleball court at 8:00 tonight so we can talk.

It sounded like Poppy was going to apologize and withdraw the lawsuit, so how could I say no? One less thing for me to worry about. I had a brief vision of Poppy kneeling at my feet and begging my forgiveness. I'd wait several minutes before I graciously replied in the affirmative. This was an offer I'd definitely not refuse.

As I started to text a reply, I heard Larry McGee's voice in my head, loud and clear, telling me to have no interaction whatsoever with Poppy or anyone else associated with the lawsuit. I was supposed to tell him immediately if anyone contacted me and he would handle it.

So that's exactly what I did, with one caveat. When Larry talked to Poppy at 8:00 tonight, I'd be right there with him.

Chapter 49

Marriage is the only union that can't be organized. Both sides think they're management.

It turned out that convincing Larry McGee to sneak out of his house for a clandestine tryst at the pickleball court was easy, even with me tagging along. The hard part was getting out of my own house. I was sure that if Jim knew what I was up to, he'd insist on coming with me. Bless him, he'd only have my best interests at heart, but he was liable to start yelling at Poppy about the lawsuit and ruin everything.

You can do this, Carol. Think about how often you've snuck out of the house and Jim was never the wiser. You got this.

I checked to be sure Jim was snoozing in his favorite chair. Lucy and Ethel were curled up at his feet. Satisfied that he was in a deep sleep, I tiptoed to the kitchen door and quietly opened it. I had one foot outside when both dogs woke up and ran to join me. Rats.

Jim walked into the kitchen, wide awake. "Where are you going at this hour, Carol?"

"It's not that late. I won't be long."

"Is something wrong?"

"No. I just realized we're out of milk. I'm going to the store to buy some so we'll have it for the morning."

"I'll come with you. CVS sells milk, and I have a coupon that expires in two days."

"No!"

"I mean, I'm also going to buy vegetables to make salad. We don't eat enough vegetables."

"I don't like the idea of you driving by yourself at night," my gallant husband said. "What if something happens?"

"For Pete's sake, Jim. What could possibly happen? Unless you're criticizing my driving. Is that what you mean?" Now I was getting angry.

"Don't lose your temper, Carol. That's not what I meant."

"I promise I'll be careful. And I'll be home before you know it." I waved my phone. "Call me if you think of anything else you want." And I raced out the door before Jim could delay me even more.

Before I even reached the rec center, I had talked myself into a first-class bad mood. Poppy wanted to talk to me tonight? Well, I had a few things to say to her, too. None of which were complimentary.

No matter what tricks she had up her sleeve, I wasn't falling for them. Poppy was the most devious, lying human being that I had ever had the displeasure to know. How wonderful people like Mr. and Mrs. P could be her parents was a mystery to me.

"Poppy Hollister is evil, through and through!" I pounded the steering wheel for emphasis. "I hate her! And I'm telling her that as soon as I walk in the rec center door!

"I hope I make her cry! I would love to see her cry. She needs to suffer, the way she's made me and my family suffer!"

There were only two cars in the parking lot when I arrived – Larry's and Poppy's infamous million-dollar white one. I had plenty of spaces to choose from, and I parked my car perfectly within the lines, just to prove that I could.

"Take that, Poppy Hollister," I said, slamming my car door. "I am a good driver. And I know how to park a car correctly!"

Larry appeared out of the darkness, startling me. I know, I was being stupid. Truth to tell, despite my show of bravado, I was a nervous wreck.

"Take it easy, Carol. I'm here with you. Let's listen to what she has to say instead of anticipating the worst, okay? And let me do the talking. That's what I'm here for, remember?"

"I know you're right. No matter what happens inside, and how much Poppy goads me, or lies to me, I promise to keep my mouth shut and not react."

"Atta girl," Larry said, holding the door for me. "Lead on. I haven't been inside this place in years."

I led Larry down a dimly lit hallway to the pickleball courts. "I don't know why it's so dark," I said, fumbling for the door. "I saw Poppy's car, so I know she's already here."

I finally found the correct switch. "Let there be light," I said. "Follow me."

I stopped walking so quickly that Larry bumped into me. "Hey, lady, your brake lights aren't working," he joked.

"Oh, dear God." I grabbed his arm and pointed to the center court, then turned away from the gruesome sight.

"I think I'm going to be sick."

Poppy was kneeling over the body of a man, sobbing. She was covered with blood spatters. And she was holding a knife.

Chapter 50

A true friend is someone who's there for you when they'd rather be anywhere else.

Larry grabbed me around the waist and held me tight so I wouldn't fall. The only thing I wanted to do at that moment was go home, but I knew that wouldn't be happening for a while. Sadly, this was not my first experience discovering a dead body.

"You okay now?" he whispered.

"I'm scared. What if she sees us and attacks us too?"

"You're sure that's Poppy holding the knife?" Larry asked.

"Yes. I'm sure."

"I'm confirming her identity because you may have to testify in court."

"Oh, lord. I hope it doesn't come to that."

"Stay right here," Larry ordered. "I'm calling 911."

"Don't leave me!"

"I won't be long. Stay back so she doesn't see you."

As I shrank against the door, I must have made a noise. Poppy screamed, "Who's there? Is someone there? Please, I need help!"

She's asking you to be her accomplice in a murder, Carol! Don't answer her!

"Carol Andrews, I know that's you. I can see your feet. You're wearing the same sneakers you wore for our pickleball lesson."

Poppy waved the knife around. "I need your help. Right now!"

Note to self: The first thing to do if you make it out of here alive is throw away these sneakers.

I stood as still as I could and didn't answer her. What was taking Larry so long?

"Carol!" Poppy screamed again. "I need you to help me!"

I found my voice. "Not unless you put the knife down." I was paralyzed with fear. Was she going to kill me too? Maybe I should have been honest with Jim about where I was going tonight.

Then he'd be in danger, too. Or he'd risk his life trying to save you. What if she stabbed him too?

I heard a clatter and prayed she'd finally dropped the knife. Poppy held up her hands to show me they were empty.

"I did it! I killed him! Oh, Lou, I'm so sorry. I never meant for this to happen." She began to sob uncontrollably.

The door behind me opened. "The police are on their way," Larry whispered.

"She saw me. I convinced her to drop the knife."

The door opened again, and I prayed the police were here.

Instead, I heard another woman screaming. "Mom! Mom! Why is Daddy on the floor? Why do you have blood all over you?

"Oh, my God. You've killed him. You've killed him!"

Charli pushed me aside and raced to her mother. She grabbed Poppy and hit her again and again. Poppy's face was bleeding from all the blows, but Charli didn't stop her brutal attack.

"We have to do something!" I screamed to Larry. "Charli's going to kill her mother if we don't stop her!"

I heard Tim's voice behind me. "What's going on here?

"Charli, no!" Tim raced to his hysterical niece and separated her from Poppy, then held her so she couldn't move.

"Let me go!" Charli screamed. "She's killed my daddy! I hate her!"

Tim held her tight. "Stop it, Charli! Stop it right now! Oh, my God. I can't believe this."

I finally heard the welcome sound of sirens, getting closer and closer. Then, I'm embarrassed to admit, I fainted.

Chapter 51

Everyone has the right to be stupid now and then. The problem is that some people abuse the privilege.

The next thing I knew, someone was shaking me awake, which made me happy, because I was having a dilly of a nightmare. I heard a familiar voice saying my name.

"Carol, it's me, Mark. You fainted. Are you able to stand up now?"

"Let me help you." My son-in-law gently pulled me into an upright position and propelled me onto a nearby chair.

"Are you feeling better now? I have to ask you some questions, starting with what the heck you're doing here at this hour when the rec center is closed." Mark handed me a cup of water and I drank it greedily. Who knew cold water could taste so good?

"Give me a second," I said. "I'll try to pull myself together."

"The victim has definitely expired," I heard someone else say. "I'd guess about half an hour ago, give or take. I'll know more after I examine him at the morgue. Cause of death appears to be a stab wound to the chest."

I saw Lou Hollister's body being loaded onto a gurney and covered with a tarp. I didn't have a nightmare. This really happened. I was an eyewitness to a murder.

"Where's Larry McGee?" I asked, looking around the pickleball court.

"The attorney? He's talking to Paul in the lobby. I was surprised to see him here. But not as surprised as I was to see you, Carol."

"Paul's here too? Oh, great. Just what I need. Please keep him away from me, Mark. You know he's bound to make a snarky comment about how he finds me at every local murder scene.

"Poppy Hollister asked me to meet her here tonight. She's my pickleball teacher."

I threw that last part in without thinking, then realized how stupid I sounded.

"Now, isn't that interesting," said the familiar voice of Mark's detective partner and my number one nemesis. "Your pickleball teacher invited you to witness a murder, Carol? Even for you, that's a first."

"Knock it off, Paul. That's not funny," Mark said.

"She knows I'm just kidding. We understand each other, don't we, Carol?"

"Perfectly," I replied.

"I'll take it from here, Paul," Mark said. "I suggest you get back to the station and take a statement from Mrs. Hollister. I'll see you when I'm finished here."

Paul was clearly not pleased about being ordered by his partner to leave the crime scene, especially in front of me, but he didn't say a word. Instead, he clicked his heels, saluted, and marched away.

"I don't know how you can stand working with him, Mark. I'd want to slug him every single day."

"Paul's a pretty good cop when you're not around, Carol. For some reason, you seem to bring out the worst in him."

His expression turned serious. "So, let's get to it. Why are you here?"

I started to answer Mark's question, then felt pressure on my arm. "I'll answer that question for Carol, if I may. I'm her attorney," Larry said.

"Pardon me if now I'm really confused," Mark said. "Are you saying you came to the pickleball court with an attorney, Carol? Were you expecting to witness a crime? Or worse, be accused of one?"

I laughed nervously. "You know me, Mark. Never a dull moment."

I felt the pressure on my arm again and knew I was being warned to be careful what I said. "Sorry. Bad joke I'm very nervous."

"Let me explain," Larry said. The poor man began to tell Mark about the lawsuit, but I kept interrupting him. I wanted Mark to know that I had not damaged Poppy's car. I also added that Poppy Hollister hated me for reasons I didn't understand, that Mike was dating Charli Hollister, that Poppy was furious about that and wanted to break them up.

Also that Jenny remembered Charli from high school and didn't like her at all. "And you know what a good judge of character your wife is, Mark," I said as I started to wind down.

Mark looked a little dazed by my explanation. I guess I'd given him TMI, even though I skipped the part about Claire and me working at Poppy's family beach house years ago.

"Carol's being unjustly sued for $2 million by Poppy Hollister," Larry said, trying to gain control of the conversation. "She texted Carol saying she was sorry she'd filed the lawsuit, and she suggested they meet at the pickleball court tonight to discuss it. Carol immediately reached out to me, and as Carol's attorney, it was important that I be present when she and Poppy met."

"Neither of us was expecting to find a dead body, though," I clarified.

Mark had been taking some quick notes while Larry and I were talking. "Exactly what did you see when you arrived here? No opinions or conjecture. Just the facts as you remember them."

"I preceded Larry going through the door onto the court." I frowned. "That doesn't sound correct. I didn't go through the door."

I paused for a minute, then continued. "I meant to say that I was walking to the pickleball court ahead of Larry. When I opened the door, it was very dark so I switched on the lights. I saw the dead body first. I stopped so quickly that Larry walked right into me."

"I apologize for that, Carol."

"That's okay, Larry. No damage done."

Mark made a "speed it up" motion with his hand, which annoyed me. He should know by now that it always takes me a while to get to the point of a story.

"I saw a man lying on the court floor, bleeding. Poppy was kneeling over him, holding a knife. There was a lot of blood, which made me nauseous. I'd never seen that much blood before."

"I was standing directly behind Carol, and because I'm taller than she is, I can verify that everything she's telling you is accurate," Larry said. "I immediately left to call 911 on my cell."

"I stayed behind, hoping Poppy wouldn't see me. But she did. She called my name and begged me to help her. I was terrified, but I convinced her to drop the knife."

"Did she say anything else?"

Oh, boy. Here it comes.

"Yes. She said...."

I started to cry.

"Don't rush," Mark said gently. "It's okay."

My next words would probably send Poppy to prison for murder. Or, even worse. But I had to tell the truth.

"Poppy called the man Lou, and I realized the man was Lou Hollister. And she said, 'I did it. I killed him.'"

"Then what happened?"

"Charli Hollister arrived and started screaming that her mother had killed her father. She hit her mother again and again. It was horrible. That's all."

"You're absolutely certain Poppy Hollister said, 'I did it. I killed him.' Those were her exact words?" Mark was wearing his serious cop face, which I always found intimidating, even though he's my son-in-law.

"Yes," I whispered. "That's what she said."

Larry grabbed my hand. "I hope that's all the questioning for tonight. Carol's very upset. So am I. Are we free to go now?"

Mark nodded. "But I'll need both of you at the police station tomorrow morning to sign statements."

Chapter 52

Some people use their phones to document the good times in their lives.
I use my phone to take pictures of labels that I can't read and enlarge the print so I can read them.

I cried all the way home. I cried for Lou Hollister, a nice man who'd lost his life tonight. I cried for Charli, who might never get over her father's shocking death. I cried for my son. Lou's death was sure to affect him, both professionally and personally. I cried for Poppy, who must have been totally desperate to commit such a despicable act.

Finally, I cried for myself. I felt horrible about telling Mark I heard Poppy admit she was a murderer. I was terrified that I'd have to testify against her in court.

But right now, I had to deal with Jim. I knew he'd be furious when he found out I was involved in another murder.

All you have to do is come up with another cleverly edited version of the truth. Think, Carol! You can do this!

I tried hard, but my devious brain was too upset and refused to cooperate. The traitor!

My phone told me it was past midnight. Maybe I could sneak into the house without being caught.

Then I had a brilliant idea, and it was actually closer to the truth than usual. I'd tell Jim that Larry insisted I let him know about any communication I received from the plaintiff, Poppy, about the lawsuit. I got a surprise text from her while I was grocery shopping, suggesting a clandestine rendezvous tonight at the rec center's pickleball court. I forwarded Poppy's text to Larry, who insisted on going with me. It wasn't our fault that when we arrived we got mixed up in a grisly murder. I was just an innocent wife who went out to buy milk. All I had to do was "adjust" the timeframe a little. Perfect.

Too bad it didn't work. I barely walked (slunk) into the kitchen when Jim stormed out of the bedroom. "Why didn't you tell me what you were really doing tonight, Carol? I could have gone with you. I should have gone with you. Why do you insist on getting yourself into these situations again and again?" He shook his head. "I'll never understand the way your brain works."

I couldn't blame the guy. I didn't understand the way my brain worked, either.

"I guess you heard from Larry," I said meekly.

"At least you called him," Jim said. His face was like a thundercloud. "You weren't going out to buy milk tonight, were you, Carol? Admit it."

"Larry insisted I call him if I heard from Poppy or her lawyer. So that's what I did."

I knew there was a subtext here, but I wasn't sure what it was. Then, I got it. Jim's feelings were hurt because I hadn't turned to him for help too.

"It was a pretty gruesome scene. Poor Lou Hollister. What a horrible way to die."

"Lou Hollister? He was the victim? I can't believe it."

"It's true. Didn't Larry tell you?"

"He didn't mention the name of the victim. He told me someone had been murdered and the two of you were there."

Jim shook his head. "This makes no sense. I saw Lou late this afternoon. He said he was leaving town tonight to look at an out-of-state property for a possible new condo development. So what was he doing at the rec center?

"Are you absolutely sure it was him?"

"For Pete's sake, Jim, I was there! I heard Poppy call him by name. And then Charli came in and started screaming that Poppy had killed her father! They had a terrible, brutal fight. Of course I'm sure it was Lou Hollister!"

Jim shook his head. "I just don't understand it."

Neither did I.

Chapter 53

Remember when people used to have diaries and got mad when somebody read them? Now people post everything on social media and get mad when people don't.

The real nightmare began before I even opened my eyes the next morning. And I'm not even counting the terrible dreams I'd had the night before.

Jim shook me awake. "You need to get up. Now. All hell's breaking loose!"

I kept my eyes closed tight and refused to budge. "If all hell is breaking loose, the Good Lord will take care of it."

My dear husband refused to take no for an answer. He returned a few minutes later with a cup of hot coffee, which he placed carefully on my nightstand.

Ah, bliss. Happiness is a husband who makes great coffee and delivers it to his sleepy wife.

As I started to reach for it, he snatched it away. "If you want the coffee, you have to get up. I'll see you in the kitchen."

I sighed. I knew I'd lost this argument, so I raced through my early morning hygiene ritual and joined my husband at the breakfast table. He was hunched over his laptop computer with a scowl on his face.

I took a quick gulp of caffeine to fortify myself. I hadn't seen that look since…well, never mind about that. I don't have to tell you everything!

Jim turned the laptop around so the screen was facing me. "Read that."

"The New York Tattler? Why are you reading that rag? You call it a disgrace to journalism."

I've been known to sneak a peek at the abovementioned source of unfounded gossip and inuendo to keep up with the latest rumors every once in a while. But please don't tell Jim that.

"I saw a blurb on the Fairport Patch first, and I followed the link."

He pointed to the laptop again. "Just read it'"

"Pickleball Princess Offs Cheating Husband," I read aloud.

I looked at the post again, and realized it included a photo of Charli that must have been taken last night. Her face was bruised, and her eyes were wild. "My mother killed my father! I hate her. Look what she just did to me! I hope she goes to prison for life!"

I took a much larger gulp of coffee. Heck, at that point, I could probably drink a whole pot and it still wouldn't help.

"The story's all over the internet. Facebook is going nuts! So are all the other alphabet sites. And Charli's being quoted in all of them."

"Facebook is always a little nuts," I said. I admit I check my page frequently every day, so I guess that makes me a little nuts too.

"That's not all. Mike's already called and texted from Florida. He's going crazy about Charli. He wants us to stop her from saying things she'll definitely regret later. She's ignoring all his efforts to reach her.

"And last but not least, Mary Alice called me."

"Mary Alice called you? Why?"

"She said she's been trying to reach you but you weren't answering. She sounded very upset. Almost hysterical."

"What in the world could she be upset about?"

"Only one way to find out." Jim handed me my phone. "Call her right now."

"It'll be better if I text her first."

"No, Carol. Call her. She insisted that she needs to talk to you."

Chapter 54

On a positive note, getting old means I'll never have another midlife crisis.

Mary Alice answered the phone after a single ring.

"I'm sorry I've been hard to....."

That was as far as I got before Mary Alice started sobbing.

I'm pretty much an expert in the crying/sobbing department, and I can tell all of you that the sobs I was hearing from the other end of my cell phone were gut wrenching.

"Carol!" Mary Alice sobbed. "Carol! I need you!"

"Mary Alice, you're scaring me. What's wrong?"

"Come!" she screamed. "Now!" And she terminated the call.

I never got dressed so fast in my life. I was so desperate to get to Mary Alice's condo that I grabbed the dirty clothes next to the washing machine, gave them the sniff test to be sure they weren't totally offensive, and wore them again. I've never done that before.

I grabbed my car keys, yelled to Jim that I was leaving, and drove like a speed demon to Mary Alice's. She sounded so desperate that I was terrified she might harm herself.

"Please, God. Please, God. Please, God," I kept repeating. "Please let Mary Alice be all right."

I arrived at the condo complex in ten minutes flat, which was definitely a Fairport speeding record. Mary Alice was standing at her door waiting for me. Her face was all red and puffy from crying.

She hugged me so hard I thought she'd break my ribs, then started sobbing again. "My life is over. I have nothing to live for anymore."

"The boys? Has something happened to one of them?"

I felt a stab at my heart. That had to be it. After her husband, Brian, died in a car wreck many years ago, Mary Alice had raised her two sons alone and done a fabulous job. Brian Jr. and Patrick were leading productive lives any parent would be proud of. And now, one of them was gone. What a nightmare.

I led a sobbing Mary Alice into her living room and settled her on the sofa. I put my arms around her and rocked her back and forth, the way I soothe my grandson when he's upset.

There was a box of tissues on the coffee table. I grabbed a handful to give to her when she was a little calmer. We sat in the same position for a few minutes (my arms were starting to hurt but I didn't dare move), and finally she pulled away. I handed her a tissue, and she dabbed her eyes.

"I'm so sorry," I said. "I wish I could find the right words to tell you how terrible I feel about what you're going through."

"Thanks, Carol. My heart is broken."

"Want to talk about it?" I asked. "If you're not ready yet, that's okay too. We can just sit here a while. Or maybe I should make some coffee."

I started to stand up, but Mary Alice pulled me down on the sofa.

"I'm going tell you something that nobody else knows. It's very personal. I'm trusting you not to share it with anyone. Okay?"

If I'd suffered the loss of a child, I'd need one person who I could absolutely trust to pour my heart out to. Not my husband, because hearing how much pain I was in would probably make his own pain even worse.

"I'm honored that you've chosen me. I promise I won't tell a soul what you tell me."

"Thank you." She paused for a minute, then continued. "I'm telling you because you knew him, too. Although not as well as I did."

"I know. I loved him before he was even born. I remember how excited you were when you found out you were pregnant," I said softly.

"Pregnant?" Mary Alice repeated. "No, Carol. You've got the completely wrong idea. My boys are both fine." She started to laugh.

"I'm so glad I called you. I never expected to laugh this morning after hearing the news. But leave it to you to misunderstand what I'm telling you and say something so ridiculous that...." And she started to laugh again.

"I'm confused. Who are we talking about?"

"I found out this morning that Lou Hollister was murdered last night." Mary Alice said, her voice shaking.

"We planned to be married as soon as his wife gave him a divorce. Instead, she killed him."

This time, there was no stopping her tears.

Chapter 55

When I was young, I was poor.
But after years of hard work, I am no longer young.

To say I was stunned by Mary Alice's outburst would be a huge understatement. I prayed she wouldn't find out I was at the pickleball court last night and bombard me with questions.

"What a horrible thing."

Mary Alice immediately jumped down my throat. "I thought you were one of my best friends. Are you criticizing me because I fell in love with a married man? I thought you'd understand and be supportive."

"I meant Lou's death, not your relationship with him. Give me a little credit for compassion, okay?"

"I'm sorry. My nerves are so raw right now. My whole world's collapsing around me and I can't do anything about it."

"I'll make some coffee," I said, giving Mary Alice a few minutes alone to pull herself together. "Even if you don't want any, I certainly do."

To tell the truth, I needed a few minutes to process her unexpected announcement. What if

Poppy found out about Lou's plans to marry my sweet friend and killed him because she was jealous? Should I break my promise to Mary Alice and tell Mark about her connection to the murder victim? What a heartbreaking mess.

I decided the most important thing I could do right now was make the coffee, let my dear friend continue to pour out her heart to me, be supportive, and keep my big mouth shut.

It would take a few minutes for the coffee to be ready, so I rummaged around Mary Alice's kitchen looking for something sweet to serve with it. Yes, I was starving. What can I say? Stress makes me hungry, and heaven knows I'd had enough of that lately to justify snarfing down an entire cinnamon coffee cake all by myself.

I opened the refrigerator and found some leftover cake on the middle shelf. Even without my glasses, I could read the writing on the top: "To my sweet Mary Alice. I'll love you forever."

I slammed the door shut. I felt like a voyeur.

Suck it up, Carol. You'll eat when you get home. You might even lose a little weight!

Mary Alice was calmer when I came back with the coffee pot and two mugs, until she grabbed one of the mugs and caressed it against her cheek.

"This was Lou's favorite," she sobbed. "He always said this one was a man's mug. My others were too small."

"Then you should use it," I blurted out. "It might make you feel close to him."

Mary Alice smiled, then poured herself some coffee. "You're right, Carol. I'm going to use it every single day. He even insisted I bring it with me last night. I used to tease him that he loved that mug as much as he loved me."

I know a cue when I hear one.

"Last night?"

"Yes. We'd planned a short getaway to Manhattan. Lou made reservations at The Plaza. We planned to leave around seven o'clock. He figured the rush hour traffic would be over by then. Like all men, he hated driving in stop and go traffic."

"Jim hates that too," I chimed in, making Mary Alice smile.

"He texted me about six o'clock, telling me something had come up and he'd be a little delayed. That was the last time I heard from him. After a while, I started to worry. I texted him back several times but he didn't answer. Then I got angry. I thought he'd dumped me but didn't have the courage to do it in person. I must have finally drifted off to sleep.

"This morning I saw the blurb on the Fairport Patch. I followed the link and read the story. I fell apart. That's the only way to describe it. Then I called you."

My mind was whirling. I wondered if Lou had received a text like mine that lured him to the rec center.

I shook my head. That made no sense. There was no way there could be a connection between Poppy's suing me and Lou Hollister.

Lou was still Poppy's husband, doofus! That's the connection! Poppy probably forced Lou to help her win the lawsuit. I bet she promised that when she got the money, she'd finally give him the divorce he wanted.

I could picture the entire scenario. Poppy texted Lou to come to meet her at the pickleball court last night to talk about the lawsuit. Her real purpose was to get him there so she could murder him for his relationship with Mary Alice. According to many of the mystery books I read, jealousy is a frequent motivation for murder.

Did Poppy lure me there so I could be the person who discovered Lou's body? Or maybe she'd planned to accuse me of his murder! That sounded exactly like something Poppy would do. But I got there earlier than she expected and caught her in the act, so to speak.

I had to share my very logical, brilliant theory with Mark right away. I was sure he'd be impressed.

But first, I had to come clean with Mary Alice.

Chapter 56

The bags under my eyes are Chanel.

I sat on the sofa with one of my dearest friends in the world, sipped my coffee, and tried to figure out a way to have such a difficult conversation. Was there a patron saint of friendship I could call on for help? I searched my usual mental roster and couldn't come up with a single one. (Just so you all know, the patron saint of friendship is St. John the Apostle, as I found out later after a more detailed internet search.)

I was so lost in my own thoughts that, when Mary Alice touched my hand, she startled me.

"You look so tired today," she said. "I don't mean to be critical, but you have circles under your eyes. As a nurse, and one of your best friends, I'm ordering you to go home and go back to bed. I feel better since I've talked to you. I'll be all right by myself for a while.

"I really appreciate your coming. Thank you. I love you, Carol."

Oh, boy. Now I really felt terrible about what I was going to say.

"I love you too, Mary Alice. If there was anything in the world I could do right now to ease your pain, believe me, I'd do it. But there's something I need to tell you, too. It'll probably upset you, but you have to know.

"I was at the pickleball court last night when Lou died. Larry McGee was with me."

"What? I don't understand." Mary Alice's eyes filled up again, and I handed her another tissue.

I took her through the whole sorry story, ending with Poppy's ridiculous nuisance lawsuit. "When I got the text from Poppy to meet her last night, I immediately called Larry to go with me. We both hoped Poppy had decided to drop the lawsuit.

"As you know, that's not what happened."

"So you actually saw Lou…murdered?" Mary Alice's voice trembled.

"No, sweetie. Thank goodness, we didn't. He was already gone when we got there.

"But here's the thing. Mark was one of the detectives who responded to the emergency call for help. He needs to know what you just shared with me. It's critical information to help convict Lou's murderer. You want her punished, don't you?"

"Of course I do!"

"I'm asking your permission to betray your confidence in the interests of seeing justice served and to tell Mark what you just told me. I'm sure the police will want to interview you, and you'll have to sign a written statement. Your name might become public knowledge as the "other woman." Are you okay with that?"

"I'm not okay with having a beautiful relationship being dragged through the mud and made to look sordid," Mary Alice said, her face flushing. "But I'm more than okay with doing whatever it takes to get justice for the man I loved. My real friends will be supportive of me, and as for anybody else, they can go to hell!"

"Atta girl, Mary Alice. That's the spirit!"

"I'd like to go with you to talk to Mark right now. Why wait? It'll make me feel like I'm doing something positive, rather than sitting around and crying my eyes out. Just let me wash my face and we can go."

"Maybe that's not such a good idea," I said. "What if Mark's not there, and we get stuck talking to his partner Paul Wheeler instead? Do you want to risk that?"

"It's going to be hard enough for me to talk to Mark about such a personal thing, but I know he'll be gentle and understanding. Talking to Paul Wheeler would make me feel worse than I already do, if that's possible. Like my love for Lou was the catalyst that caused his death.

"You're right, Carol. It's better for me to stay home and wait for you to tell me what happened at the police station."

"I promise I'll call as soon as I'm finished." I kissed her on the cheek. "Meanwhile, try to eat something. You need to keep up your strength. And don't answer the door or take any phone calls or texts unless you're sure they're from me."

Mary Alice sketched a salute. "Okay, you're the boss."

"And don't you forget it," I said.

Chapter 57

"Your call is very important to us. Please enjoy this violin solo from my grandson's kindergarten concert while we keep you waiting for at least forty-five minutes."

A quick shower and clean clothes did wonders to brighten my mood. I fired off a text assuring Jim that Mary Alice was feeling better and I'd be out for a while "doing errands."

My heart was breaking for my dear friend, who'd finally found true love again, only to have it snatched away from her by a violent act committed by someone so despicable. I vowed to do everything I could (that was legal) to be sure Poppy Hollister spent the rest of her life paying for her crime.

I thought about checking with Jenny about what Mark's schedule was today, then decided against it. Because my daughter and I are so close, I was afraid I'd be tempted to share Mary Alice's heartbreak with her—a definite no-no.

If I had to deal with Paul Wheeler instead of my wonderful son-in-law, so be it. I'd just be super cautious about what I told him. Or, even better, I could leave and come back when he wasn't there.

On my way to the police station, I had a sudden brainstorm guaranteed to ensure me a "glad to see you" greeting from Fairport's boys in blue. I made a quick stop at the best donut shop in town for a dozen assorted goodies for Mark and his fellow cops, plus an extra one for me. Few things put a smile on my face (and an inch on my waistline) faster than a yummy lemon-filled piece of heaven. And lemon is a fruit, so it's a healthy choice, right? Of course, right.

By the way, National Donut Day is celebrated in the United States every year on the first Friday of June. The event was originally created by the Salvation Army in 1938 to honor those members who served donuts to soldiers during World War 1. (This may be a clue on Jeopardy! soon, so try to remember it. You're welcome.)

I found the perfect parking space in the police station parking lot, next to an odious neon green sedan. (What idiot would buy such a horrible color car?) The space had plenty of wiggle room, so I'd be able to open my door safely.

The driver was taking his sweet time getting items out of his car, which normally would bug me. Instead, I took advantage of the delay by sampling my donut. It was even yummier than I'd remembered. So I finished the whole thing, and enjoyed it thoroughly.

My sugar high and positive attitude mood came crashing down when I realized the driver of the repulsive green car was Paul Wheeler. I turned my face away as quickly as I could, but it was too late.

"What are you doing here, Carol? Why don't you stay home and be a good little housewife instead of pretending you're a master detective and bothering the police with your crazy theories?"

Good lord. I hadn't even walked into the building and I was already being insulted.

"Good morning, Paul," I said with saccharine sweetness (probably thanks to the donut). "What a terrible tragedy at the pickleball courts last night. You may recall that I was there. I was asked to come today to sign a statement about what I witnessed. Therefore, as a law-abiding citizen of Fairport who, incidentally pays part of your salary through my taxes, here I am." I picked up my box of uneaten donuts, turned, and marched into the police station before he could think of a reply.

"Detective Mark Anderson asked me to sign a statement about last night's incident at the pickleball court," I announced to the receptionist, whose name badge identified her as Sharon.

I ordered my baby blues to well up, then lowered my face so I was eyeball to eyeball with her. "I'm Mark's mother-in-law, Sharon. I'm very nervous." I allowed my voice to tremble for effect. "I only want to talk to him. I hope he's here."

"Of course, Mrs. Andrews. You can go right back. I'll let him know you're on your way."

"That won't be necessary," Paul said, elbowing his way past my new pal Sharon just as we were getting along so well. "I have your statement right here, Carol." He shoved the document in my direction and pointed to the bottom of the page. "Sign here and you can be on your way home to do all those important female household tasks like dusting and vacuuming."

Sharon flinched at Paul's rudeness, and I wanted to smash the bullet-proof glass and knock the smug expression off his ugly face. Only knowing I'd hurt myself stopped me.

Suddenly, Paul's face turned white, like he'd seen a ghost. (Where was one when I really needed one? But I digress.)

"Apologize to this woman right now, Detective Wheeler," I heard someone say.

I turned to say thank you and came face to face with Fairport First Selectwoman (a.k.a. Mayor with a fancier title), Carla Grimaldi.

Chapter 58

Wanted: Someone to brush their teeth with me because nine out of ten dentists say brushing alone isn't good enough. No weirdos, please.

"How dare you speak to a respected member of the Fairport community in such an insulting, degrading manner?" she continued. "I'm reporting your outrageous behavior to the chief and demand you be demoted to permanent traffic duty. I wish more of our town's citizens were as vigilant and supportive of the police as Carol Andrews is.

"And be warned, if I hear even a whisper of another incident like this, you'll be fired. I'm not kidding."

"I'm sorry, Ms. Grimaldi." Paul stammered. "Please don't tell the chief and have me demoted. Carol and I joke around a lot. She knows I was just kidding."

His pleading look almost made me feel a little sorry for him. Almost.

"Then why am I not laughing, Paul."

"The person you need to apologize to is Mrs. Andrews, not me. Right now, so I can hear you do it."

"I'm sorry," Paul mumbled.

"I'm sorry who?"

"I'm sorry, Carol."

The First Selectwoman shook her head. "Not good enough. Only one more shot at getting it right, and then you're out of chances and on your way to traffic duty."

"I'm sorry, Mrs. Andrews."

"And? Continue."

Boy, Carla Grimaldi was one tough cookie. I was glad she was on my side.

"And I promise it will never happen again."

The First Selectwoman sighed. "I guess that's the best you can do. But don't forget, I'll be keeping an eye on you."

"Yes, ma'am." Paul looked totally humiliated. It was a good look for him. "Here's the statement for you to sign, Mrs. Andrews."

"Thank you," I said, snatching the document from his outstretched hand before he "accidentally" dropped it on the floor in front of me. Knowing the little twerp as well as I did, anything was possible.

The First Selectwoman took my arm like we were dear friends. "If Sharon will buzz us in now, we can walk back to the offices together."

As soon as the door closed behind us, I grabbed her hand. "I'm so lucky you happened to walk in at exactly the right moment, Ms. Grimaldi. I can never thank you enough for standing up for me the way you did."

"Please, call me Carla," she said. "And it wasn't luck that I happened to be here." Her face was scarily serious. "I have an emergency meeting with the chief right now. Could you delay your talk with your son-in-law and sit in on it with me? I'd really appreciate it."

I was torn. My first loyalty was to Mary Alice. I had to share what she'd told me with Mark as soon as possible.

On the other hand, I was flattered that the First Selectwoman and I were now on a first name basis, plus she'd invited me to her important meeting with the chief of police. Definitely a first for me.

Usually the powers-that-be (Jim) insist I mind my own business and let the police do their job. He's conveniently forgotten that the first time I was involved in a murder was because he was number one on the police suspect list and I had to save him. I hope some of you remember that. If you do, feel free to remind Jim when you see him. Thank you.

"I need to see Mark first," I answered. "It's very important. How about if I text you when we're finished talking to see if you're still meeting with the chief?"

The First Selectwoman frowned. I guess she wasn't used to anyone saying no to her. Finally, she tapped out a number and texted it to me. I was puzzled that she already had mine, but didn't dare ask her how she got it.

"Our town's in big trouble, Carol. I'm hoping you can help make it right."

She turned and walked away without any explanation.

Chapter 59

As I grow older, I find that pleasing everyone is impossible, but offending everyone is a piece of cake.

I tapped lightly on Mark's office door. Receiving no answer, I took a chance I'd be welcome (especially because I was carrying fresh donuts), eased the door open, and found Mark snoozing in his office chair. Poor guy. He probably didn't get any sleep at all last night. I wondered if he'd even made it home.

What if the police chief or Carla Grimaldi found Mark sleeping on the job? That'd be terrible. Maybe he'd even lose his job. But the poor guy looks so exhausted. He really needs his rest.

Who was I kidding? I wanted to let my son-in-law sleep a little longer so I could go to the meeting with Carla Grimaldi and the police chief.

Carla Grimaldi said she needed your help. You know you're dying of curiosity to know why. Isn't it your civic duty to attend that meeting? You can check back with Mark when that meeting is over.

Satisfied I had justified my hasty retreat to myself, I slipped my unsigned statement onto Mark's desk and, quiet as a little mouse, inched toward the door.

"I see you, Carol," Mark murmured, startling me into a quick change of plans.

"I'm sorry I woke you up. You look exhausted."

"I wasn't really asleep. I was just resting my eyes."

"You were pretty convincing."

"I've become an expert at quick power naps, thanks to CJ's teething. He seems to favor late night hours when I'm home to express his displeasure. Jenny insists that he's an angel during the day." Mark yawned. "I think she's just kidding me."

Picking up my statement, he gave it a quick perusal. "You haven't signed it yet. That's good."

I started to tell him about my earlier interaction with Paul Wheeler at the reception desk, but Mark interrupted me. "I don't need or want to know any details about you and Paul. We have more important things to talk about."

Uh oh. Mark's face had changed from loving son-in-law to scary cop in the blink of an eye. I could feel my heart beating faster already.

He handed me back my formal statement. "Read it carefully. No rush. Then we'll talk."

My hands were shaking as I held the document. "Am I in trouble? Do I need to call Larry McGee?"

Mark's face softened. "No, Carol. You're not in any trouble. I just want to be sure everything in your statement is completely accurate. Feel free to make any changes you feel are necessary. I know how upset you were last night. That's why I'm giving you this chance to review your statement privately with me. If you're satisfied it's completely accurate, and you're willing to swear to its contents in court, if necessary, then go ahead and sign it."

I fumbled in my purse for my reading glasses and slowly read my statement. Satisfied that it was accurate, I signed it with the Lilly Pulitzer ball point pen I'd also found in my purse. Seeing the bright colors of the pen almost cheered me up. Almost.

Mark glanced at it quickly, then placed it carefully in a folder. His scary cop face was still visible. "Now I want to know exactly why you went to the pickleball court last night."

"I already told you the reason. Why do I have to go through it all over again?"

Mark continued wearing his scary cop face. "Humor me, Carol. Please."

"I got a text from Poppy asking me to meet her at the pickleball court last night at eight o'clock. She said she was sorry about the lawsuit and wanted us to talk."

I squirmed a little in my chair. Mark's scary cop face made me feel like I was the person who'd murdered Lou Hollister, not Poppy.

Stop it, Carol. Get hold of yourself. You have nothing to hide. And it's Mark asking the questions, for heaven's sake. You know he loves you. He's just doing his job.

"Go on. Please."

I took the next ten minutes to give my son-in-law all the details about my car's supposed encounter with Poppy's car in the rec center parking lot and her resulting, ridiculous $2 million lawsuit.

"I'm completely innocent. I am a very good driver, and I know how to park a car!"

"Just to clarify," Mark said patiently, "you received a text from Poppy Hollister asking you to meet her at the pickleball court last night. Are you absolutely sure she was the person who contacted you? If necessary, are you willing to swear to that in a court of law?"

"Of course, I am. I still have the text." I dug into my purse again and pulled out my phone. "Do you want to see it?"

Now I was getting angry. Did Mark think I was lying?

He examined the text, photographed it, then handed my phone back. "And I thought this was going to be an open and shut case. Boy, was I wrong.

He waited a beat, then said, "Poppy Hollister showed me a text on her phone about the meeting last night at the pickleball court. But it was sent from you to her, not the other way around."

Chapter 60

I am responsible for what I say, not what you understand.

I was speechless. But not for long.

"Let me be sure I understand this. You're telling me that Poppy Hollister and I received texts from each other about meeting last night? I swear I never texted her. This makes no sense."

"You're right," Mark agreed. "It makes no sense."

"I have a massive headache coming on." I rubbed my temples and closed my eyes, neither of which helped relieve the pain.

"I don't blame you. So do I," Mark said. "And if the chief finds out I'm telling you all this, he'll probably fire me.

"Poppy signed a statement swearing that the only reason she was at the pickleball court last night was to talk to you about the kids," he continued. "When she got there, she found her husband with a knife in his chest. And you were there, too."

"Is she accusing me of stabbing him? That is a complete lie! You know I'd never do anything like that, Mark! You have to believe me!"

I was verging on hysterics now, envisioning the rest of my life spent behind bars for a murder I didn't commit. Plus, I look horrible in orange. It drains all the color from my face. I started to sob uncontrollably. And I thought today couldn't possibly be any worse than yesterday.

In an instant, I felt Mark's strong arms around me. "Of course I don't believe you murdered him. Poppy didn't accuse you of murder."

"Well," I said, "I guess I should be grateful for that."

"Poppy insists that when she found Lou, she immediately started screaming for help. She removed the knife from his chest, thinking that would help. She was trying to save him."

"Do you believe her?" I asked.

"At the moment, I don't know what I believe," Mark answered. "All I know is the chairman of the Fairport Recreation Commission has been murdered. His wife, who happens to be a member of one Fairport's most prominent families, may be the murderer. There's only one witness—you, Carol—who saw Poppy holding the murder weapon."

"Larry McGee and I walked into the rec center together," I reiterated. "He's my attorney for the lawsuit, and since I thought that's what we were meeting about, I asked him to come with me.

"I opened the pickleball court door and saw Poppy before Larry did. When he realized what had happened, he immediately left me and ran outside to call 911, so she didn't see him. I've told you all this before."

Mark scribbled a few more notes. "The timing is very important. We need to clarify your signed statement. I'll have it redone, but you don't have to stay. I can drop by the house later and you can sign it then. Thanks for coming in. I'm sorry this took so long."

Mark stood up, ready to escort me to the door. In his mind, our meeting was over. But not in mine. A lightbulb had just turned on in my brain.

"Lou Hollister received a similar text. That's why he was at the pickleball court last night."

Mark sat down with a thud. He looked angry. "Just out of curiosity, I'm wondering why it took so long for you to share this valuable piece of information with me. Or are you just guessing that's what happened?"

I started to explain, but Mark wouldn't let me talk.

"How did you come by this so-called information?" His voice was getting louder. "You didn't do anything illegal, did you?"

That did it. No way was I taking insulting questions like that from someone I'd known since he was 9 years old.

I sat up straight in my chair, despite the fact that my back was now killing me. It was a very uncomfortable chair, not that I'm complaining. Most people probably don't stay in Mark's office as long as I do.

"I came to the police station to sign my statement about last night's murder, just like you told me to," I said, matching Mark's angry look with one of my own. "But first, you went over it with me, line by line, which took a while. Then you told me Poppy'd received a similar text to mine. I'm still trying to process what that could possibly mean."

Mark nodded impatiently. "Go on."

"The most important reason why I came here this morning was to tell you I'd just found out what Lou Hollister's original plans were for last night. I got here as quickly as I could."

Mark started to speak, but I ignored him and kept on talking. Points for me, right?

"You have to let me tell the story my way.

"My source for this information," I continued, "is Mary Alice Costello. She called me early this morning and begged me to come to her home as soon as possible. She was crying hysterically so naturally I went right over."

"Mary Alice Costello," Mark repeated. "I'm having trouble figuring out how a sweet person like Mary Alice could have anything to do with Lou Hollister's murder."

I sighed. "If you stop interrupting me, I'll tell you. Mary Alice and Lou had been in a secret relationship for quite a while. They planned to marry as soon as his divorce was final.

"Lou and Mary Alice had plans for a romantic getaway last night. She was packed and waiting for Lou to pick her up when he texted telling her something important had come up and he'd be delayed, but he'd be there as soon as he could. Of course, he never came, and she couldn't figure out what happened. This morning, she found out he'd been murdered and called me.

"She agreed to come in and sign a statement after I convinced her that her information could helpful to the police."

At that point, I couldn't hold back my tears anymore. "You probably don't remember when Mary Alice's husband Brian was killed in a car accident years ago. You and Mike and Jenny were just little kids then."

Mark nodded. "I remember. One of her sons was in my class." His eyes filled up, too. We were quite a pair.

"After Brian died, Mary Alice never thought she'd find true love again. But she did. And now, Lou's been taken from her too."

"Did Mary Alice actually say that Lou had received a text?"

He had me there. But I was sure I was right.

"Everyone communicates by text these days," I said, not willing to admit she hadn't exactly said that. "All you have to do is check Lou's cell phone and you'll find the text. Why haven't you done that already?"

"We went through everything Lou had on him when he was murdered," Mark said. "There was no cell phone."

Chapter 61

I'm not going outside again until the temperature is my age.

I couldn't wait to get home. After the day I'd had, I wanted nothing more than to put on a pair of my favorite jammies, hang a "Do Not Disturb" sign on the bedroom door, and sleep for about a year.

Too bad it was only 11:00 in the morning.

I drove three blocks out of my way home to avoid passing by Town Hall. I wasn't taking any chances that Carla Grimaldi would recognize my car and flag me down.

After I parked in the safety of my driveway, I began to relax for the first time since Mary Alice's phone call. After securing the gate to ensure the dogs wouldn't scamper onto Old Fairport Turnpike (one of my worst fears), I grabbed my purse and headed toward the side door.

Claire was sitting on the steps waiting for me. She looked like she'd been crying.

Claire and I have been dear friends since the second grade. In all those years (and I'm not telling you how many), I had never, ever seen her shed a tear. Not even when either of her parents passed away.

I touched her shoulder, and Claire slowly got to her feet. "I've been waiting for you for half an hour, Carol," she said. "Where have you been? Your steps are very uncomfortable."

"That's the Claire I know and love," I said, giving her hug. "Come inside and we'll talk. Maybe we can make each other feel better."

After taking quick care of doggie needs, I suggested she freshen up while I made fresh coffee. "I don't even mind if you use my good guest towels," I called after her.

I heard her laugh. All my family and friends know that the embroidered white hand towels in the master bathroom are only for show. Woe be it to anyone who breaks that rule without asking my permission. Only one person did, and she turned out to be a murderer. But that's another story.

"That helped a little," Claire said, making herself comfortable at the kitchen table. "But I'm still sad."

"I guess you've talked to Mary Alice."

"She called me right after you left," Claire said. "I didn't know what to say to comfort her.

"I also didn't know you'd asked Larry to represent you in a lawsuit. Nor that you were the client he went to meet last night at the pickleball court. I had to hear all this from Mary Alice."

Good grief. No way was I going to worry about Claire's hurt feelings just because she was out of my lawsuit loop. So, I did what I always did when she backed me into a corner: I pretended I didn't hear her and changed the subject.

"I've forgotten if you like cream and sugar for your coffee," I said, falling back on my hostess role. "I don't think I have either. I need to get to the food store."

"I'm sorry."

"I forgive you," she said, looking mollified.

I realized she thought I was apologizing for not filling her in about the lawsuit. I certainly wasn't going to correct her. Nor was I planning on giving her any more lawsuit details.

"Larry's in terrible shape." Claire continued. "Witnessing Lou Hollister's murder has really shaken him to his core."

"Neither one of us actually witnessed the murder, Claire," I corrected. "I was ahead of him walking into the pickleball court so I saw what had happened first. Larry immediately went outside to call the police."

"Oh, Carol," Claire said, looking guilty. "I should have asked right away how you're holding up. I was totally fixated on my husband. But you'd had a traumatic experience last night too."

I waited for Claire to add one of her usual zingers, probably suggesting me that, since I frequently find dead bodies and Larry doesn't, this one upset him more than me. To my surprise, the zinger didn't come.

"It was a pretty gruesome scene. I can understand why Larry's so upset. There was so much blood."

"I hope you didn't tell Mary Alice about that!"

I ignored Claire's comment, which took a lot of self-restraint.

"I had no idea that Mary Alice was seeing anyone," I said. "Did you?"

"Nope." She looked thoughtful. "If Lou mentioned it to Larry, he wouldn't betray his confidence. I'm learning that my husband is very good at secrets."

"I'm having trouble keeping up with you," I said. "Why would Lou Hollister have confided something so intimate about his personal life to Larry?"

"They were business partners. And very close friends."

My brain was about to explode. Was Larry representing me in Poppy's lawsuit a conflict of interest, since he and Poppy's estranged husband were business partners? Shouldn't Larry have shared this information with me when I asked for his help? Why didn't he?

I was beginning to have doubts about the professional ethics of Larry McGee.

"That's really interesting," I said, trying to think of an innocent way to pump Claire for more information. I fell back on what I figured was a safe subject to begin my inquisition.

"I remember the good old days when Larry and Jim commuted to Manhattan together. Larry's been very helpful in several little emergencies since he retired," I said.

"You mean, like getting our dear friend Nancy off the hook when she was almost arrested for murder? Or going to the police station with Mary Alice now so she could give a statement about Lou Hollister? I'd hardly call those little emergencies, Carol."

Trust Claire to correct me, although my memory of Nancy's recent predicament was more accurate than hers. I hope some of you remember that I was the one who figured out what really happened and cleared Nancy's name. And I was also the one who persuaded Mary Alice to share her information about Lou Hollister's original schedule with the police.

Not that I'm bragging.

"Just between us," Claire continued, "it's a good thing for Nancy that her case didn't go to trial. Larry's specialty is corporate real estate law, not criminal law. His expertise is in the purchase and sales of large-scale properties like office buildings and shopping malls."

Claire took a sip of her coffee. "I hope I'm not boring you. If this is too much information, please feel free to stop me."

"On the contrary, I think it's really interesting," I said with total sincerity. "I never knew there were different kinds of lawyers."

"When Larry retired a few years ago, it didn't take him long to become totally bored. I know you understand what living with a retired husband with not enough to do is like. Heaven knows, you complained about it enough when Jim retired."

I couldn't deny it, so I let her remark pass.

"Anyway, Larry was thinking of starting a private law practice to keep busy, assuming he could get enough clients here in Connecticut. He and Lou Hollister happened to meet when Lou was buying property for a new condo community. Long story short, they became business partners and very close friends."

I thought of another potential conflict of interest, which scared the living daylights out of me.

"What about Lou's divorce from Poppy? Was Larry representing him?"

Say no. Please, say no.

"I'm sure he referred Lou to an attorney who's an expert in divorce law," Claire said. "As far I know, Larry and Poppy have never met."

I noticed how carefully she'd framed her answer. And how nervous she suddenly seemed. Was she telling me she didn't know the answer to my questions? Or that she knew the answer and wasn't telling me? I was silent for a few seconds, which Claire knew was unusual for me.

"I'm sure that Larry would have told me if he'd met Poppy," she finally said. "He knows we went to the same high school."

"And that we spent one summer at her family's beach house," I added. "I'll never forget the look on Poppy's face the first time I walked into the dining room wearing a maid's uniform and carrying a dinner tray. That summer experience taught me I was not cut out to be a domestic goddess. I hope I remember to tell Jim that when he complains I haven't made a real home-cooked meal for a while."

"It's wonderful to talk about the old days and Larry's career, but we haven't figured out a way to help Mary Alice," Claire said.

"Why are you smiling?"

"Because I just thought of something that might cheer her up a little," I said. "Offer Mary Alice your Florida condo to use for a short vacation. I'm sure the hospital can find another nurse to take over her private duty patients with enough advance warning. A change of scene may be just what she needs."

"That's a fabulous idea, Carol. I wish I'd thought of it myself." Claire grinned to show she was only kidding, then grabbed her phone. "I have to text Larry right away. I hope I can stop him."

"Stop him? From what?"

"We're thinking of selling the Florida condo. Larry planned to talk to a realtor about listing it, but we haven't made a final decision yet. The last thing Mary Alice needs is strangers knocking on the door wanting to see the unit when she's supposed to be relaxing."

I grabbed Claire's phone and put it next to my coffee mug. "Hang on a minute. Let me get this straight. You're thinking of selling the condo that you absolutely love, that you look forward to living in when the temperature here dips below sixty degrees for more than two days in a row. You're giving up basking in the warm Florida sunshine on a sandy beach or by a beautiful pool. You're giving up that amazing view. You're giving up the opportunity to entertain your closest friends in paradise. Is that right?"

Claire nodded.

"For Pete's sake, why? Are you nuts?"

"Maybe I am," Claire said. "But Larry pointed out that neither of us enjoy living in Florida as much as we used to. It's so crowded now. The traffic is horrible. Our HOA fees were really low years ago when we bought the condo, but now they've tripled and will probably go up again after the recent hurricanes. We don't go out to restaurants nearly as much as we did, either. I cook most of our meals at the condo or have meals delivered. We don't go to the beach anymore, and if we go to the pool twice the whole winter, it's a big deal.

"I didn't agree with him at first. But the more I thought about what he was saying, the more I realized he was right. We can always rent a condo for a month or two in the winter, instead of owning one. Plus, when I'm not here, I miss Nancy, Mary

Alice, and even you, Carol. Believe it or not. I'm lonely."

She picked up her phone again. "I'll text Larry right now and ask him to delay talking to a realtor. If I'm too late, I'm blaming you."

Chapter 62

Never leave the house without a kiss, a hug, and saying, "I love you."
Then remove the dog hair from your mouth as you walk to the car.

The next few days were fairly quiet by my standards. No more murders, no more lawsuits, no more command performances at police headquarters. Jenny was teaching at the college most of the week, which allowed me several babysitting opportunities.

Mike's plans to return to Fairport were now uncertain due to an unexpected complication: Both his chefs were leaving Cosmos's to start their own restaurant and finding replacements was proving difficult. His decision to let Jim handle things at Picklelilly's while he was away was turning into a longer gig than either of them anticipated. It was a good thing my husband was enjoying himself being the Man in Charge. I just hoped he and Mike were in frequent communication so Jim didn't make any major decisions on his own.

Having Jim out of the house on a daily basis should have been a dream come true for me. Unfortunately, my life was currently overflowing with crisis after crisis, so I couldn't enjoy the break in our routine.

According to what I gathered from what Mike did (and didn't) say, his relationship with Charli was on the mend. I knew he was trying to be supportive, but I suspected he felt lucky to be far away from her daily drama right now.

I was relieved when the First Selectwoman reached out to explain our recent interaction at police headquarters. One of her staff had just alerted her to several billboards on local highways dubbing Fairport "The Murder Capital of New England." I assured Carla (she insists I call her by her first name, and who am I to argue?) that her anger was completely understandable and that I was flattered she thought I could help. I also thanked her for defending me against the odious Paul Wheeler.

As part of our newly forged friendship, when she asked me to try to find out who was behind the negative publicity, I agreed. It took a little convincing on her part; you may recall I also had a few other crises on my plate to deal with and juggling is a skill +that I've never mastered. It wasn't until Carla insisted that I was the only person in the entire town she trusted to carry out such a sensitive task discreetly and successfully that I finally said yes.

Flattery will get you everywhere with me. I wish Jim understood that.

I knew just where I'd start my undercover investigation. If I was lucky, I'd get the answer by crossing to the opposite side of Old Fairport Turnpike and knocking on Phyllis Stevens's front door.

Chapter 63

When older people say, "Enjoy them while they're young," they're talking about your knees and hips, not your kids.

I snuck a quick peek across the street from my dining room window, to be sure Phyllis was home from her early morning prowl around the neighborhood, checking to see if all the now-empty garbage cans had vanished from the front of each home. Her vintage Ford Taurus station wagon was parked blocking the sidewalk—a clear message that anyone daring to walk close to the Stevens home was trespassing. On a public sidewalk! It was so ridiculous that it made me laugh.

The curtain on the living room window moved, and I figured Phyllis was watching me watch her. Note to self: All the drapes on the windows in the front portion of my house must always be closed tightly.

I tossed the two dogs two biscuits each and reassured them I'd be back soon. They both ignored me and settled down for an unexpected snack.

"You don't scare me, Phyllis," I said in a loud voice. I marched to the creaky front door, which we rarely use. I wanted her to have an unobstructed view of me walking across the street in her direction. Once I showed up at her house unexpectedly and interrupted Phyllis and her long-time suffering husband Bill cavorting in their hot tub. No way did I want to repeat that experience, no matter how desperate I was for information.

"Ready or not, here I come."

I wrenched the door open and came face to face with my former high school English teacher and now (usually) good friend, Sister Rose.

My planned interrogation of Phyllis would have to wait.

Chapter 64

Yesterday my husband thought he saw a cockroach in the kitchen. He sprayed everything down and cleaned the kitchen thoroughly.
Today, I'm putting the cockroach in the bathroom.

"Thank heavens you're home," the good sister said. "I knocked on the side door and called to you, but the only ones who answered me were the dogs."

I was immediately on the defensive. Sister Rose has that effect on me.

"I wasn't trying to avoid you," I said, my face flushing. "I was on my way across the street to talk to a neighbor, and I didn't hear your car."

"I didn't drive here. I walked from the thrift shop."

"But that's over two miles!" And you're even older than I am.

"I needed to think, and the walk helped me. But you seem to be leaving now. Perhaps I should come back when it's more convenient."

"Of course not, Sister," I said, leading the way to the kitchen where Lucy and Ethel raised their heads briefly at the unexpected intrusion, then continued napping. "I'm sorry if I seemed inhospitable. I was surprised to see you. That's all."

Sister Rose sniffed. I hoped that meant I was forgiven. She took my usual seat at the kitchen table, and I pretended not to notice.

"Would you like something to drink? I can make a fresh pot of coffee in a jiffy. Or a soft drink?"

"Just a glass of water. This is not a social call. I'm here on official Mount St. Francis Academy business. We have a crisis."

For a split second, I thought Sister Rose was losing her grip on reality. For those of you who didn't have the privilege of attending Mount St. Francis Academy like I did, there's no way you could know that the school has been closed for over twenty years and now is an assisted living facility.

No comments, please.

I handed Sister Rose her water, took a seat at the table, and waited for her to explain. I had a sneaking suspicion I knew what her "Mount crisis" was, and hoped I was wrong.

"I had a visit today at the thrift shop from Poppy Hollister," she said. "I'm sure you know why."

"How are things at Sally's Place?" I asked, hoping to steer the conversation into another direction.

"We're extremely busy these days, and the shop is desperate for more volunteers, Carol." Sister gave me a look. "Thank you for asking.

"I didn't come here to lay a guilt trip on you about volunteering at the shop, so please don't try to change the subject."

I folded my hands in my lap and waited. A list of terrible possibilities popped into my mind, none of which I wanted to share with Sister Rose.

"I want to talk to you about that horrible murder at the pickleball court. Poppy told me you're involved, Carol. I was shocked to hear that a nice girl like Mary Alice Costello was trying to break up Poppy's happy marriage. It sounds like a very bad soap opera, not that I've ever watched one of those. And now Poppy's daughter is accusing her mother of murdering her father."

I bit my lip so hard it hurt.

"Sister Rose," I said, trying to keep my temper under control, "Mary Alice was not breaking up anybody's marriage. What Poppy told you today is a complete lie. She and her husband were separated and getting a divorce."

"I know that, dear," Sister Rose said, patting my hand. "You didn't think I fell for that story Poppy told me, did you? I know Mary Alice would never involve herself in anything so unsavory. That's what I told her when we met a few hours ago. I wasn't quite this blunt, but I think she got the message."

"How did Poppy react?"

"As you'd expect. Let's just say, she wasn't happy and leave it at that, all right?"

I was dying for details, but let it go.

"However, after speaking with Poppy, I honestly believe she's suffering too. Placing so much blame on Mary Alice for the failure of her marriage may be Poppy's way of dealing with her husband's tragic death. Especially if she feels partially responsible."

She's completely responsible, in my opinion.

"I tried to comfort Mary Alice as well," Sister Rose said, "but I have no personal experience in this type of romantic situation."

I pretended to look shocked. "I should hope not, Sister," I said, making us both laugh.

"You mentioned that Lou Hollister's murder is a crisis for Mount St. Francis Academy. I don't understand why."

"Mary Alice and Poppy are both graduates of the Mount," Sister Rose replied, looking at me like I was stupid. "Having them both involved in something so sordid reflects very badly on the school."

"But the school is closed," I said. "I'm sorry, I'm not following you."

"Many current donors to Sally's Place associate the high school, even though it is closed, with the thrift shop and the battered women's program it supports. We have enough trouble raising money to support the program already. This scandal could really hurt our ability to serve women and families who desperately need our help."

"I'm sorry, Sister Rose. I think you're overreacting."

There was no verbal response from the good sister. The icy look she gave me was response enough.

"Poppy extended an olive branch to Mary Alice and asked for her help in planning Lou's funeral," she continued. "Mary Alice refused and hung up on her."

"I don't blame Mary Alice for reacting that way! Poppy was doing everything she could to stall the divorce. She was making Lou's life miserable. Mary Alice's, too."

Sister Rose sighed. "I'm trying to remain impartial and give Poppy the benefit of the doubt, but I can't fault Mary Alice's decision."

"Thank you, Sister. You and I both know that Mary Alice Costello is one of those rare people who radiates love and kindness. She always looks for the good in people, unlike me, who's always so quick to condemn. I've tried to emulate her, but I don't think I was born with the forgiveness gene."

"My dear Carol," Sister Rose said with a sad smile, "I believe that we are all born with the forgiveness gene. We should remember to use it more often."

We sat in silence for a few minutes. Sister Rose had her eyes closed, and I knew she was praying.

"You're right, Carol," she finally said. "My concern that a tragic murder would negatively impact fundraising for the battered women's program was selfish and unreasonable. I hope you and the Good Lord will forgive me."

I knew it took a lot for Sister Rose to admit she was wrong. "I'm sure He will. I certainly do."

My eyes began to tear up again. I don't know how people can complain about dry eye. That's never been a problem for me.

"What else can I do to help Mary Alice, Sister Rose? I hate to see her in such pain."

"I know you'll do your best to be there for her whenever she needs you. She may prefer being alone right now to grieve, and if that's what she decides, I know you'll respect her wishes. Often solitude can be as precious a gift as love and friendship.

"Perhaps you should reach out to Poppy right now. She's feeling very much alone."

No way! Not ever!

"Sister Rose, I understand that you mean well," I began. "My relationship with Poppy has never been very friendly, even when we were in high school. It's even worse now. Poppy is suing me for $2 million for a tiny dent on her expensive car, which she claims I caused. I am completely innocent!"

My face was getting hot just thinking about Poppy's outrageous treatment of poor little me.

"I know all about the lawsuit," Sister Rose said softly. "Poppy confessed to me that she was angry and bitter about her husband's relationship with Mary Alice. She knew you two were very close, so she took her anger out on you. She's instructed her attorney to withdraw it immediately."

"I'll believe it when my attorney tells me the lawsuit's been withdrawn, not before. I don't trust her."

"I also know you were at the pickleball court and think Poppy killed her husband," Sister Rose said. "Perhaps you're mistaken."

"I know Poppy killed her husband," I said. "She was holding the bloody knife in her hand and I heard her admit it! With all due respect, Sister Rose, you weren't there.

"I think it's time we ended this conversation."

"Carol, dear," Sister Rose said, "I'm sorry I've upset you. But Poppy explained to me that when she arrived at the pickleball court, she found her husband had been stabbed. She pulled the knife out of the wound, thinking that would help him. But instead, her action made the bleeding worse. She knew immediately she'd done the wrong thing. She should have called for help. She said you misunderstood what you saw and heard.

"We all make mistakes, Carol. Especially when we're under a great deal of stress. Perhaps this time, you have."

With that parting shot, she was on her way, leaving me with too many conflicting issues to ponder.

Chapter 65

I've figured out why I always look so horrible in pictures. It's my face.

Sister Rose's visit had shaken me more than I was willing to admit, even to myself. Then I reminded myself what a manipulative, horrible woman Poppy Hollister was.

You know what you saw and heard. Poppy admitted she'd killed her husband. She's using Sister Rose to make you doubt your own eyes and ears.

"Very clever move involving Sister Rose, Poppy," I said aloud. "But I know you much better than she does. Your lies won't work with me."

My phone pinged with a brief text from Larry McGee.

Larry: Poppy's withdrawing the lawsuit! Congratulations!

Me: Thank you for all your help. I'd like a framed copy of the withdrawal document, please.

Larry: I'll see what I can do.

I was feeling positive about my life for a change until I re-read Larry's text. He clearly stated that

Poppy was withdrawing the lawsuit, not that she had actually withdrawn it. Sister Rose said that Poppy had instructed her attorney to withdraw the suit. In neither case was there confirmation that the lawsuit withdrawal had actually happened. Call me paranoid, but the difference in semantics was a red flag as far as I was concerned.

I shared the lawsuit update with both dogs, who immediately began to dance around the kitchen in celebration. Skeptics may think they were excited because I was tossing dog biscuits their way. Not me. Lucy and Ethel instinctively know my moods better than most humans, including the man I married. (Please don't tell Jim that.) If they were celebrating, maybe I should, too.

"That's enough snacks for now," I told them. "You both have to watch your weight. You're not getting any younger, you know."

Lucy gave me a dirty look, clearly suggesting I should take my own advice instead of criticizing my canine companions. Ethel kept her eyes riveted on the floor. She hates to take sides when Lucy and I have a disagreement.

"I miss Nancy," I said aloud. My best and closest non-canine friend since first grade was a critical part of my support system, despite the fact that our joint childhood escapades usually landed me in hot water while she escaped scot-free. Plus, being a local real estate agent gave her an impressive contact list and intel I'm not allowed to share. All this musing led me to wonder if Nancy knew anything about Lou's and Poppy's business dealings.

You're such a dope, Carol. All you have to do is ask Larry. Who'd know better than one of his colleagues?

I rejected that idea as soon as it bubbled up in my brain. Although Larry and I now had a better meaningful relationship thanks to the lawsuit—easy to accomplish since we'd never had any meaningful relationship at all—I still didn't really know him as a person.

I sent off quick texts to Jim and Mike with a lawsuit update and a "fingers crossed" emoji. They both replied immediately, and Jim even included a smiley face emoji.

I'd been treading carefully with Jenny since her volatile reaction to Mike's current love interest. On the surface, everything seemed fine between us. But underneath, I didn't think it was. I'd already told Mark about Poppy's lawsuit. Jenny had a right to know about it too, but whenever I told her, I had to emphasize that Poppy was now dropping the suit. I didn't want to be accused of hiding things from my daughter, so I hoped she didn't ask me any questions about Lou Hollister's murder or Charli's accusations against her mother. Gosh, this was all so complicated.

I was in the middle of drafting a quick invitation to a mother-daughter catch-up lunch when I heard knocking on the side door. Lucy and Ethel immediately began barking like crazy. The only people who use the side door are family and very close friends, none of whom bother to knock first.

Imagine my shock when my side door visitor turned out to be Phyllis Stevens. This was turning out to be a humdinger of a day.

Chapter 66

The price of gas is so high that the mailman has started working from home.
He called yesterday to read my bills to me.

"Here's today's mail," Phyllis said, handing me several pieces of obvious junk mail. I prayed there was nothing embarrassing or confidential in the bunch, since I was sure my oh-so-helpful nosy neighbor had already checked out every piece.

Phyllis took a step back and bumped into the side door. "Can't you control those animals?"

I realized she wasn't being nasty. She was really afraid of the dogs.

"Lucy and Ethel are very gentle," I said as I snapped their leashes on. "They're just suspicious of strangers."

"Humph," Phyllis said, looking unconvinced. "I'm a neighbor, hardly a stranger. Bill suggested I wear one of his sweaters so your dogs would recognize the smell. I understand he comes here to play with them once in a while."

I smiled. "That explains why they're so excited. Lucy and Ethel are just saying hello." I reached in the treat jar and handed Phyllis two dog biscuits. "I'll hold their leashes tight and make them sit. You give them the treats."

"Are you sure they're not going to bite me?"

"I'm sure."

It took a lot more coaxing (of Phyllis) and a little more obedience (from the dogs), but finally the canines and the suspicious neighbor became tentative acquaintances willing to give their new relationship a chance.

"Now that we've settled them down, Phyllis, you obviously didn't stop by just to bring me today's mail. Plus, you didn't use the front door, the way you always do. So...."

"So, what am I doing here?" Phyllis finished. She pulled out a kitchen chair and settled herself in it. After my emotional visit with Sister Rose, I needed a break, so I remained standing, hoping Phyllis would get the hint.

She did not. Or if she did, she decided to ignore it.

I realized that if Phyllis Stevens and Sister Rose ever decided to team up, they'd be a formidable twosome.

"I came to collect the signed petition banning pickleball I gave you a few days ago. You promised to give the petition to Jim to look over and sign, too, and that he'd write a feature story about it for the local newspaper." Phyllis folded her arms, sat back in her chair, and waited for my response.

"Your memory and mine aren't exactly the same," I said, choosing my words carefully.

Phyllis stiffened, and I knew she was going to argue with me.

Lucy emitted a low growl. For once, she was on my side. I stroked her head, and she relaxed. (Lucy's head, not Phyllis's, in case you were confused.)

"I had planned to stop over to see you today to talk about a few things that were on my mind. Jim also had some questions about the petition, but I was detained by Sister Rose." Okay, you all know Jim and I had never discussed the petition. I bent the truth a little. Again.

"Several personal things have happened, and I'm feeling overwhelmed." To my utter embarrassment, my baby blues filled with tears, which then dribbled down my cheeks.

"I'm sorry," I sobbed, unable to control my emotions while what was left of my rational mind ordered me to control myself.

Phyllis grabbed my hand so hard she almost broke it. "Carol, dear, I'm the one who should apologize to you."

"Please, that's not necessary," I said, gently withdrawing my hand from Phyllis's vicelike grip. "It's been a very hard time for people I love, and I don't know how to help them."

"And here I am, adding to your woes by barging into your home about this silly petition." She actually looked embarrassed.

Please remember how embarrassed you felt when you're tempted to barge in again.

"To tell you the honest truth," Phyllis continued, "the only people who've signed the petition are Muriel Anderson, Bill, and me. Muriel lives next to the recreation center. She's the one who started the whole petition thing. She complains to me about anything she views as wrong in town and expects me to fix it." Phyllis rolled her eyes. "You know the type. She has nothing going on in her life, so she sticks her nose into everybody else's business."

Since this was an accurate description of how my across-the-street neighbor chose to live her life, I refrained from comment. With effort.

"I hate to burden you," I said, frantically trying to remember what I originally wanted to talk to Phyllis about. Veering from the truth as often as I do makes my life so confusing.

"I want you to know you can talk to me about anything, Carol," Phyllis said. "Even though I never had a daughter, I've often thought of both you and Portia that way."

"Portia?" I repeated. "Do you mean Poppy? Poppy Hollister?"

"Poppy may be what she calls herself now, but she'll always be Portia to me," Phyllis said.

"Years ago, I volunteered in the children's room of the Fairport Library. Portia's mother brought her to Storytime several days a week so she could help out at her husband's restaurant. I didn't mind if the child stayed longer after Storytime was over. She was such a sweet little thing." Phyllis smiled at the memory.

"I assume you know that the Fairport Diner was originally owned by Portia's family," she continued. "That was long before Mr. P started his first fancy restaurant in Manhattan." Another disapproving look. "He was making a lot more money by then, but his rapid success went to his head. He had no time for his family anymore. He was too busy impressing his New York City pals."

I didn't know any of this, but there was no way I'd admit my ignorance to Phyllis.

"Portia was only four years old when her mother died of a heart attack. Poor little thing. If you ask me, when Mr. P opened that hoity toity restaurant, he broke his wife's heart and that's why she died so young.

"It didn't take long for Mr. P to get married again," Phyllis added. "He and his new wife had several children together, all girls. Portia always felt like an outsider among all her blonde, blue-eyed half-sisters.

"She had dark brown hair and brown eyes when we were in school together! That's one reason why I didn't recognize her at the pickleball court. She looks so different now."

"I didn't realize you two were friends," Phyllis said, looking miffed that not only had I interrupted her story but also had my own connection to Poppy.

"We both went to Mount St. Francis Academy many years ago," I said. "We reconnected recently, but I wouldn't call us friends. Not yet, anyway."

Not ever. But Phyllis didn't need to know that.

"I haven't talked to Poppy in several weeks. I'll reach out this afternoon. I know she's going through a very difficult time, and she always values my advice."

I started to tell Phyllis that perhaps she should wait a while before reaching out to Poppy, but I stopped myself. For all I knew, she had experience counseling women who might have murdered their husbands.

Chapter 67

I want to be 14 again and ruin my life differently. I have new ideas.

To tell you the truth (and I usually do), what Phyllis shared about Poppy upset me more than my conversation with Sister Rose. Poppy's mother died when she was a little girl. My father died before I was born.

Poppy's father married again soon after his wife's death and had several other children. It was just my mother and me until I met and married Jim.

I wondered how I would have felt if my mother married again. Would I have accepted her new husband as my dad? What if she'd had children with him. Would I be happy to have siblings? Or would I be bitter because now I had to share my mother's love with others?

I always tell my friends that I'm a selfish only child and don't share well. Then, we all have a good laugh. Even me.

Suddenly, that joke didn't seem funny anymore.

Are you starting to feel different about Poppy, Carol? To understand her better? Or even feel sorry for her?

My phone announced an incoming text from my darling husband, interrupting my examination of conscience.

Jim: Heard the good news about the lawsuit.
Me: Fingers crossed.
Jim: Want to celebrate tonight?
Me: How? Where?
Jim: I'll surprise you.
Me: No more surprises, please. Where are we going? How will I know what to wear?

My phone was silent. Rats.

My current series of life crises all began when my son decided to surprise me. And now Jim was doing the same thing.

Maybe your life is coming full circle and your troubles will magically disappear.

I was amazed to see it was still morning. How so many crises could intrude in my life before noon was beyond me.

My phone pinged again. "Whoever you are, go away and leave me alone! I'm running away from home, and I'm not taking you with me. So there." I tossed the device onto the bed and smothered it with a pillow.

Ethel—sweet Ethel, who never criticizes me—raised her head and gave me a Look, telling me loud and clear that I was in danger of losing my status as her Perfect Human and I'd better get my act together. Or maybe she was pointing out, politely, that the idea of my running under any circumstances (except being threatened with bodily harm) was laughable.

I sighed. She was right, of course. I should be grateful for all the information that had dropped into my lap this morning. Unfortunately, everything I'd learned from Sister Rose and Phyllis had only confused me more. I needed expert help sorting out my thoughts before I said or did something I'd regret.

Fortunately, I knew exactly where to find it. In less than fifteen minutes, I was on my way to my scheduled appointment at Crimpers, Fairport's best (and my favorite) hair salon. The fact that Crimpers is also the town's go-to place for reliable local gossip thanks to Deanna, salon owner and my dear friend, is merely a happy coincidence.

With any luck at all, I'd pick up a clue or two about Lou Hollister's murder, find out if Poppy had a homicidal streak, or discover who was behind the campaign dubbing Fairport "The Murder Capital of New England." And even if I didn't accomplish any of those things, my hair would be returned to its "natural blonde" color, making me look ten years younger.

Multitasking is my passion.

Chapter 68

I can't decide if I want to be a hair stylist or a novelist, so I decided to flip a coin: heads or tales.

My good mood vanished in a millisecond when I saw the CLOSED sign on the salon front door. What the heck? I was sure my appointment was today.

You didn't confirm it, though, did you, Carol?

I was heartbroken. I felt like a little kid who'd just found out there was no Santa Claus. (I hope you knew that already. If you didn't, I'm really sorry to be the one who spilled the beans.)

There were lights on inside, so I knocked on the door.

No answer.

I knocked again, even louder, and pressed my face against the glass. There was definitely someone in there.

I heard footsteps. The door opened, revealing a woman who was definitely not Deanna. "Crimpers is closed right now," she said, pointing to the sign.

"I'm sure I had an appointment today. Is Deanna here?"

I heard Deanna's voice. "Don't leave, Carol. I'll be right with you."

"I guess you're expected. My apologies." The mystery woman stepped aside. "Be careful walking," she cautioned. "The floor is still wet."

"Okay," I said, more relieved that I'd remembered my appointment correctly than concerned about watching where I was walking. At my age, my short-term memory isn't always accurate. But ask me to name which film won the Academy Awards in 1963, and I'll dazzle you with my knowledge.

(To save you all from checking the internet for the correct answers, *Lawrence of Arabia* won the Best Picture award, Anne Bancroft won the Best Actress Oscar for *The Miracle Worker,* and Gregory Peck was chosen Best Actor for his performance in *To Kill a Mockingbird.* What a year for movies!)

I navigated my way through the salon to Deanna's station without a major mishap. I was glad to see that the salon's business had improved enough that my favorite stylist could afford to hire a cleaning woman. I toyed with finding out how much the woman charged. But as soon as the thought had flickered into my brain, I heard Jim's objections, loud and clear.

Oh, well. It was a nice fantasy.

Deanna appeared carrying a smock to protect my clothing, which she ordered me to put on. "I'm proud of you, Carol. Not only did you remember your appointment today, you came early.

"I'm running away from home right now," I confessed, making myself comfortable in the salon chair. "Crimpers is my temporary refuge from reality."

"Always happy to oblige," Deanna said as she began applying her magical goo to my locks.

"I see you've met Harriet."

"We didn't officially meet," I clarified.

"I know who you are," Harriet said as she walked past me carrying her mop and pail. "You're a cheeseburger well done, one side of French fries, one of onion rings, and a Coke. You ordered a cheeseburger medium rare for your friend, plus a Coke, and you both shared the two sides."

My eyes widened. "That's my favorite meal. How did you know?"

"Between cleaning gigs, I work at the Fairport Diner. I was your server a few days ago when you and your friend came in for lunch.

"Usually, there are four of you, not two," Harriet continued. "That threw me off for a few minutes, until you placed your order. Then I knew who you were. What happened to your other two friends? Everything okay with them?"

I started to reply that I only invited Claire, but stopped myself. Harriet was even nosier than I was!

Deanna sensed that I was uncomfortable with Harriet's cross-examination, so she intervened. "Okay, that's enough chit chat for now. Carol, stop turning your head to talk to Harriet and let me get your highlights done. My whole afternoon is jam packed with other clients."

"Sorry, Deanna," Harriet said. "It isn't often that I get to actually talk with a diner customer beyond taking their order." She checked her phone. "I better be on my way. My shift starts soon and I can't be late."

"Before you leave," I said, "how did you remember exactly what I ordered a few days ago?"

"That's easy," Harriet said. "You always order the same thing. You may start by ordering something different, especially if your friend the nurse is with you, but you always come back to the same food. I've been waiting on you and friends for years.

"I can tell from that way you interact with each other that you're really old friends. So, what happened to the other two? I'm always concerned when regular customers change their habits."

Honestly, the woman would not let this go until I gave her an answer. Sheesh.

"They couldn't make it," I shot back quickly. Maybe a little too quickly, because Deanna shot me a questioning look.

"You're right, we've been friends since grammar school, and there's no way I'm telling you how long ago that was," I said in a friendlier tone. "Let's just say we met sometime in the last century and leave it at that, okay?"

"Works for me," Harriet said. "You're blessed to have friendships that go back that far."

"I know I am. Although I don't always feel that way. Especially when one of them brings up an embarrassing incident from my misspent youth in a public place. And there are many to choose from, believe me."

"I have the opposite problem," Harriet said, now wearing her Fairport Diner server uniform. "People I went to school with come into the diner all the time and don't ever say hello. Either they don't recognize me in my uniform, or they recognize me and are embarrassed they do. That used to hurt my feelings, but I finally learned to just let it go. I've worked hard to support my family, and I'm proud of what I've accomplished in my life.

"One of the worst offenders is Poppy Hollister. She's in and out of the diner all the time because she owns the place. Or rather, her family does."

"Did you go to school with her too?" I'd feel terrible if Harriet was a fellow Mountie and I didn't recognize her.

"No, but I've known her since she was a kid. I don't like waiting on her because she always says there's something wrong with her order and sends it back. But I need the money, so I suck it up.

"She doesn't ever leave me a tip, either."

"I'll be sure to ask for you whenever I'm at the diner," I said. "And maybe I'll change my regular my order, too, just to surprise you."

"Try the BLT on whole wheat toast," Harriet said as she headed toward the door. "It's my favorite."

Chapter 69

It only takes one slow-walking person in the grocery store to destroy the illusion that I'm a nice person.

"The conversation with Harriet was a real wake-up call for me," I said. "I've eaten at the Fairport Diner so often over the years. Harriet must have been my waitress some of those times, and I didn't even remember her. I feel terrible about that. I bet I didn't even look at her when I was ordering my food, like she was invisible."

"Don't go beating yourself up, Carol. Most people are like that with service people. It's not right, but it happens more often than you can imagine. Even to me, believe it or not. I often see a salon customer when I'm out food shopping and say hello, and they have no idea who I am. It's like I only exist for them within the salon walls, and I don't have a real life like everybody else."

Deanna whipped off my plastic cape and turned my chair around so we were facing each other. "We have a little time before my next client is due, so let's catch up. What's new in your life?"

My mood darkened in a millisecond.

"Oops. I can tell from your expression that all is not well in Carol-land," Deanna said, sympathy written all over her face. "You don't have to tell me anything if you don't want to. I didn't mean to pry."

Having someone show me such no-strings-attached kindness caused the waterworks to start (of course). Soon we were both crying, even though Deanna had no idea why I'd reacted so emotionally. That's the thing about a really good friend: if one of us is sad, the other one is automatically sad too. No explanation is necessary.

"Give me a sec to pull myself together," I said, mopping my eyes with an old tissue I'd found at the bottom of my purse. "You go first. What's new with you?"

"Same old, same old," Deanna said. "I'm still waiting for my prince to come and sweep me off my feet, just like Jim did with you." And she winked to show she was kidding.

"Ho ho. You are so funny," I said. "I could tell you stories about my so-called wedded bliss that would make your hair stand on end, figuratively speaking."

"You already have," Deanna replied, a deadpan expression on her face.

"You always cheer me up," I said, laughing. "Sorry to be such a Debbie Downer today. I have a lot on my mind."

"Of course you do," Deanna said. "I'm worried, too. I feel terrible that someone we both care about is going through such a tough time."

"I'm glad you talked to Mary Alice. She needs all her friends around her right now."

"I don't mean Mary Alice," Deanna clarified. "We haven't been in touch for a few weeks.

"I'm talking about Claire."

Chapter 70

The older I get, the tighter manufacturers put lids on jars.

It's a good thing I was sitting down when Deanna shared that bombshell. The salon floor is tile, and an intimate encounter between the hard floor and my aging body would've crippled me for life.

"It's not true," I said. "I was there and saw everything that happened. No way is Larry to blame. He's not on the police suspect list, either. Claire is completely wrong." I couldn't understand how Claire could suspect her own husband of murder. It boggled the mind.

"Carol," Deanna said, talking slowly like I was a child, "there's no way you could have been there when Larry sold their Florida condo without talking to Claire first. I know you would have stopped him from doing something so stupid. And why in world would the police be involved? What Larry did was wrong, but not illegal."

"We're talking about two different things, thank goodness," I said. "It's my fault for overreacting quickly without giving you a chance to explain what you meant. I was afraid Claire thought Larry had done something much worse."

"I don't think you understand what I just told you," Deanna replied. "I'll repeat it again, slowly. Larry sold their Florida condo behind her back and she's absolutely livid. She's talking about divorcing him, and I don't blame her. What would you do if Jim ever pulled a stunt like that?"

"What Larry did was horrible," I said, pulling out the family credit card to settle my hair appointment bill. "If Jim ever tried something similar, I'd simply hire my regular hit man to teach him a lesson."

Deanna's eyes widened.

"I'm only kidding. I don't really know a hit man."

I thought for a minute, then came up with a perfect plan. "Instead of a hit man, I'd change all the locks on the house and force Jim to make alternative living arrangements."

"Maybe you should suggest that to Claire."

Chapter 71

When I ask for directions, please don't use words like "East."

I decided to take a big chance and drive to Claire's house without texting her first. Claire is the only one of my besties who forbids drop-in visits, despite the fact that she feels free to stop by everybody else's house whenever the mood strikes her. Especially mine.

I took back roads to avoid early afternoon traffic jams on Fairport Turnpike. All those years of carpooling kids all around town has given me a black belt in short cuts.

Unfortunately, a tractor trailer backing into a convenience store parking lot collided with a small delivery truck right in front of me. Thank goodness I slammed on my brakes in enough time to avoid being part of the collision. Nobody was hurt, but both drivers refused to move and were now screaming at each other. A traffic nightmare.

My first instinct was to bang my head on the steering wheel in frustration. Instead, I took deep cleansing breaths and told myself I was lucky my car was spared.

My escape to the hair salon hadn't been filled with as much fun as I'd hoped. Even a quick glance at myself in the rear-view mirror (I didn't have much else to do) to admire my shiny, naturally blonde hair failed to cheer me up, the way it usually did.

"Face facts, Carol Andrews. You are an old woman. An old, depressed woman. And you look like it."

Plus, I now had another person in my life to worry about. Claire was preparing to end her long marriage to Larry because he'd done something really stupid and, in her opinion, unforgiveable.

Note to self: Be sure Jim understands that if some bozo should show up at our beautiful antique house with cash in his hand and offer to buy the aforementioned beautiful antique house that very day, Jim is to run inside immediately and lock the door without uttering a single word.

Best to be prepared, right? Of course, right.

On the positive side, my surprise encounter with Harriet today reinforced my negative opinion of my former schoolmate/current pickleball instructor. However, just because Poppy was a mean, nasty, cheap woman who treated the diner employees (and me) badly didn't necessarily mean she was a murderer.

Not that I'm always right about people. I've made several snap judgments over the years that I've ended up regretting. Listening to what both Sister Rose and Phyllis Stevens told me about Poppy's early life had made me wonder if I was guilty of another snap judgment I'd eventually regret. Sister Rose's parting comment about how a person should be presumed innocent until proven guilty stuck in my mind, and I couldn't get rid of it.

The more I thought about the statement I'd signed at the police station, the more paranoid I got. Did Larry also see Poppy holding the knife before he left to call the police, or was I the only one? The bloody knife was already on the floor when he came back.

I didn't want to be the sole person responsible for sending Poppy to prison for a crime she might not have committed. What if I was wrong about what I saw? Did I want that possibility haunting me for the rest of my life?

The only thing I was absolutely positive of was that Larry McGee had morphed from brilliant lawyer to worst husband in Fairport, and I wanted Claire to know I was on her side.

A blast of a horn from an impatient driver behind me brought me out of my musings and sent me on my way to Claire's. Too bad I didn't check out the two people in the delivery truck as I inched past them. If I had, I would have seen Charli, my possible almost daughter-in-law, in the passenger seat, cozying up to the driver, a guy who definitely was not my son.

Chapter 72

The best murder weapon would be a Tupperware lid because the police would never find it.

Claire's car was in the driveway so I knew she was home. I also knew that she was in a terrible mood because she and Larry are overly meticulous about the way all cars are parked. Woe to any of us who accidentally allow a single tire to be anywhere near the precious McGee lawn. Today, her car was positioned sideways, so the front wheels rested on one part of the lawn and the back wheels on another.

Oh, boy.

I marched up to the front door and leaned on the bell. Then, just for the heck of it, I did it again.

The door flew open, revealing my furious friend holding a heavy frying pan. When she saw it was me, she relaxed. "I thought you were Larry."

"I heard a rumor you're looking for a divorce lawyer."

Claire gestured me inside. "Enter at your own risk."

"I have a hit man on speed dial," I said, waving my phone. "He comes very highly recommended from people I'm not allowed to name. And he takes credit cards."

"Good one, Carol." Claire made herself comfortable in Larry's recliner. "You actually cheered me up."

Her good mood didn't last long.

"What a mess. I never in my wildest dreams figured that good old reliable boring Larry would do something so horrible to me. He's completely betrayed my trust, and if one partner in a marriage can't trust the other, what's left?"

I was smart enough to realize that Claire wasn't expecting an answer to that question, which was a darn good thing. Since I've been known to be creative in what I share with my own dear husband, I kept my mouth firmly shut and waited for her to continue.

"You know what the worst part of this is?" Claire asked.

"The worst part is the way I found out about what he'd done. The sneaky son-of-a-you-know-what only confessed when I asked him if Mary Alice could use our condo for a few days."

"You did tell me you were thinking of listing it for sale," I reminded her softly.

Her face turned bright red, and I was afraid she was going to have a stroke right there in front of me.

I punched 911 into my phone and had my finger on the "send" button, just in case.

"Listing a property for sale is one thing. Actually selling it is completely different. And I was already having second thoughts about whether we should list it in the first place!"

"But Larry didn't know that, did he?"

Claire ignored me and continued her tirade. "I asked him if Mary Alice could use our condo. Like I needed his permission or something. What a dope I was. I wonder what else he's been hiding from me after all these years. He probably has a secret bank account in the Bahamas loaded with cash he's stolen from unsuspecting clients. And a villa with a sexy mistress there to share his new life."

"I don't think..."

"We had a terrible fight last night. The worst one we've ever had. I ended up throwing him out of the house and told him to sleep in the garage with his precious cars.

"Today, I have a locksmith coming to change all the locks on the house. And I'm not giving Larry the keys. He can stay out there and rot for all I care."

"What about food? You don't want him to starve to death, do you?"

"Ha! Let him order take-out. Or cook for himself in the garage on a hot plate. I'm not feeding him anymore.

"Larry changed completely when he teamed up with Lou Hollister," she continued. "Lou always seemed to have large supply of cash to throw around."

"Lou was a property developer," I said "Wouldn't he need access to cash for business? I don't know how that all works."

Claire dismissed my comment with a wave of her hand. "Lou's also the one who got Larry interested in collecting antique cars.

"Correction. Larry doesn't just collect antique cars. He's obsessed with them. I told him that he loves his cars more than he loves me. I was kidding when I said it, but now I know it's true. Because now I know about the villa and the sexy mistress in the Bahamas."

"Claire, I'm positive you're imagining things."

"Whose side are you on?" she screamed at me. "I thought you were one of my best friends."

"I am. Always."

I waited a few beats to be sure it was safe for me to talk.

"May I ask you a question without you biting my head off?"

Claire nodded. "I'm sorry for taking my anger out on you. What do you want to know?"

"How many antique cars does Larry actually have?"

"Guess."

"Two?"

Claire burst out laughing. "Two! Ha! I know he has five. But he may have more hidden all over town that he hasn't told me about."

"That's a lot of cars."

Claire gave me a withering look. "Ya think? "Larry loves his cars. He even has nicknames for each one of them. He never gave me a nickname! Those damn cars mean more to him than I do."

"I'm sure that's not true. You're just upset right now."

"Ha! I mean it because it is true! I'll never forgive Larry for selling our condo without discussing it with me first. How could he betray me like that?"

Every now and then, a thought pops into my head from out of nowhere that is so absolutely, positively brilliant that it even amazes me. I know, hard to believe, right? I was about to plant one in Claire's mind that would give her the last laugh on Larry.

"I don't think Jim would ever have the nerve to try something that sneaky with me. But even if he did, it wouldn't work. Our house is in both our names. If he wanted to sell it, I have to sign the sales agreement too."

I sat back and waited to see Claire's reaction.

"Have I ever told you that you are brilliant, Carol?" she asked, a huge grin on her face.

I opened my baby blues wide. "Why, no, Claire. In all our years of friendship, I do not believe you have ever described me as brilliant."

She jumped up and gave me a huge hug.

"Am I right? The condo is in both your names?"

"You're absolutely right. I can't wait to give Larry the news."

Her face clouded.

"Now what's wrong? I thought we'd solved your problem."

"Thanks to you, the condo sale problem has been solved. Or at least, delayed until we get a chance to talk about it and make a joint decision.

"But I'm afraid there might be a much bigger problem. Why is Larry so desperate for cash? Are we having serious money problems and he's afraid to tell me?"

Chapter 73

A penny for your thoughts seems a little pricey.

I'd been away from home way longer than I expected to be. Or, more importantly, way longer than Lucy and Ethel usually allowed me to be. Praying they hadn't punished me by leaving a few souvenirs around the kitchen to show their displeasure, I made it home in record time.

I'd expected to be greeted by two canines racing past me to get outside. Instead, I saw two canines looking annoyed because I'd disturbed their naps.

I checked the kitchen for clues and found an open bag of kibble and two used food bowls, sure signs that Jim had been home and taken care of the two now contented canines.

If this was the way Jim decided to surprise me, fine. It certainly was preferable to a midnight madness sale at CVS.

Still, it would've been fun to have my husband announce he'd won the Mega Millions jackpot and he was taking me on a cruise around the world to celebrate. Just thinking about a trip that glamorous cheered me up.

Except that I'd worry about leaving the house for so long. And I'd miss the kids. And seeing our grandson. What if we were gone so long that CJ didn't remember who we were when we got home?

And who would take care of Lucy and Ethel?

"Nope, an around-the-world cruise is out of the question," I informed the dogs. "I don't want either of you to worry about it."

Instead of indulging in any more ridiculous fantasies, I decided that what I needed most was to treat myself to a quick afternoon snooze. I set the alarm on my phone for 20 minutes. I was just beginning to relax when I had a horrible thought. Did I set the alarm to ring at 4:00 A.M. or P.M.?

I knew I'd never get any rest until I was sure I'd done it right. So, I had to find my glasses, leave my cozy bed, and walk back into the kitchen, where the phone was charging, to check.

The good news was I had indeed changed the wakeup reminder to P.M.

The bad news was that I had muted the phone when I was in the hair salon and hadn't turned it back on. As a result, I'd missed a series of frantic texts from Jim telling me an emergency had come up at the restaurant and he didn't know when he'd be home.

His last message, sent about half an hour ago, was the scariest of all.

Jim: If you hear from Mike, don't tell him anything. I'm handling it.

To text him back or not, that was the question.

On the one hand, I wanted to know what was going on. On the other hand, I was afraid to find out. I made a decision to reach out after a quick prayer to St. Jude, to be sure he agreed with me.

Me: What's going on?

Jim: I texted Maria Lesco and she was very helpful.

Me: ???

Jim: Dinner tonight at her restaurant. Will pick you up at 6:30. We'll talk then.

Me: OK.

I was relieved Jim sounded much better. It was a lucky break for me that I missed all the earlier texts. I would have been drawn into even more drama, and my capacity for drama-dealing today had reached capacity and then some. Plus, instead of worrying about how Jim planned to surprise me tonight, I was getting a free pass from kitchen duty due to circumstances I wasn't responsible for and knew nothing about.

Cue Carol clapping both hands and heading back to the bedroom to continue her well-deserved nap.

Chapter 74

Some things are better left unsaid, which I generally realize right after I've said them.

I was ready to leave for dinner at 6:27 sharp, feeling refreshed and rejuvenated after a power nap and a quick shower. It occurred to me while I was washing today's troubles away that perhaps I should start taking daily naps like the dogs do. Maybe I'd have a better disposition if I had more rest. I resolved to give my new theory a try at the next available opportunity.

Jim arrived home at exactly 6:30 to pick me up for dinner, and I was ready to go for once in my life. It was the least I could do for a guy who'd apparently had a terrible day (not that I hadn't).

"I appreciate your punctuality, Carol. Thank you."

"You're welcome," I said, giving Jim a quick smooch.

"My day had its ups and downs, including interesting conversations with Sister Rose and Phyllis Stevens. But I'm in a good mood because I also had my hair done today, and my dear husband is taking me out to dinner."

Jim laughed. "And you're in a good mood after talking to both of them? I'm impressed with your fortitude."

He turned into the driveway at the rear entrance of Maria's Trattoria and parked the car. "We're here."

"Why are we going in this way? Aren't we having dinner? We don't have to cook it too, do we?"

I hoped I was kidding.

Jim pointed to the EMPLOYEES ONLY sign. "Maria asked me to use this entrance. She didn't explain why."

I shrugged, opened the door, and we walked into complete chaos. Orders were being plated for impatient servers, two sous chefs and one pastry chef were toiling away on the other side of the kitchen, and Maria was barking orders at everyone. I'd hadn't seen this side of her since her long-ago days terrorizing students at Fairport Middle School. Her required parent-teacher conferences were no picnic for the adults, either.

Maria turned, caught sight of us, and immediately smiled. "Welcome to the madhouse," she said loudly, gesturing around the kitchen. "This is where the magic happens."

"If you say so," I replied, trying to stay clear of two servers on their way to deliver dinner orders to hungry customers.

"I had no idea a functioning restaurant kitchen was like this," Jim said, looking a little dazed.

"Just wait until Picklelilly's opens," Maria said. "You'll find out fast enough."

She gestured us toward the back of the kitchen. "Head down that hallway and on the left there's a door that has an OFFICE sign on it. Make yourselves comfortable inside. I'll meet you there with our dinners in a few minutes, and we can talk in private."

Maria's office was small and tidy, just like the woman herself. We had barely settled ourselves in two straight-back chairs facing her desk when Maria and one of the servers appeared, bringing our meal.

I still had no idea why we were eating in her office, but I trusted that all would be explained soon. In the meantime, we ate in companionable silence for several minutes, and I concentrated on enjoying my dinner.

The mood was broken by the sound of a cell phone. I scrambled to find my phone and silence it, mortified that I had neglected to turn it off.

"It's my phone, not yours, Carol," Maria said. "As delightful as it is to share a private meal with two good friends, I have to be back in the kitchen in a few minutes. I set an alarm to remind me.

"So, Jim, what's going on and how can I help?"

"That's the problem," Jim answered. "I don't know what's going on. There's no pattern to any of the problems at Picklelilly's. We've had some building supplies stolen, and I found another broken window yesterday. Supplies have been ordered and never arrived, or the order arrives and it's wrong.

"On top of all of this, whenever any town inspector comes to check out the restaurant, he finds another problem that has to be fixed before it can open. It's just one thing after another."

"Don't forget about the kitchen fire a few weeks ago when Mike was still here," I added.

"He assured me that small fires like that can happen in any restaurant kitchen," Jim said, giving me a "be quiet" look. "Isn't that true, Maria?"

"I honestly don't know," Maria answered. "All I can tell you is we've never had a kitchen fire here. It's odd to have one in a restaurant that isn't even open yet."

"Right now, I'm wondering if it will ever open," Jim said, shocking the heck out of me.

"Have you contacted the police?" Maria asked.

"Yes. I talked to Mark, and he said all the incidents seem to be a series of unfortunate coincidences. There's nothing the police can do unless an actual crime is committed."

"Running a successful restaurant is hard work," Maria said. "I can't imagine how difficult it's going to be to juggle managing two restaurants in two different parts of the country. Mike's taken a tremendous burden on himself. I hope it works out for him and for our town. When will he be back in Fairport to take over from you?"

I shot Jim a questioning look. I hoped he knew what our son's travel plans were, because I had no clue.

"Hopefully he'll be back by next week," Jim answered.

"For now, how about hiring a nighttime security guard for Picklelilly's?" Maria suggested. "I have a local firm I've used in the past, and I'd be glad to give you the contact information."

Jim's eyebrows shot up. "Have you had problems like this too?"

"Like I said, running a restaurant is hard work," Maria answered without giving specifics. "And speaking of that, I have to get back to the kitchen. Heaven knows what's been going on while I've been here talking with you."

"I'll text Carol the security firm information. I already have her cell number in my phone."

"What do we owe you for this delicious feast?" I asked.

"Let's call it professional courtesy from one restauranteur to another," Maria said. "I'll be in touch later tonight."

After expressing gratitude for the valuable information (Jim) and a promise to return soon for another delicious meal that we would pay for (me), we said our goodbyes and headed to our car.

Chapter 75

Host at restaurant: "Do you have a reservation?"
Guest: "Yes, but we decided to eat here anyway."

Jim and I were both silent on the way home. Yes, even me! I was bursting with questions, but my husband looked so worn out that I kept my mouth firmly shut.

Was I shocked at what he'd revealed to Maria? Did I wonder why he hadn't mentioned a word about what he was dealing with to me? Was I annoyed with Mike for allowing his father to shoulder all this responsibility and stress when they were really his problems?

You betcha' to all of the above, especially the last question.

We were walking toward our kitchen door when I couldn't contain myself any longer. As Jim fumbled for the house key, I used mine, stalked into the kitchen, and turned to face him.

"I don't usually criticize our son, but I'm angry at his current cavalier attitude about Picklelilly's. Piling so much stress onto you when it's really his job to handle these problems is unforgiveable in my book. When he finally shows up, I'm going to tell him so."

I knew that Mike was also dealing with hiring two new chefs for Cosmo's, but if he planned to run two successful restaurants, he had to figure out a way to do that without involving his father.

"There's more to this story that I haven't shared, Carol. Since the dogs seem to be sleeping right now," Jim pulled out a kitchen chair and gestured for me to sit, "I'll tell you what else is going on. But you have to promise me not to interrupt with questions until I'm through."

"I promise."

"I didn't want to talk about any of this in front of Maria."

"Why? Maria is the soul of discretion."

Jim glared at me. "You promised not to interrupt."

"Sorry," I said meekly. "I won't do it again."

"Mike discovered that a large amount of money from Lou Hollister's business was paid to a marketing company for a national public relations campaign. He thought it sounded fishy, so he texted me to see if I'd ever heard of the company."

I started to ask for the name, but stopped myself when Jim gave me a look.

"I hadn't. But I was curious, so I did a little more digging. The company is called Major Marketing Solutions. Good name, right?"

I nodded. What did I know about marketing company names? "So, what's the problem?"

"The problem is that there's no such company. But I was able to find a hefty bank account under that name in George Town."

"Georgetown is such a pretty part of D.C.," I said. "There are so many beautiful shops and restaurants to check out. I wish Jenny had gone to college there."

"No, Carol. Not that one. The other one."

"You've lost me."

"George Town is the capital city of the Cayman Islands. The primary account holder of the bank account in question is Lawrence McGee. Do you understand what I'm telling you?"

"This can't be true," I protested. "You must be wrong."

Jim shook his head. "I wish I were, Carol. The sources I used are the same ones the police use. They don't make mistakes.

"It looks like Larry McGee, Claire's husband and our friend, has been siphoning off thousands of dollars from Hollister Construction and stashing it in a bank account in the Cayman Islands."

"I don't believe it!"

Jim looked miserable. "How do you think I feel? I never expected to find anything like this."

"There must be a logical explanation. Larry's not a crook!"

"I wish I could agree with you, but it sure looks like he is."

"Did you tell Mike?"

"I had to since he's the one who asked me to check the company out for Charli."

"Charli! What does she have to do with this mess?"

"She's a minority stockholder in Hollister Construction. Since her father is now deceased, and her mother is...."

"I know. Her mother is suspected of murdering him," I finished.

"Yes. That. Anyway, Charli's taken over more responsibility for the company, and she asked Mike to help her."

My head was spinning. "You mean, Mike and Charli are completely back together?"

"Carol, focus! Our son's current love life is not the most important thing we're talking about here."

"Okay, okay. Sorry I interrupted you," I said again.

Although our son's current love life was pretty important to me. Moving on.

"I'm trying to remain calm about this latest bit of news, but it's hard," I said, biting my lip and forcing myself not to cry.

"You can see now why I didn't bring this up at Maria's Trattoria."

"Since Mike's the person who got you involved in the first place, he should be here now, not still hanging out in Florida." Just like he shouldn't have asked you to shoulder the burden of Picklelilly's.

"He's not hanging out in Florida like a beach bum, Carol. He's working."

"I know he's having staff problems in Florida. But right now, he should be here! This is all his fault."

"Only you could come to that conclusion."

Humph.

"For your information," Jim continued, "Mike's found two people to fill the open positions at Cosmo's, and he's taking a red eye flight from Miami tonight. He'll be here tomorrow morning."

"If all this Cayman Islands bank information is true, why would a stand-up guy like Larry McGee do something so crooked? I can't figure it out."

Jim just shook his head.

"I'm sorry to dump all this bad news on you. You have enough to deal with already."

I managed a smile. "That's okay. I'd rather know what's going on than not know." I guess.

Suddenly, my brain kicked into overdrive. Claire told me Larry was obsessed with antique cars, and she figured that's why he wanted to sell the Florida condo. I realized Larry could have stolen all that money from Hollister Construction and hidden it in a secret bank account so he could use the money to buy even more of them. Maybe Lou Hollister discovered the thefts and confronted him at the pickleball court before I arrived. So Larry murdered him.

No way, Carol. Larry McGee is not an embezzler and a murderer. You are way off base.

"Do you think you can handle one more piece of bad news tonight?" Jim asked.

I came back to earth with a thud. "I guess I zoned out for a minute. Did you say something?"

"I don't blame you," Jim said. "I'm laying a lot on you all at once. And there's more."

He took both my hands and held them tight. "There's an additional account holder named on the Cayman Islands bank account.

"Claire."

Chapter 76

There are some days when I wish I could wear a "Do Not Disturb" sign around my neck. Today is definitely one of them.

I had only one item on my To Do list the following day: Confront Poppy and force her to confess that she'd killed her husband, set up the Cayman Islands bank account to incriminate Larry and Claire, or was behind the negative publicity campaign nicknaming Fairport "The Murder Capital of New England."

I was prepared to be flexible, if necessary, but I was really hoping she'd break down during my relentless cross-examination and confess to all three. I had no firm plan as to how I was going to accomplish such a feat, but I was confident one would come to me when I needed it, hopefully right before I opened my mouth.

Chugging the rest of Jim's delicious coffee straight from the pot earned critical stares from both dogs, which I ignored. It was a surprisingly freeing experience, and I didn't even spill a drop on my pajamas.

While in the shower, I tried to plan my strategy. I finished my shower squeaky clean but strategy-less. Maybe I needed more caffeine.

You have to do better than this, Carol. Find an accomplice to come with you. Two sets of ears are better than one, and it's always good to have a witness in case things go wrong.

In situations like this—and there have been many, as I'm sure most of you already know—my favorite accomplice is my bestie, Nancy Green. She's always up for an adventure if it doesn't conflict with her busy real estate business. Since she and her off-again/on-again husband were still away on a cruise, I crossed her off my list. Claire was out, too, for obvious reasons, which was a shame. She could have been really handy if Poppy became violent, since she's a large woman (don't tell her I said that) and packs a hefty punch when necessary.

Mary Alice was also out, and if I have to explain why, you haven't been paying attention and shame on you.

I nixed Deanna because she was busy at Crimpers all day, and I wanted to get this confrontation/interrogation/possible confession over with during daylight hours. I wasn't comfortable asking Maria Lesco, so I crossed her name off my list. Somehow involving Sister Rose seemed inappropriate, even though she can strike terror into anyone with a single glance.

Phyllis Stevens was an interesting thought, but I nixed that idea too. She's a real gossip, and I needed an accomplice I could trust completely to keep her mouth shut.

All this perusing brought me to the last possible person on my list, my daughter Jenny. I hated to involve her, especially since she was married to the detective in charge of solving Lou Hollister's murder. I didn't want to take the chance of ruining her marriage.

I wondered if there was a saint who was in charge of decision-making. A quick Internet search revealed the answer: St. Ignatius Loyola, who developed a way of decision-making while he was convalescing from a cannon ball injury during the Battle of Pamplona, a 1521 territorial battle between France and Spain.

I'd never reached out to him before, but I figured it was worth a try. His method involved using your imagination to pretend you've already made the decision you're struggling with. Live with that pretend decision for a while and assess what your heart and head are telling you.

Confirmation that you've made the right choice may come through interaction with another person or through opportunities that arise or doors that will open once you've moved forward with that decision.

I let the information roll around in my head for a few minutes, trying to decipher how his advice could be used in this case. I finally decided I should just go for it, sent up a silent prayer that I was doing the right thing, and texted my daughter.

Chapter 77

I don't like making plans for the day because then the word "premeditated" can be thrown around the courtroom.

"We've never done this before," my daughter said as I made myself comfortable in the passenger seat of her SUV.

"We've had plenty of adventures together," I corrected.

"True. But none like this."

"Like what?"

"Oh, Mom, you're being deliberately obtuse. You've never taken CJ and me along with you when you were investigating a murder."

I winced. "Since you put it that way, you're right. And if my husband and your husband find out, they're both going to be furious. Especially about bringing CJ along with us." I turned to gaze at the most perfect grandson ever born, who winked at me. I swear, the little dickens knew exactly what we were talking about. And he was up for the adventure.

"Is contributing to the delinquency of a toddler punishable by law?"

Jenny burst out laughing. "I don't think it is if the toddler is accompanied by his mother and grandmother. And CJ's just starting to crawl, so he's not officially a toddler yet. Stop worrying and tell me where we're going."

"Poppy's address is 68 Pine Knoll Drive. According to the navigation app, it's about eight miles from here, close to the Westfield town line."

"What's your plan when we get there?"

"The best thing I can come up with is to tell Poppy that I'm following up on Sister Rose's visit yesterday. She insisted I reach out to Poppy and hear her side of the story, and that's what I'm doing."

It suddenly occurred to me that, for once, I was telling the truth. Unbelievable.

Jenny gave me a quick glance. "So, you're blaming the nun, right? Do you think Poppy's going to believe you?"

"If she doesn't, she can text Sister Rose and ask her. So there."

"Okay, okay. I believe you, Mom. And what's your reason for bringing us with you?"

"I haven't figured that part out yet."

"You better figure it out fast," Jenny said, pointing to the house number on the nearby security gate. "We're here. How do we get in?"

"Rats," I said, squinting at the call buttons on the gate. "I didn't anticipate this. There are probably cameras here too. I'll have to text her. I hope I have her number."

As I was rooting around in my purse for my phone, I heard a disembodied voice. "Drive through to the main house, Carol. I've been expecting you." The gates slowly opened, and we followed the long driveway over the river and through the woods (no kidding, we really did) to Poppy's house.

"Good thing I had a full tank of gas, Mom. This is the longest driveway I've ever seen."

"I guess Poppy likes her privacy," I said as I exited the SUV without mishap and took a close look at the house. "And her space. I wonder if this is the largest house in Fairport."

Jenny joined me on the front steps, a squirmy baby in her arms. "Ready, Mom?"

"As I'll ever be." I squared my shoulders and rang the doorbell.

"I wonder if there'll be a butler," Jenny whispered, giggling. "Or a maid."

"Behave yourself," I said. "Remember, this is serious business."

The door swung open at the exact moment my darling grandson let out the loudest wail I'd ever heard. Timing is everything, right?

"Here, Mom, take him please." Jenny thrust the baby into my arms. "I'll get his pacifier and a bottle. I just realized I'm late with his feeding."

"This is a surprise," Poppy said, eyeing CJ like he was from another planet. "I didn't realize you were bringing anyone with you."

"This is CJ, my grandson," I said, turning him toward Poppy so she could see how cute he was despite the squirming and screeching.

Miraculously, the baby calmed down when Poppy smiled at him.

"He's adorable."

"No argument from me there."

"Follow me," Poppy said. "We'll sit in the conservatory. Will the girl...?" her voice trailed off.

"The girl is my daughter, Jenny. She's CJ's mother."

"So I gathered."

Don't let her get to you so soon, Carol. Keep your cool.

"Jenny will find us without any problem. She's a very bright girl."

"I'm glad we have a few minutes just to ourselves," Poppy said, gesturing CJ and me to a wicker sofa that probably cost more than my entire living room. "I have a sensitive question to ask you that you might not want your daughter to overhear. And I want the absolute truth.

"How long did you and my father have an affair?"

Chapter 78

*I've got to stop asking, "How stupid can you be?"
Too many people are taking it as a challenge.*

A loud gasp behind me from my daughter brought me to my senses. Good thing. I was so shocked by Poppy's question I almost dropped the baby.

"I'll take CJ back now, Mom. It's going to be all right."

I was sure Jenny meant the baby would be all right, not me. I had a long way to go before I got over Poppy's accusation. Possibly the rest of my life.

"That is the most insulting, ridiculous, disgusting thing anyone has ever said to me. What is wrong with you? Are you hateful or just stupid?" I was standing over Poppy with both my fists clenched. Trust me, if she didn't apologize right away, I was going to smack her face.

Poppy looked at me defiantly, her eyes brimming with tears. "You can't lie your way out of this one, Carol," she screamed. "I saw you and my father making out in the kitchen like two teenagers that summer you worked for us at the beach. That image has haunted me since I was sixteen years old."

I was shaking so hard I felt like I was going to vomit. I started to say something, but the words wouldn't come. Besides, I was smart enough to know that anything I said wouldn't help at this point. She was totally out of control.

"He was always talking about what a wonderful girl you were. So bright. So pretty. So smart. And my poor mom agreed with him. I wanted to tell her what was going on, but I didn't want to break her heart. So I kept it to myself all these years. Until now."

I collapsed on the coach with a thud. Jenny and CJ joined me in a show of Andrews family solidarity. My daughter grabbed my hand. "Whenever you're ready, Mom, we'll leave. Just say the word."

I shook my head.

"Thanks, sweetheart, but I have to get this...accusation...straightened out right now."

Poppy was now sobbing uncontrollably, but I was determined to find out what the heck she was talking about.

"At least now I know why you hate me so much," I said.

"I want to know what you saw, or think you saw, that gave you this completely crazy idea. Every single detail. Because if your father and I were having the torrid affair you say we were, why don't I remember it?"

"You blocked it out of your mind because you felt guilty about it," Poppy said. "And you should!"

She closed her eyes and said, "I remember every single detail like it just happened. I woke up extra early one morning, and I couldn't get back to sleep. I decided to grab some cereal and then go for a bike ride. I got as far as the kitchen doorway, and I saw you and Daddy kissing passionately. It was disgusting."

"How long were you there?"

"Not long. Just a couple of seconds. Then I ran back upstairs to my bedroom and cried until everyone else got up."

"That's it? That's what you saw?"

"Yes. That was enough."

"Too bad you left so soon," I said.

"Huh?"

"It's too bad you didn't stick around for more than a couple of seconds. You missed the part where I slapped your father's face and told him if he ever tried anything like that with me again, I'd report him to the proper authorities. And that's the truth!"

"Would you really have reported him to the police?" Jenny asked.

"Nope. Even worse. I would have reported him to the nuns!"

Poppy stared at me, and then started to laugh.

You might remember, if you were paying attention in an earlier chapter (and if you don't remember, shame on you!), that hearing Poppy's laugh made me cringe. But it didn't bother me this time. Go figure.

Be careful, Carol. This could all be an act to throw you off balance. And she still may have murdered her husband. That's what you came here to find out, remember?

I took a quick glance at Jenny. CJ was now blissfully asleep in her arms. She pointed to her cell phone, and I realized my smart daughter was recording the entire conversation. Just in case it was needed in the future.

Poppy's laughter trailed off, and suddenly she didn't look as friendly as she did a few minutes ago.

"I still have a few more questions, Carol. Why did Daddy give you a job in New York? He never did that for me. And why did he set you up in your cushy apartment and pay your rent? He never did that for me or anybody else in the family."

Oh, brother. Here we go again.

"When I moved to New York after college, I was sure I'd get a job right away," I answered. "I didn't. I was living in one room at a cheap hotel, and I could barely afford that. I was almost broke, but I kept it a secret. I was too proud to admit I was a failure to anyone. I was finally so desperate that I contacted your father. He was nice enough to give me a job in his restaurant kitchen until I could find something better. I spent the next four months cutting up vegetables and peeling potatoes.

"He did not set me up in my first apartment, either, unless you mean that I was able to afford the rent because of my salary at the restaurant. I also got all my meals there for free. Your dad was a great guy, and he didn't want me to starve. He also told me that nothing valuable ever came easy, to work hard, and not give up."

Poppy started to interrupt me, but I steamrolled right over her.

"It's my turn to talk, now. So please don't interrupt.

"In case you didn't know this, your dad was also known among all his female employees for stealing a quick kiss or two every now and then. When Claire and I got those summer jobs at your family's beach house, the maid who was leaving—I can't remember her name now—warned me against him. She said his passes were innocent but annoying. So, I was prepared when he tried to kiss me.

"Do you remember the bruise he had on his right cheek for a few days? I did that. I think he respected me because I stood up to him. That's why he was so good to me later when I turned to him for help."

"Oh, my gosh. I remember when he had that bruise!" Poppy said. "He told us he'd walked into a refrigerator door at the restaurant."

I raised my right hand. "Say hello to the refrigerator door."

"I'm so glad we finally talked," Poppy said. "Once you confessed to the affair, I hoped I could forgive you. Instead, I'm asking you to forgive me."

It would take me at least a year before I'd be able to forgive Poppy. Maybe even longer.

Then I realized how long she'd been consumed by her mistaken interpretation of what she saw happen between her father and me. Perhaps she'd never be able to let that go. I felt very sorry for her.

I knew there was only one thing for me to do.

"I forgive you," I said slowly.

"Thank you," Poppy said. "That means the world to me. I used to be young and stupid and jealous. Now I'm older, still stupid, and in a lot of trouble."

She reached over and grabbed my hand. "I didn't murder my husband, Carol. I tried to save him. You completely misunderstood what happened. You have to tell the police that I'm innocent!"

I stood up so fast I almost tripped on my own feet. "I should've known you had an ulterior motive for all this sweet "let's forgive each other" talk. And to think I almost fell for it. You haven't changed a bit.

"Come on, Jenny. Let's get out of here."

As I stormed to the front door, I heard Poppy's voice. "I admitted I misunderstood what happened between you and my father. Just like you misunderstood what you saw happening at the pickleball court. I did not kill my husband!

"Please, Carol, you have to help me! Nobody else can!"

Chapter 79

My favorite childhood memory is my back not hurting.

Poppy's words haunted me on the drive home. I tossed them over and over in my mind. If she'd wanted to lay a major guilt trip on me, she'd done a fabulous job. Her desperate cry for help was so perfectly expressed it was like she'd rehearsed it in advance. Not only was I depressed, I no longer trusted my own judgment where she was concerned.

I turned my head (with some effort) and gazed at my wonderful grandson, blissfully asleep. His innocent face made my heart burst with love.

"I wish I could sleep like CJ."

"I think you'd be uncomfortable in one of those car seats," Jenny said as she pulled into our driveway.

"You're right, of course." I made a half-hearted attempt to smile. "Thanks."

"Want us to stay with you for a while? Maybe it would help if we talked through what happened."

"As tempting as your offer is, I'm going to pass. My mind is complete mush right now. I have a lot to think about. I promise I'll call you later. Okay?"

"Sure, Mom. Whatever you say." She held up her phone. "I recorded most of the conversation. I can text it to you if you feel up to listening to it. Please don't make a decision about whether or not to help Poppy until you and I've talked."

"I won't, and thanks, sweetie. For everything." I leaned over and gave Jenny a smooch. "How did I get such a wonderful daughter?"

"I think Dad had something to do with it."

"Very funny," I said, waving Jenny and CJ on their way. "I'll thank him when he gets home."

Lucy and Ethel greeted me warmly, and I attended to their needs. "You're lucky your lives are so easy," I told them as they chomped on their snacks. "Maybe I'll get lucky and come back in another life as a dog. Then somebody will wait on me the way I wait on you."

I was considering if the best use of my time was to satisfy my hunger cravings or vacuum the entire downstairs. When a quick perusal of the refrigerator revealed nothing was there for lunch, which is what happens if a person hadn't been food shopping in several days, the choice was made for me.

I awakened the vacuum cleaner from its catatonic state in the front hall closet, feeling extremely virtuous and confident I'd lose a pound or two if I did some housecleaning.

I was paying attention to whatever was visible without my glasses and ignoring everything else, like under furniture (why bother?), when I felt a hand on my shoulder. I turned to defend myself with the vacuum cleaner hose and almost smacked my dear husband in the face. Holy cow. That was close.

"What are you doing? Trying to kill me?"

I lowered my weapon and glared at him. "Why did you sneak up on me like that? I thought you were a burglar."

"At one o'clock in the afternoon? This is when most burglars get some shuteye. You should know that already, after reading so many mysteries."

"Why are you home so early?" I countered. "And you should be praising me for vacuuming the house, not scaring me to death."

I forced a single tear to appear, then slowly inch its way down my cheek. "I have to do all the housework myself since you insisted we couldn't afford a cleaning woman anymore. And you know I have a bad back. Don't you care?"

We were heading toward a full-blown domestic about…what? One of us had to stop acting so childish and the other one had to stop being so bossy. Take your pick as to who was who.

I switched off the vacuum cleaner and mentally promised myself that sometime before next year, I'd take it out again for a nice spin around the whole house.

"In the interest of family harmony, I am relinquishing my weapon," I said, dragging the machine back into its resting place in the closet. "You are completely safe."

I followed my husband into the kitchen. "You still haven't told me why you're home and not at Picklelilly's."

Jim ignored me and headed straight to his favorite household appliance, the refrigerator. "I'm hungry and there's nothing to eat in here," he said.

I glared at Jim. "I haven't had a spare minute to go food shopping. My life has been pretty hectic the last few days, in case you've forgotten that I recently witnessed a murder. Or I thought I did. I'm very confused and I desperately need to talk to someone. Even you.

"I'm sorry you've been having problems at the restaurant. If there's anything I can do to help you, you know I will. But you haven't even asked me how I'm doing! Don't you care?"

I was truly proud of myself. Nobody can throw a husband off balance quicker than I can.

Jim didn't look me in the eye because he knew I was right. Guilt trip accomplished.

"I'm here and ready to listen," he offered. "I promise I won't criticize you, tell you you're overreacting, or interrupt you with suggestions constantly, the way I usually do. I understand we look at things differently."

"And don't forget we're both positive we have the perfect solution to each other's problems, especially when we can't solve our own," I threw in, just for fun.

"You may be on to something, Carol," Jim said. "I never realized that."

"I just realized it myself," I said, laughing. "And caring is sharing, right?"

"You know what I'd like to share with you right now, my dear wife?"

I figured he'd point toward the bedroom and wriggle his eyebrows, like he usually does. Not this time.

"I have a proposition for you," Jim said. "Each of us will share something on their mind, and the other one will react to it in a positive, helpful way. What do you say?"

"I'm willing to give it a shot," I said cautiously. "You go first."

"Great." Jim cleared his throat and looked me straight in the eye. "I have an important announcement to make. It may upset you at first, so please keep an open mind. Okay?"

I nodded. "You're making me nervous."

"I got fired today. I am no longer employed at Picklelilly's."

"How could you possibly get fired? Our son runs the place."

"He's the one who fired me."

Chapter 80

You can tell a lot about a woman by her hands.
For instance, if she's holding a gun, she's probably angry.

"I figured phrasing my news this way would distract you from your own problems," Jim said, grinning. "And I was right.

"Maybe I went a little bit too far, though. I was only kidding, Carol."

I looked at him. Silently. For several seconds. Maybe more.

"Some joke. Not funny."

"We're both concerned about Mary Alice. And Claire and Larry. And Mike." Jim said in his defense.

"But I know what's bothering you even more. You're obsessing about whether or not Poppy murdered her husband because you don't want your statement to send an innocent woman to prison. You're not obsessing about that right now, so my idea worked."

Jim looked very pleased with himself.

Thoughtful person than I am, I chose my response carefully.

"You're absolutely right, dear. Now I'm obsessing about how I can bump you off without being caught. I may have to do some online research to figure out the answer, so be warned."

Jim laughed, although I was pleased to see he also looked a little nervous.

Give the guy a break, Carol. He was only trying to help you. It's not his fault that he's a clueless male.

Instead of rummaging in the cutlery drawer for a convenient sharp object, I sat quietly in my chair and stared at him for a little while longer.

"Okay, I admit I was stupid," Jim finally said. "But I meant well. "

"I suggest trying a different approach next time."

"Okay."

"Part of what I said was true, though," he continued. "Mike and I agreed that my services at the restaurant were no longer needed. Technically, I am unemployed, thanks to our son. He didn't get to Picklelilly's until almost noon, even though he flew in late last night.

"He and Charli had a long talk, then Mike grabbed a few hours' sleep at his rental condo," Jim continued, correctly anticipating my next question. "I wasn't comfortable asking him for details of their talk, and he didn't share any.

"I brought Mike up to speed on what's been happening at Picklelilly's while he was in Florida. He agreed with Maria Lesco that hiring a security company was an immediate priority. I think it's finally dawning on him that running two restaurants in two different parts of the country isn't such a great idea."

I'd been completely silent while Jim talked. Trust me, it was one of the most difficult things I'd ever done, but I wanted to prove to him—and maybe to myself—that I could control my motor mouth if I tried.

"Did Mike mention Lou Hollister's murder?" I finally asked.

"We only talked about Picklelilly's. He didn't mention the murder, and neither did I. I'm sure he and Charli talked about it, though."

"What about Larry McGee? I hope you found something to clear up that ridiculous situation."

"I was hoping you wouldn't ask me that. But since you did, I'll tell you what I found out today."

He gave me a stern look. "This is not to be shared with anyone, Carol. Under any circumstances. Do you agree?"

I crossed my heart and nodded.

"In addition to the phony marketing campaign, it appears that every Hollister Construction real estate transaction has included a hefty extra charge for closing costs. These funds were then transferred to another Cayman Islands bank account with Larry and Claire's names on it. As of now, the combined total of both accounts is over $1 million.

"In other words, money was being stolen from the company two different ways: for extra closing costs and for a phony marketing campaign. And all the evidence points to Larry as the thief," Jim said.

"If Larry needed money and didn't want Claire to know, why did he try to sell the Florida condo? She was bound to find out eventually. Why didn't he just take money from the stash he supposedly has in the Cayman Islands instead? Claire's convinced they're having financial problems because of his antique car obsession and he's afraid to tell her.

"This whole thing makes no sense. And as for Claire's name being included on the Cayman Islands bank account, that's totally ridiculous."

"I know why Larry wanted to sell the Florida condo," Jim said, looking guilty. "But I can't tell you. Larry swore me to secrecy."

"Jim Andrews, you better tell me what you know right now if you know what's good for you. I'm not kidding!"

"Okay, okay. Larry found out that the condo unit next door to theirs was being taken over by a mortgage company because the owners couldn't make their payments. He bought it right away as a surprise for Claire, and listed their old for sale. The new unit is twice the size of their current one with three bedrooms and three full bathrooms. There's plenty of room for guests.

"Claire's always complaining that she loves being in Florida but misses all her friends in Fairport when they're away. With a bigger place, we can all visit them. Larry got an offer on the old condo right away and took it. Don't you think this is great news?"

I sat back in my chair and silently glared at Jim.

"Why are you looking at me like that? Did I do something wrong?"

"You didn't. But Larry certainly did."

I could tell Jim had no idea what I was talking about.

"Remember the old saying about the road to hell being paved with good intentions?" I asked.

"Sure. Everybody's heard that one."

"Larry's intentions were good ones. I'm not arguing with that. But because he decided to surprise Claire, and she didn't give him a chance to explain why he was selling their condo without telling her, she got furious and threw him out of the house. Now she's decided they must have a secret financial crisis because it's the only reason that makes sense to her. Just wait until she finds out about the Cayman Islands bank account in both their names with all that money that she also knows nothing about!"

I took a minute to catch my breath, then steamrolled on before Jim could say anything.

"We both agree that somebody must be framing Larry for fraud, embezzlement, grand theft, and who knows what else, right? That's the only thing that makes sense. And on top of that, because of Larry's stupidity, now his own wife doesn't trust him. He should have been honest with Claire from the beginning about buying the bigger Florida condo instead of deciding to surprise her. Secrets between husbands and wives are never a good idea. Even though men and women look at things differently, if they just discuss them openly, they could learn from each other, and maybe there'd be more happy marriages."

My own words ricocheted right back at me.

What a hypocrite you are, Carol Andrews! Maybe you should remember another old saying about the pot calling the kettle black. How can you criticize Larry McGee for not being honest with Claire when you've been hiding things from Jim since the day you were married?

"You're right as always, Carol," Jim answered. "Claire and Larry should be more honest with each other, the way we are."

The guilt I was now feeling after more than 40 years of successful deceptions was threatening to choke me. Or was my dear husband putting me on and I wasn't smart enough to catch on?

Nope. The serious expression on Jim's face told me he was completely sincere. I resolved to be more honest and up front with him from then on.

"In the interest of full disclosure, though," Jim added, "I need to confess something to you."

On the other hand, if he'd been sneaking around behind my back, my above resolution was hereby cancelled.

"I saw Carla Grimaldi in Town Hall yesterday. She wanted you to know that all the billboards have been changed, and to thank you for your help. I just remembered to relay the message now."

"That's okay. Don't worry about it.'" I could afford to be magnanimous since I had done absolutely nothing about finding out who was behind the negative publicity for our town. Something else for me to feel guilty about.

I put my head down on the kitchen table for a second or two, hoping to clear my mind. It didn't help,

"Right now, I'm feeling overwhelmed and confused. I don't know what's true and what isn't. And I don't even know where or how to start figuring everything out. It's like a puzzle with hundreds of random pieces that don't have anything in common with each other. But something in my mind keeps telling me there's a connection between Lou's murder, the billboards, Mike and his new restaurant, Poppy and Charli, Mary Alice, the lawsuit, Larry and Claire, and who knows what else?

"I'm hungry too. I didn't have lunch."

"I have an idea," Jim said. "Sit tight. I'll be right back."

He returned in a flash holding a wine glass in one hand and a coffee mug in the other. "How about we sit down with some liquid refreshment and you share your thoughts with me. Your choice. Wine or coffee?"

"Definitely coffee for a clear head. Let's save the wine for when we figure everything out."

"We're only doing this together," Jim said. "You're not allowed to include Deanna, Claire, Mary Alice, Sister Rose, or any other members of your usual posse. It's just you and me this time. Agreed?"

"Agreed." And just to be sure, I reserve the right to eliminate any details that might possibly incriminate me.

Chapter 81

*Never be afraid to try something new. Remember,
amateurs built the Ark.
Professionals built the Titanic.*

The next few hours were excruciating and because I like you, I'll spare you the gory details. I was clear, concise, and extremely organized in my thought process, thanks to an infusion of caffeine so huge I knew I'd be awake for the next several days.

I started with Mike's surprise of my pickleball lesson and ended by playing Jenny's cell phone audio of Poppy's disgusting accusation against me. I included Mary Alice's secret romance with Lou Hollister, my (non) car accident and the resulting lawsuit, Lou's murder and my seeing Poppy holding the murder weapon, the negative billboards, Mike and Charli's romance, Larry and Claire and their problems, the conversations I had about Poppy with Phyllis Stevens and Sister Rose, and a partridge in a pear tree. (I didn't actually mention the partridge. I threw that in just for fun, and to see whether all of you were paying attention.)

Jim scribbled copious notes while I was talking, which I was sure he wouldn't ever be able to decipher. Not that I'd tell him that, of course.

I finally shut up and downed the glass of water Jim had thoughtfully placed at my elbow. "So, what do you think?" I asked.

"I finally understand," my husband said, thrilling me beyond belief.

I jumped up and gave him a passionate kiss. "You can't believe how happy that makes me. You're wonderful. I wish I'd talked to you sooner. Tell me what you figured out so I can understand it too."

"I understand why you're so confused," Jim said, bursting my brief bubble of happiness. "I am too. I can't believe anyone would hold a grudge for over forty years."

He yawned, then checked his phone. "It's after nine o'clock. We've been at this for hours and we're both starving. Do you think it's too late to go to Maria's?"

"Honestly, Jim, here I am pouring my heart out to you, and you tell me you're also confused and hungry. That's it?"

"You know I think better when my stomach is full."

"We shouldn't impose on Maria after taking advantage of her hospitality last night."

"Good point. So, do you want to order takeout?"

"Not really. Let me think for a minute."

Inspiration came in the form of a cheeseburger and French fries. "I have a great idea. Give the dogs a snack and a quick run in the yard. I'll meet you at the car in five minutes."

"Where are we going?"

"The Fairport Diner. It's open twenty-four hours."

You've probably figured out that I had an ulterior motive for suggesting that particular restaurant. Besides indulging in my favorite high cholesterol meal, I hoped Harriet would be our server. With any luck, I'd be able to get more inside information about Mr. P and his family.

Multitasking is my passion.

When we arrived at the diner, there were only two cars in the parking lot.

"Are you sure they're still open?"

I pointed to the OPEN 24 HOURS" sign that was clearly visible despite the darkness. "Neon signs never lie. It's a law. And besides," I added as I unfastened my seat belt, "I'm sure they'll be glad to see two customers, so we'll get great service. As I recall, slow service is one of your pet peeves." My husband's complaints about service when dining out have been a cause of major embarrassment for me on more occasions than I care to remember.

"Humph," Jim responded, not willing to admit that I was right. He gallantly held the door open for me. "After you, my dear."

The woman at the hostess station was hidden behind a magazine and barely acknowledged our presence. "Sit anywhere you want."

"Thank you," Jim said, shooting me an "I knew this wasn't a good idea" look.

"I know that voice," the woman said, ditching the magazine and looking at us directly. It was Harriet. She had a welcoming smile on her face, which was surprising since we'd just met.

"I guess you remember me," I said, then realized she wasn't talking to me; she was talking to Jim.

"Hello, toasted cinnamon raisin bagel with cream cheese and a large black coffee to go. How've you been? It's been a long time since you've been in here."

Jim matched Harriet's smile with one of his own. "I started my day that way for almost twenty years. I can't believe you still remember me."

"And this is your wife?" Harriet asked.

Jim put his arm around me and nodded. "This is Carol."

"Not to me," Harriet corrected. "She's a cheeseburger well done with sides of fries and onion rings. And a Coke."

"I only order two sides so I can share with my friends," I clarified, lest Jim get the wrong idea about my dining habits. "I don't eat both of them all by myself."

Harriet gestured around the almost empty diner. "Pick a spot, and I'll bring you over some menus."

We slid into a booth near the diner entrance (Jim's choice so he could keep an eye on the car). Harriet was back in a flash with two menus and two glasses of water. "I'll give you a few minutes to decide. No rush."

"I already know what I want," I said, not bothering to even glance at the specials. "I always stick with a sure thing."

"I figured as much," Harriet said, making a note on her order pad. "What about you?" she asked Jim. "Are you ready to live dangerously, or are you going to stick with your usual bagel and cream cheese?"

"No way," Jim said, snapping the menu shut. "I'll have what she's having," he said, pointing to me. "I always wanted to say that."

"Good choice," Harriet said, making another note on her pad. "We're known for having the best burgers in Fairport. I have a story about that you'll both get a kick out of. I'll put your orders in and be right back."

"I'd also like…"

"A side of fries and a side of onion rings," Harriet said. "Already noted."

Before I could even check the messages on my phone, she was back with two chocolate milkshakes. "On the house," she said.

"I could get used to this special treatment," Jim said.

"So, what's the story about the burgers?" I asked.

"If you'd been here last night about this time," Harriet said, speaking in a low voice, "you would have seen a screaming match between the First Selectwoman and my boss. It was a dilly."

She leaned a little closer to us. "Did you hear about the billboards near the highway? The ones calling Fairport the Murder Capital of New England? Turns out the boss had ordered billboards to advertise the diner as the Burger Capital of New England. Tim swore up and down that he'd checked a proof of the sign and it read Burger Capital so the change in wording had to be the printer's mistake. The First Selectwoman checked with the printer, who swore there was no mistake. The billboard order he got clearly read Murder, not Burger. Since both Tim and the printer had already deleted their copies of the order, there was nothing to prove which one was lying. Who knows what really happened?

"Anyway, after a lot of screaming, Tim agreed to reimburse the town for the cost of new signage, and that satisfied the First Selectwoman. After she finally left, Tim couldn't stop laughing. He thought the mistake was hilarious."

"Tim?" I repeated. "The only person I know with that first name is a lawyer."

"That's him. He's Poppy Hollister's first cousin."

Chapter 82

I don't trust coffee that requires 10 or more words to order.

I would have slapped myself for being so stupid if I hadn't been sipping a delicious chocolate milkshake at the time. I had totally forgotten that Poppy and Tim were related. Harriet's casual comment convinced me she was a gold mine of information she was willing to share about Mr. P's family without any nosy or sneaky questions from me.

In the interests of historical research, to broaden my local knowledge, and to solve a recent murder, I was ready, willing, and eager to listen to every word she said.

Jim's milkshake was already a distant memory, so he started eyeing mine. "Are you going to drink that?"

"The rest is all yours," I said, pushing my glass in his direction. "I'll stick to water."

I wasn't being selfless. So far, Jim hadn't commented on the fact that I hadn't secured the top button of my jeans for the last several days. But I was sure he'd noticed.

Smart man. One of the secrets to a long marriage is knowing when to keep your mouth shut.

Promising myself to begin counting calories tomorrow, I was already salivating when Harriet arrived with our sumptuous repast. "Enjoy," she said.

"Don't worry, I plan to do exactly that."

Jim finished his cheeseburger light years before I did (slight exaggeration) and pointed his fork at what was left of mine.

"Not a chance, buster," I said, moving my plate out of his reach. "This is all mine. You can have the rest of the fries and onion rings."

I heard the sound of a cash register, then Harriet's voice. "Thanks for stopping in tonight, folks. Hope to see you again soon."

"We'll definitely be back," a man said. "Good night."

I was conscious of the diner door closing, and realized that Jim and I were currently the sole diner customers. A perfect opportunity to have a chat with Harriet, and I had no intention of wasting it.

I wondered if there were such a thing as diner server/customer etiquette. Would she think it was weird if I invited her to sit and join us?

I was plotting the best way to continue our conversation when Harriet appeared. "Who'd like dessert?"

"Not me. I couldn't eat another bite," I admitted. "My jeans are protesting already." I shot Jim a don't comment look.

"I hope you won't be offended if I say you look tired," I continued. "Are we your only customers?"

"You are until the hospital night shift folks come by on their way home from work. Another half hour and the place will be hopping."

"You're not here all by yourself, are you?" Jim asked. "That's not safe."

"There are others slaving away in the kitchen," Harriet said. "Someone's always in screaming distance if I need any help. I'm perfectly safe.

"Although I wouldn't mind a short break right about now to rest my feet." Hint, hint.

"Then please join us, Harriet," my gallant husband said, correctly zeroing in on my wave length for once.

"Well, just for a minute," she replied, looking pleased at the invitation. "This is the first time that any patron was really nice to me. Most folks just want quick service and then they're out of here. Nobody's ever called me by name, either, even though I wear a badge that clearly shows it. Thank you."

She sank down beside me, then jumped right up again. "Are you sure you don't want dessert? We have some cherry pie that would be the perfect way to top off your meal. And there's always a fresh pot of coffee brewing."

"I thought you wanted a break," I said, looking stern. "Don't you ever sit still?

"Harriet and I first met at Crimpers," I explained to Jim without giving Harriet a chance to answer my question. "She was cleaning the hair salon for Deanna. And doing a terrific job, too."

Left unspoken was an obvious hint to my spouse that we should hire Harriet to clean our house, too. Of course, Jim ignored that part.

"Deanna and I have a deal," Harriet clarified. "I don't charge her for cleaning the salon every week, and she does my hair for free. Sometimes we trade local gossip, too." At my stricken look, she added, "Never anything about you and your friends. No need to worry about that."

Now that Harriet and I were getting chummier, I needed to steer the conversation back to Tim, Mr. P, and his family before another patron arrived. Jim was already sending me signals that he wanted to go home. I had to work fast.

"Deanna and I have known each other for years," I began. "Not as long as I've known Poppy, though. She and I went to the same high school. And one summer, back in the eighties, my friend Claire and I worked for her family at their beach house. Claire tutored the younger girls, and I was the maid. It was a wonderful experience." Mostly.

I hoped Harriet would accept me as someone who also had a connection with Mr. P's family and share more things about them. Tit for tat, as it were.

"Mr. P had an older brother, Demitri, who's Tim's father," Harriet said, answering the first question I had without my even asking. "Mr. P's real first name was Dominic. The brothers bought this diner together. Tim inherited his dad's share of the diner when he died, and when Mr. P passed, he left Tim his share, too. Tim was furious."

"I must be missing something here," I said. "Why was Tim so angry? The diner must be worth a lot of money. If he didn't want it, he could just sell it."

"That's because there were strings attached to Tim's inheritance. According to the terms of Mr. P's will, Tim can't sell the diner without Poppy's approval, and she won't allow it."

I waited for Harriet to continue, and she didn't let me down. I had a feeling she'd had all this information bottled up inside of her for a long time, waiting for the right person to share it with. And here I was.

"There was bad blood between the two brothers. It started when Dominic wanted to open a restaurant in New York City, and his older brother Demitri provided money for the down payment. The restaurant was a huge success, and Dominic was suddenly a rich celebrity nicknamed Mr. P.

"Demitiri asked his brother to pay him back the money he loaned him. Mr. P refused, claiming it was a gift. They quarreled and never spoke to each other again."

"Mr. P repaid the loan by giving Tim the diner," I said, defending the man who'd been so good to me. "He was a very generous man."

"Then why didn't he just leave the diner to Tim free and clear, without involving Poppy?" Harriet asked. "Think about that for a while, Carol. If you come up with an answer, I'd love to hear it."

Chapter 83

I don't understand why people have to "get ready for bed." I'm always ready for bed.

I bet you're all expecting me to tell you that I didn't get a wink of sleep that night. That I tossed and turned, keeping Jim and the dogs awake until dawn.

Surprise! I was so exhausted when we got home that I tumbled into bed (after performing my regular pre-sleep ritual) and slept soundly through the night. Jim woke me the next morning with a quick kiss, told me he'd be out for a while, and ordered me to stay out of trouble. I appreciated the kiss, said goodbye, and planned to ignore the order, the way I always did.

My little gray cells must have been working overtime while I was sleeping, because before I'd finished my first cup of coffee, a complete scenario about how Lou's murder could have happened popped into my mind.

One the one hand, it was outrageous and I couldn't prove a thing. On the other hand, if I spent today confirming my suspicions, by dinner time I'd have enough information to figure out whodunnit.

My plan was to talk to Phyllis first, followed by a visit with her friend Muriel Anderson, the woman who'd started the petition to ban pickleball. I also might stop by Claire and Larry's to see whether they were still married (only kidding). I had a few questions about the corporate structure of Lou Hollister's construction company I figured Larry could answer. I might also innocently drop the information about his possible Cayman Islands bank account to see how he reacted. Or not.

I had to check on Mary Alice. I felt terrible that I'd been neglecting her. If I guessed correctly, she had evidence hidden at her condo that would help me solve the murder of the man she loved and give her some peace.

Oops. I made a little slip there. What I meant to say was, I'd find enough evidence at Mary Alice's to turn over to my detective son-in-law so the police would solve the murder. Please forgive me. I got carried away.

Inviting Jenny, Mark, and CJ (the best guest ever!) to dinner tonight and presenting my brilliant solution was my big finish.

"Which reminds me," I said to the dogs. "I have to arrange for a meal delivery too." I added that to today's list in bold letters so I wouldn't forget.

You didn't think that, with all I had to do today, I'd actually cook dinner too, did you?

A quick text to Jenny gave me the glad news that Mark was enjoying a well-deserved, two-day break from his detective duties, and they'd love to come for dinner.

A second text from Jenny suggested that she'd be happy to provide dessert.

A third text from Jenny suggested she order takeout from our favorite Chinese restaurant as a special treat, and I didn't have to do anything but set the table.

My daughter knows me so well.

After a quick shower and doing whatever else it took to make myself presentable, I was ready for my talk with Phyllis. My plan was to invite her here for coffee, and after a few minutes of neighborhood chit chat, steer the conversation to Lou Hollister's murder.

I made a fresh pot of coffee, took the dogs for a quick run, then called Phyllis. She answered on the second ring and accepted my invitation immediately. In less than ten minutes, she was sitting at my kitchen table with the dogs snoozing at her feet.

"The dogs have certainly accepted you," I said. "Consider yourself honored."

"Bill suggested I bring a few dog biscuits with me," Phyllis said. "I'm sure that helped.

"Don't bother with the coffee, Carol. Let's get right down to business. How can you and I work together to solve Lou Hollister's murder?

"We'll be just like Watson and Holmes," Phyllis continued, oblivious to the shocked expression my face was wearing, "Or maybe we should both be Holmes, since neither one of us have a medical degree. Anyway, what's your theory about the murder, and how can I help you prove it? Two heads are better than one, right?"

Not these two heads. No way.

I searched my mental filing cabinet for how I could reject her offer without hurting her feelings. "What an interesting thought, Phyllis."

"It was Poppy's idea that you and I team up to clear her name." Oblivious to my silence, Phyllis prattled on about how our new partnership would work.

If this was Poppy's idea, she must be nuts. Or maybe she was looking forward to spending the rest of her life in prison. For all I knew, the women's penitentiary in Danbury had a pickleball court so she could keep up her game.

I forced myself to look sad. "But it's not going to work. I've been ordered to keep my nose out of this case. If my son-in-law catches me interfering with police work again, it will cause major problems on the marital front. I can't risk forcing Jenny to choose between saving her marriage to Mark and being loyal to me. I might not even be allowed to see my precious grandson. I simply can't take that risk. I'm sure you understand."

Okay, you all know I was deviating so far from the truth that my nose should have grown several inches longer, just like Pinocchio's. But desperate times call for desperate measures, and I was desperate.

"Oh, my goodness, Carol. That never even occurred to me. I only wanted to help Poppy." Phyllis looked like she was going to cry, which made me feel guilty.

"Perhaps Mark wouldn't go that far," I said, trying to smooth over the imaginary crisis I had just created. "I can't help thinking about the murder, though, especially since I was there."

Phyllis brightened up. "Do you want to talk about what you saw? Perhaps that would help you. I promise I won't repeat anything you tell me, even to Bill."

"Well..." I said, then I pretended to make a decision. "Maybe you're right." I spent the next few minutes telling Phyllis everything that had already been reported by the local media.

"I keep wondering if someone other than Poppy could be the murderer," I added. "I wish the police could find another witness. Perhaps someone who lives near the pickleball court might have seen something that night and didn't realize it was important."

I sat back and waited for Phyllis's response.

"I know just the person. Muriel Anderson. She's the one who started that ridiculous petition to ban pickleball in town. The woman has nothing but time on her hands and a vivid imagination, if you ask me. Always sticking her nose in her neighbors' business. And she complains about everything."

Since this was an accurate description of Phyllis herself, I remained silent.

"She lives on Mayberry Lane in a bright yellow house. It's a true eyesore on such a lovely street. That would never be allowed on Old Fairport Turnpike! Her property backs up to the recreation center property. The pickleball court is so close, it's practically in her back yard.

"I'd be glad to talk to her, dear, if you think that would help."

"Actually, Phyllis, I just thought of something much more helpful you could do. Only if you want to, of course. No pressure."

Phyllis leaned forward in her chair, quivering like Lucy and Ethel do when I have treats in my hand.

"Do you know anyone at the Fairport Patch?" I asked. I'd always suspected that Phyllis was a secret contributor to what I've nicknamed the Fairport Snitch, and wondered if she'd finally admit it.

"I may know someone there," she said, pretending to think. "Why?"

"I'm wondering who tipped the Patch off about those billboards calling Fairport the Murder Capital of New England. There could be a link between the billboards and Lou Hollister's murder. Does the staff keep a record of sources in case there are follow-up questions?"

"Do you think the murderer sent it?" Phyllis looked both thrilled and nervous.

"Maybe. Can you find out?"

"I'm sure I can," Phyllis said. "Oh, my goodness. What if I'm the one who solves the murder? Wait until I tell Bill."

"No! You can't tell Bill. This has to be just between us. Do you promise?"

"I promise. And I won't let you down. I'll report back as soon as I can."

Chapter 84

With the end of daylight-saving time, now we can enjoy watching the sunset while we eat lunch.

Mayberry Lane was a cul de sac of older, small colonials mixed with a few ranches and split levels. Finding Muriel's house was easy. All the other homes were painted in typical New England colors of white or gray, and while they were well kept, there was nothing unusual about any of them.

I pulled up in front of a two-story house painted mustard yellow with white shutters. For once, I agreed with Phyllis. It was a real eyesore, for sure.

The front door opened before I had a chance to knock, revealing a petite woman of senior vintage, a welcoming smile on her face. "You must be Carol Andrews. Phyllis said you want to talk to me about the pickleball courts." She gestured me to follow her.

As we walked toward the back of the house, I heard irregular thwacking sounds. They'd stop, then start again. The noise was really loud and really annoying.

"Horrible, isn't it?" Muriel asked. "How would you like to hear all that noise every day?"

"It's enough to drive a person batty. Not that I'm implying you are," I added quickly, my face crimson with embarrassment.

Muriel cackled, which I assumed was a laugh. "Not to worry, honey. I've been called a lot worse than that."

"Now I understand why you started that petition to ban pickleball in Fairport," I said.

"Then you're the only one who does. I tried to get the First Selectwoman over here to listen to what I have to deal with every day, but she blew me off like a piece of lint."

Muriel leaned closer. "I've showed her. Yes, I have." She cackled again.

I had no idea what the woman was talking about, but I figured if I humored her a little, I might learn something useful. Or not. My mother always told me to be polite to my elders, and since my elders are in shorter supply these days, I couldn't be picky.

"I've decided to close the whole rec center down," Muriel continued, "not just the pickleball court. I got the idea when I heard there was some fancy restaurant being added. Well, I couldn't have that. I'd have to deal with pickleball noise all day and party people all hours of the night.

"It was the kitchen fire that gave me the idea. Of course, that was an accident, but..." she leaned forward, "have you heard about the restaurant windows being broken and graffiti on the walls? I've even damaged a few cars in the parking lot. When you're an old lady, like me, nobody pays any attention to you. I can get away with anything and not get caught."

"That's very interesting," I said, working hard to keep a poker face. "Thank you for telling me." I really wanted to throttle this deranged woman who had caused my family so much trouble, but I restrained myself.

"Will you tell the First Selectwoman for me what I've been doing and why? Phyllis said you two are good friends. Maybe you could convince her to listen to me. I love this town. I was born here. I don't like having to do these things. People may get the wrong idea.

"I'm trying to save Fairport!"

"What you've been doing is very serious." I answered. "You could even be arrested for damaging public property."

Muriel's lower lip quivered. "But I didn't mean any harm. You have to believe me. I don't want to be arrested! I'd be so embarrassed."

"I hope you understand that I have to give the police this information. My son-in-law is a Fairport detective. I'll tell him, and he'll take it from there. I'm sure he'll want to talk to you. Mark's a good guy. You'll like him."

My phone vibrated with an incoming text, and I reached in my purse to silence it. I still wanted to know if Muriel had seen anyone at the pickleball court the night of the murder.

Focus on your original goal, Carol!

"There was a murder at the pickleball courts a few nights ago," I began.

Muriel burst into full-blown hysterics. "I didn't do it! Dear heaven, don't tell me you think I'm guilty of that, too!"

"No, Muriel. That's not what I meant. I was wondering if you happened to notice anyone at the pickleball courts around the time of the murder."

"I remember that night I had a splitting headache and went to bed right after supper," Muriel said. "All the police activity woke me up a little while later, and I couldn't figure out what was going on. I didn't know what happened until I heard about it on the local news."

A dead end, pardon the pun.

I checked my phone and my priorities changed instantly. The text was from Mary Alice, and she wanted to see me right away.

"I have to leave right now."

"Before you go, I have something to give you." She led me to a desk in the living room and handed me a flash drive. "I have hidden cameras outside the house in case anybody tries to break in. I live alone, and I have to protect myself. I change the videos every few days and date them. This one is from the camera at the back of the house, the one that has a full view of the pickleball courts. It includes the night of the murder. Maybe you'll find something helpful on it."

As much as I wanted to be the one who checked that video footage, I forced myself to give it back to Muriel. "You should turn this over to the police, not to me. My son-in-law, Mark Anderson, is the lead detective on the case, so ask for him."

I could tell by Muriel's face there was no way she'd go to the police station, so I came up with a better offer. One she couldn't refuse.

"Do you like Chinese food?"

Chapter 85

I don't always go the extra mile. But when I do, it's because I missed my exit.

A part of me was thrilled that I was getting closer to helping the police solve the murder. As a bonus, I now also knew who'd been causing the problems at Picklelilly's. If I hadn't been driving, I would have patted myself on the back. Not that I'd want any public credit for my brilliance. You all know that I'm a very modest person.

Right now, my primary focus was on Mary Alice. I let her know that I was on my way, and she replied with a thumbs-up emoji. Still, I wasn't prepared to find her pacing outside her condo, waiting for me to arrive.

"I got here as soon as I could," I yelled out the window.

She nodded, then removed an orange cone from the nearest parking space. "I saved this spot for you."

I eased the car into my V.I.P. spot with only one attempt, then followed her inside.

"Thank you for coming so quickly."

"I haven't been in touch for a few days, and I'm really sorry. I should have been more supportive. I know how much you loved Lou. Please forgive me. I feel so guilty."

Mary Alice gave me a big hug. "I needed to be alone to grieve, and you gave it to me. I appreciated that. And I knew that I could always reach out for help and you'd come running. Or driving."

I took a good look at my dear friend. "Did you just make a joke? I can't believe it."

"Well, it wasn't a very good one." Mary Alice admitted. "But I feel better now than the last time I saw you.

"Anyway, I decided to go through Lou's...things today." Her eyes brimmed over, and she wiped the tears away. "He used the spare bedroom as an office, and he kept his clothes in that closet. He used to kid me that after we were married, we'd have to find a place with a lot more closet space."

The tears really started then, and Mary Alice made no effort to stop them. "We had such wonderful plans for a happy life together."

"This is so unfair," I said. "Nobody should be forced to suffer through such a heartbreaking loss twice."

"Brian's death was a senseless accident," Mary Alice said. "He happened to be in his car at the wrong place at the wrong time.

"Lou's death was a cold-blooded murder, and I have the proof. I can't wait to show you what I found today."

I followed Mary Alice into the small guestroom. Lou's clothing and shoes were arranged neatly on the bed.

She pointed me toward a pile of files and assorted papers heaped on top of a small rolltop desk. I figured it would take me the rest of the afternoon to go through it all.

"I know it looks like a lot to deal with," Mary Alice said. "Once I realized what I was looking at, I tried to put the most important information on the top of the pile."

Pulling out the chair, she gestured me to sit down. "I want you to read the first few documents and tell me what you think. Try not to jump to any conclusions right away. And if you think I'm wrong, please tell me. I trust your judgment."

"You're telling me not to jump to any conclusions," I repeated after a quick look at the top document. "Are you kidding? The first name that jumps out at me is Larry McGee's. What's this all about?"

"When I saw Larry's name, I couldn't believe it. Especially because these papers were in this manila envelope." Mary Alice held the envelope up so I could read the label.

"It's marked EVIDENCE." I pushed the documents away. "I don't want to do this."

"I understand. I had the same reaction when I saw Larry's name. All I could think of was that someone we thought we knew so well was really a crook. Poor Claire. I put the papers back in the envelope and locked them in the desk. I almost burned them without reading them.

"After a while, I calmed down and forced myself to read all the documents. Then I texted you. I'm counting on you to tell me what to do now."

Then she left me alone.

I cleaned my glasses and got to work. I have no idea how long it took me to read everything in the manila envelope.

When I was finally finished, thanks to Lou Hollister's meticulous record-keeping, I was sure I had enough evidence for Mark to arrest Lou Hollister's murderer.

Chapter 86

Here are two tips to make any day better: Stay off the bathroom scale, and don't watch the news.

Please accept my apologies for not inviting all of you to my big-reveal dinner. I don't have enough matching silver and dinnerware to set a proper table, and when I entertain, even if it's a takeout meal, presentation is very important to me.

The final attendees, in addition to Jim and me, Jenny, Mark, and CJ (who slept through the entire meal), included Mike, Mary Alice, Claire and Larry, Phyllis, Bill (Phyllis insisted he come with her and she brought an extra dessert so I had to agree), Sister Rose, Muriel, and Harriet (who brought extra food from the diner). It was a tight fit around my dining room table, even with the addition of two extra extensions.

I didn't prepare an agenda, which turned out to be a huge problem. I tried to keep order, but whenever I called on one person to give his or her report, others interrupted with opinions, questions, and objections. So, in the interests of trying to decipher my notes and failing, I'll just skip to the big finish.

Lou Hollister's murderer turned out to be Tim Peterson, who was never on my suspect list. The evidence Lou had collected was a real eye opener.

Tim had been embezzling from Hollister Construction for years. When Larry joined the company, he noticed unusually high amounts charged as company closing costs and asked Lou for clarification.

To cover his crimes, Tim set up Larry (and Claire!) with phony Cayman Islands bank accounts as the thieves. You should have seen Claire's face when she found out!

Of course, Lou didn't believe that. When he began researching the thefts on his own, he finally realized all the evidence he was finding pointed to Tim. Tim realized the jig was up, so to speak, lured Lou to the pickleball court with a phony text and killed him. Tim's plan was to set Poppy up as Lou's murderer with me there as the witness. But it didn't work out that way, thank goodness.

The footage from Muriel's outdoor camera clearly showed Tim arriving at the pickleball court several minutes before Lou Hollister and the rest of us did. By the way, Lou's missing cell phone was finally found under a pile of leaves in Muriel's back yard.

Please know that I'm only giving you the bare bones of what was revealed at my dinner party.

Some information is privileged and my lips are sealed. I don't want to do anything to jeopardize the murder case against Tim.

A police search of Tim's law office revealed the burner phone he'd used to lure everybody to the pickleball court the night Lou was killed. Phyllis had a moment in the spotlight when she announced that the same phone number was used to report Lou's murder to The Patch before Larrry called the police to report the murder. She'd found that out all on her own, and I realized I'd better watch my step with her if she ever wanted to help me investigate another murder.

Not that I'm expecting to investigate another murder! However, I do believe in planning ahead. Just in case.

The crowning touch was that Tim stole Poppy's priceless antique car to make his getaway and was caught before he made it to the New York state line.

It seemed logical (to me, anyway) that Tim had also deliberately ordered the Murder/not Burger billboards as his secret way of bragging about his newest addition to the local fatality count. Mark didn't believe me, and it couldn't be proved, anyway.

Harriet provided background information about the feud between Mr. P and Tim's father, which was the original spark that fueled Tim's desire for revenge. I suspect that Tim's attorney, whoever he or she may be, will use it in his client's defense.

Charli and Mike broke up. My smart son finally admitted that running two restaurants so far away from each other was too much and bowed out of the rec center project. Future plans for a restaurant there are still being discussed, but no matter what's decided, I'm sure the place won't be called Picklelilly's.

I was (selfishly) relieved I didn't have to worry about Poppy becoming part of our family. I don't think she hates me anymore, but it doesn't pay to take any chances.

I heard through the local grapevine that she and Charli have pitched an idea for a new reality show to a few national media networks: The Bachelorette and The Golden Bachelorette Search for True Love, with them in the starring roles.

It sounds so ridiculous that I'm sure it'll be snapped up immediately.

Nancy finally came back from her cruise looking tan and relaxed. We met at the Fairport Diner for very long lunch while she entertained us with details of her cruise.

After she finally ran out of things to tell us, Nancy asked, "So, what's up with all of you? Did I miss anything exciting while I was away?"

I looked at Claire and Mary Alice. They looked back at me.

We all said, simultaneously, "Not a thing."

*Enjoy this introduction to the
Baby Boomer Mystery series!*

RETIREMENT Can Be MURDER
Every Wife Has A Story

A Carol and Jim Andrews Baby Boomer Mystery
First in the Series

Susan Santangelo

Chapter 1

The hardest years of a marriage are the ones following the wedding.

Here's an amazing weight-loss tip for all the women in America: an out-of-body experience makes you look thinner. Forget about vertical vs. horizontal stripes. I'm telling you, an out-of-body occurrence does the trick. Plus, it can be quite a pleasant sensation to look down and see a movie starring... you. What's not to like?

Of course, there's a downside to my weight-loss tip. Out-of-body experiences are triggered by a traumatic event, like the panicky phone call I'd just gotten from Jim, my husband of thirty-six years, telling me he'd found his retirement coach, Davis Rhodes, dead at his kitchen table.

When Jim said that the police were grilling him like he was a prime suspect in a crime, rather than an innocent person who happened to be at the wrong place at the wrong time, I could feel my mind and body separate. This was immediately followed by an overwhelming sense of guilt.

Because the whole rotten mess Jim found himself in was my fault. Don't get me wrong. I didn't murder Rhodes, although I will admit I'd often harbored dark thoughts about the guy because of the havoc he caused in our lives. However, I was responsible for getting Jim and Davis Rhodes together in the first place.

Well, to be honest, I manipulated Jim into consulting Rhodes about his impending retirement. The thought of having my dear husband around the house 24/7, with nothing to do except sit in his recliner with the television remote clutched in his fist, appealed to me as much as a root canal without novocaine.

On second thought, I'd definitely take the root canal. So, I made the decision to stall Jim's retirement as long as I could. By whatever means I could come up with.

How was I to know that the chain of events I'd innocently set in motion a few weeks ago would end up this way?

About the Author

Susan Santangelo is the author of the best-selling Baby Boomer mystery series. The humorous mysteries follow the adventures of a typical Boomer couple, Carol and Jim Andrews, as they navigate life's rocky road toward their twilight years.

Susan is a member of Sisters in Crime, International Thriller Writers, and the Cape Cod Writers Center. She divides her time between Clearwater, Florida and Cape Cod, Massachusetts, and shares her life with her husband Joe (not Jim). A dog lover all her life, her two English cocker spaniels, Boomer and Lilly, are featured on the books' covers. She is also a two-time breast cancer survivor and credits early detection through mammograms for saving her life twice.

www.ingramcontent.com/pod-product-compliance
Lightning Source LLC
LaVergne TN
LVHW091528060526
838200LV00036B/528